CW01263454

THE MONASTIC GATEHOUSE
And Other Types of Portal of Medieval Religious Houses

THE MONASTIC GATEHOUSE
And Other Types of Portal of Medieval Religious Houses

Roland W. Morant

The Book Guild Ltd
Sussex, England

In memory of Ethel Margaret Haines

This book is sold subject to the condition that it shall not, by way of trade or otherwise, be lent, re-sold, hired out, photocopied or held in any retrieval system or otherwise circulated without the publisher's prior consent in any form of binding or cover other than that in which this is published and without a similar condition including this condition being imposed on the subsequent purchaser.

The Book Guild Ltd.
25 High Street,
Lewes, Sussex

First published 1995
© Roland W. Morant 1995
Set in Times
Typesetting by Poole Typesetting (Wessex) Ltd.
Bournemouth.
Printed in Great Britain by
Antony Rowe Ltd.
Chippenham, Wiltshire.

A catalogue record for this book is
available from the British Library

ISBN 0 86332 994 2

CONTENTS

List of Photographs	vii
List of Figures	ix
Acknowledgements	xi
Preface	xiii
Introduction	1
Chapter 1 Functions and Types	5
Chapter 2 Precinct Plan and Portal Location	26
Chapter 3 Structure (1)	56
Chapter 4 Structure (2)	79
Chapter 5 The Gate-hall	97
Chapter 6 Survivors and Adaptations	118
Inventory The Portals Classified in Groups	137
Appendix 1 Monastic Houses Mentioned in the Text	202
Appendix 2 A Survey of Surviving Gate-halls	208
References	218

Errata page 97 line 4 from top insert **55** instead of " 56 "
              line 12 from bottom insert **55** instead of " 58 "
        page 173 line 3 from top insert **Benedictine** instead of " Augustinian "

LIST OF PHOTOGRAPHS
(between pages 96 and 97)

1   Great Gate, Staffordshire
2   Lenton, the White Hart Hotel
3   Maxstoke Priory, example of precinct wall
4   Usk Priory, gatehouse to front
5   Kidwelly Castle, main gatehouse to front
6   King's Lynn Carmelite Friary (Whitefriars), gateway to front
7   Dunfermline Abbey, gatehouse (The Pends) to rear
8   Bury St Edmunds Abbey, gatehouse (Great Gate) to front
9   Hyde Abbey, one-storeyed gatehouse to front
10   St Osyth Abbey, Bishop's Lodging hall to front
11   Battle Abbey, three-storeyed gatehouse to front
12   Thornton Abbey, front façade of gatehouse showing principal niches and original statues
13   Kirkham Priory, gatehouse to front
14   Peterborough Abbey (now cathedral), Prior's Gateway to front
15   Peterborough Abbey (now cathedral), Abbot's Gatehouse to front
16   Leiston Abbey, west range porch north turret fragment

17	Burnham Norton Friary, gatehouse to rear flushwork
18	Monk Bretton Priory, gatehouse gate-hall interior showing chase where main gates were fitted
19	St Albans Abbey (now cathedral), gatehouse to front
20	St Albans Abbey (now cathedral), gatehouse to rear
21	Bristol Abbey (now cathedral), Abbey Gatehouse showing interior wall arcading of vehicular gate-hall
22	Wetheral Priory, gatehouse to front
23	Evesham Abbey, North Gate to front
24	Alnwick Abbey, gatehouse to front
25	Ely Cathedral-priory, Palace gatehouse to front
26	Letheringham Priory, gatehouse to front
27	Forde Abbey, Abbot Chard's Tower to front
28	Oxford, St Bernard's College (now St John's College), gate-tower to front
29	Wigmore Abbey, inner gatehouse to front
30	Chester Abbey (now cathedral), Abbey Gateway to front
31	Norwich Cathedral-priory, watergate (Pull's Ferry) to front
32	Coventry Charterhouse, postern to front

LIST OF FIGURES

1	Norton Abbey, sketch of destroyed gatehouse attributed to S. & N. Buck, 1727
2	Tupholme Abbey, sketch of destroyed gatehouse by William Stukeley, *c.*1710–20
3	Typical ground plan of a medieval monastery
4	Types of portal
5	Table of monastic portals showing for each its (a) approximate distance and bearing from the conventual church, and (b) orientation
6	Summary of locations of portals
7	The cross-placed portal
8	The facing portal
9	The Benedictine one-portal plan
10	The Benedictine two-portal plan
11	The Cistercian one-portal plan
12	The Cistercian two-portal plan
13	The friary portal plan
14	Portal dimensions
15	Gateways, conjectural development
16	Gatehouses, Type 1
17	Gatehouses: lean-tos, wings and ranges
18	Bridlington Priory, ground-plan of gatehouse

19	Niche types
20	The undivided gate-hall
21	The divided gate-hall
22	Thornton abbey, storey plans

ACKNOWLEDGEMENTS

I am greatly indebted to the *Buildings of England* series which appears under the founding editorship of the late Sir Nikolaus Pevsner and which are published by Penguin Books. A number of the portals referred to in the text of this monograph might have remained unidentified had it not been for a mention in the appropriate county work.

More specific acknowledgements are due to the following who are owners of the illustrations and have kindly permitted their use:

J.P. Green, *Norton Priory* (1989), published by Cambridge University Press for Figure 1.

English Heritage for Figure 22.

J.R. Earnshaw and the North Wolds Borough Council, Bridlington, for Figure 18.

Though the sketch in Figure 2 is out of copyright, an acknowledgement is made to Lincolnshire Museums for its use.

PREFACE

During the medieval period a number of monastic houses belonged in turn to more than one religious order. Indeed, several abbeys and priories belonged in turn to more than two different orders. To avoid confusion, in this book all references have been made to the final order that a particular house belonged to before the Dissolution.

The status of several monastic houses changed in the course of their histories, usually from priory to abbey as happened at Norton and Kenilworth. Their later status has therefore been given when referring to such houses.

The locations of all abbeys, priories and other monastic establishments have been identified within the setting of the historic counties. Apart from a few exceptions, the latters' boundaries conformed with the pre-1974 pattern.

To make it easier for readers to visualise individual architectural features of portals, the practice has been adopted throughout the book of describing such features in terms of their left-hand or right-hand position as the viewer observes the building to its front.

INTRODUCTION

When King Henry VIII finally closed the abbeys and priories in England and Wales in the middle of the sixteenth century, his officials enforced a policy of rapid destruction which speedily eliminated most of the conventual churches and nearly all the claustral and other domestic buildings. This phase of rapid destruction, which was emulated in Scotland a few decades later, was followed by a period lasting several centuries in which those buildings that had not been pulled down in the immediate aftermath of the Dissolution, suffered slow decay and neglect.

As a standard feature individual abbeys and priories included one or more gatehouses which were often designed as elegant structures and frequently enriched with much ornamentation, especially religious symbols. We should therefore have expected such buildings to have received from Henry VIII's demolition-men the destructive treatment that was meted out towards most other monastic buildings.

Many gatehouses were indeed pulled down, frequently leaving nothing visible to show where they had stood, as at Croxden in Staffordshire where, incidentally, the lingering memory of the gatehouse is preserved in the name of a hamlet near the abbey ruins called Great Gate (Photograph 1). Sometimes a totally vanished gatehouse is represented by a picture in a book or manuscript, as are the gatehouses at Norton (Figure 1) in Cheshire and Tupholme (Figure 2) in Lincolnshire; while at Lenton near Nottingham the White Hart Hotel (Photograph 2) is said to have been built on the foundations of the priory gatehouse.

Nevertheless a number of pre-Dissolution gatehouses and other portals do remain standing, sometimes as undamaged and complete as they were when finally vacated by their

Figure 1   Norton Abbey, sketch of destroyed gatehouse attributed to
S. & N. Buck, 1727

Figure 2 Tupholme Abbey, sketch of destroyed gatehouse by William Stukeley, c.1710–20 (from the Lincolnshire Museums Information Sheet, Archaeology Series No. 10 [Sept. 1979], Tupholme Abbey)

conventual owners. In crude terms, approaching two hundred portals have survived as recognisable medieval buildings of their type, that is, approximately as many portals as abbey and priory churches.

Sometimes gatehouses remain standing near the abbeys now ruined, to which they were designed to control access (as at Bury St Edmunds and Glastonbury), or near conventual churches which are still used for worship (e.g. Bromfield, Cartmel and Carlisle). At a few sites such as Michelham and Stoneleigh the gatehouse, largely bereft of its abbey or priory buildings, now commands access to a mansion constructed from or built over the remnants of one or more of the former claustral ranges. The situation equally exists where the church and other monastic buildings have been completely swept away, leaving the gatehouse standing in isolation (as at Alnwick, Kingswood or Wetheral).

What makes monastic gatehouses exceptionally interesting and thus a subject worthy of study is the varying degree of design and size that the survivors display. They range from buildings constructed on the grand scale that sometimes served as medieval mansions (as at Thornton) to small and insignificant structures (for example at Calder and Llanthony). They range from the great blocks of masonry redolent of castle keeps (such as the Porta Gate at Ely) to modest gateways which were designed solely for regulating traffic, such gateways (as at the King's Lynn friaries) apparently not being provided with inclusive living accommodation.

Though much has been written *en passant* about monastic gatehouses within larger works on abbeys and priories, the topic has not been directly or fully addressed in its own right. Given the wealth of surviving architectural material that abounds in England, and to a much lesser extent in Wales and Scotland, this account seeks to fill the void by supplying a general description of them.

Chapter 1 deals with the functions and types of monastic gatehouse and other portals. In Chapter 2 their locations are considered in respect of the typical precinct of conventual houses, and differences in location dealt with, in so far as there tended to be contrasts between the houses of some of the various religious orders. The historical development of portals and their structure, including accommodation and external ornamentation, is covered in Chapters 3 and 4. In Chapter 5 the design and ornamentation of the gate-hall and other types of internal accommodation are considered, while Chapter 6 reviews the surviving specimens and adaptations of gatehouses in Great Britain, as well as providing an indication of their geographical distribution. These six chapters are followed by an Inventory which lists and briefly describes all the surviving portals of England, Wales and Scotland classified in six groups according to their present material condition. The work concludes with two appendices, one identifying every monastic house referred to in the text and the other providing a structural survey of surviving gate-halls, and a set of bibliographical references.

1

FUNCTIONS AND TYPES

BACKGROUND

From early Christian times, men and women have been motivated to withdraw from the world in order to attain the higher ideals of the Gospels. Broadly speaking this withdrawal took two forms. Some became hermits or eremites (from the Greek word *eremos*, meaning desert), living in the wilderness among the rocks and bushes, and in caves. Some hermits lived as anchorites or anchoresses, especially in the twelfth and thirteenth centuries when a parish church would support such an individual in a cell attached to the chancel of the building (Lawrence, 1989, p.152). Solitary existence never appealed to more than a few individuals, however, all of whom must have possessed an unshakable determination and an abundance of self-sufficiency, both qualities requisite for leading lives of this kind.

Men and women are social beings, and many more people wishing to withdraw from the world instead chose to become cenobites rather than eremites. A cenobite (the term being derived from the Greek *koinos bios*, meaning the life in common) was a member of a self-governing and disciplined religious community, normally acting under a rule. With reciprocal support provided by the membership of a community, monks or nuns were thus able to follow their personal vocations in the seclusion of a monastery where there was a strictly controlled or regulated environment. Above all, the cenobites were able through this mutual support to practise the Christian commandment of loving one's neighbour, a criticism often levelled against the eremitical way of life.

A community of men or women seeking to accomplish similar religious vocations and sharing a common life within the same set of monastic buildings would nevertheless have been prone to external interference unless basic precautions were taken. Obstruction with the smooth running of a monastic house could have had a number of causes, of which the chief might have been the unauthorised entry of individuals from the outside, everyday world. Such people, ranging from thieves and vagabonds to well-meaning but harmless cranks, making loud or uncouth noises (such as whistling, singing or shouting) could have disturbed the quiet atmosphere unless strict precautions were taken. Even servants going about their duties in the outer court may have been a potential nuisance unless schooled into acceptable modes of behaviour. The fostering of privacy and seclusion among a community's members was therefore essential, not only to protect them from external disturbances but also to ensure their own good order and discipline.

A number of cases are reported, for example by Midmer (1979) of nuns being found outside their priories apparently without permission or having been able to give an acceptable reason: at Cook Hill, a small Cistercian priory in Worcestershire, the nuns were found wandering in both the thirteenth and fifteenth centuries (op. cit., p. 118); at Thame, the visiting abbot of Waverley rebuked the monks for their love of archery and feasting in taverns (op. cit., p. 303); while at Exeter Polsloe, injunctions were issued in 1319 and 1376 concerning the nuns' 'wanderings' and freedom (op. cit., p. 140). All this behaviour represented the other side of the coin where it was necessary for monastic houses, also in the interests of good order and discipline to have the means – not always successfully employed – of preventing monks or nuns from leaving the monastic premises.

THE MONASTIC PRECINCT AND BOUNDARY

The monastic buildings consisted of:

1. *The conventual church*, partly bounded by the monks' cemetery;

2. *The domestic buildings* (such as refectory, chapter-house, etc.), ranged round the cloister;
3. *The service buildings*, placed at the perimeter of the great court; and
4. *Several detached buildings*, especially the infirmary and possibly the superior's lodging and/or guests' accommodation.

The buildings (Figure 3) together with the cloister, great court, monks' cemetery and, occasionally, other open spaces (e.g. gardens, orchards) occupied the abbey or priory ground area known as the precinct. As we should anticipate, a precinct varied considerably in size from monastery to monastery, the chief factors being the availability of land and the building requirements of a new community. A list of some monastic houses with the size of their precincts expressed in acres illustrates this variation:

Jervaulx (Cistercian abbey)	100
Furness (Cistercian abbey)	73
Fountains (Cistercian abbey)	70
Glastonbury (Benedictine abbey)	60
Westminster (Benedictine abbey)	40
Canterbury St Augustine's (Benedictine abbey)	30
St Andrews (Augustinian cathedral-priory)	30
Cleeve (Cistercian abbey)	28
Tintern (Cistercian abbey)	27
Battle (Benedictine abbey)	20
Leicester St Mary's (Augustinian abbey)	15
Pluscarden (Benedictine cell)	10
Dunwich (Franciscan friary)	7
Monk Bretton (Benedictine priory)	7
Michelham (Augustinian priory)	6
Mount Grace (Carthusian priory)	5
Hulne (Carmelite friary)	2

Information on the acreages of precincts is difficult to obtain except in the case of a small number of monastic houses, as many of the boundary markers such as walls and moats have been destroyed.

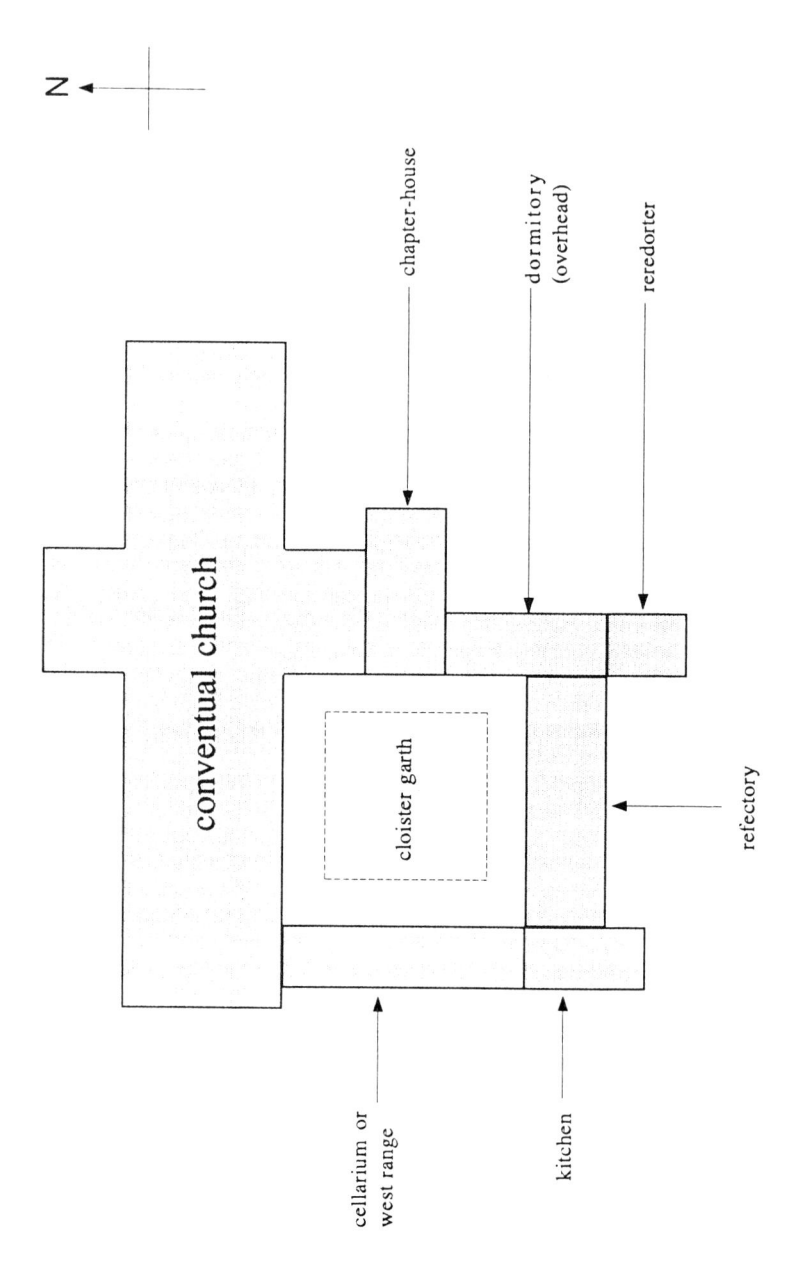

Figure 3 Typical Ground Plan of a Medieval Monastery

The larger, richer, rural houses had precincts that were planned on an expansive scale. In towns and cities, precincts tended to be smaller, especially when occupied by latecomers such as the mendicant orders or friars who often had to make do with unsuitable urban sites, which were frequently placed immediately outside the city walls or squeezed in between existing buildings.

The limit or boundary of a monastic precinct was always marked by a clearly visible physical barrier. With the majority of houses this was a high precinct wall of stone or brick. However, some abbeys and priories (such as Kirkstead, Michelham), especially if located in low-lying rural areas, relied on a moat. Very occasionally a dry ditch was used (probably the method used at Breedon-on-the-Hill which was first founded $c.700$); at Iona in Scotland, which was established in 563, the house was surrounded by a bank, and at Oundle (also pre-Conquest) the house had a hedge (Gilyard-Beer, 1958, p. 11).

A number of monasteries (Alnwick, Kirkstall, Shap, Whalley, for example) were sited on the bank of a river. This apparently often obviated the need to have an artificially contrived barrier on that side of the precinct, the landward or opposite side being protected by a wall. The riverbank at St Benet's Abbey in Norfolk clearly exhibits the remnants of a precinct wall, a situation indicating that at least this house did not rely on the width and depth of the river alone for protection.

One or two houses in Scotland such as Inchmahome Priory, were situated on an island in a remote loch where the breadth of water around the island provided an adequate barrier. However, a great monastery sited beside the sea, if otherwise unprotected, would always have been vulnerable to sudden attack by foreigners from afar. The precinct wall at St Andrews, which is constructed on the shoreline, demonstrates the stress that the canons of the cathedral-priory placed on being well protected.

The use of barriers of more than one kind was employed at some other monasteries too, for example Ulverscroft where the site was walled and moated because of its location in a wild wood at Charnwood (Bottomley, 1981, p. 234).

The precinct wall, river boundary, moat, ditch and so on

were normally selected to deter all but the most resolute of potential intruders. A wall was normally about eight to ten feet tall (higher at the great abbeys and priories) and constructed of large, well-fitting blocks of ashlar which would deny hand- and toe-holds. On its top was an overlapping cope-stone usually carved or bevelled, designed to throw off rainwater and to act as an additional disincentive to climbers. Though nearly all the surviving lengths of precinct wall (Photograph 3) are made of stone (this being the commonest building material), one or two consist of brick, as at Thornton.

As would be expected, the precinct wall was normally continuous between gatehouses, gateways and various buildings such as the conventual church that may have been placed on the perimeter of the precinct, the masonry of the wall normally being keyed-in at the points of meeting with such buildings. Though in many cases the precinct wall has been removed, there are several surviving instances where the meeting-points between gatehouse and wall may still be seen, for example at Battle, Malling and Maxstoke.

Though most precinct walling has been dismantled and removed for use as a convenient supply of post-Dissolution construction material, at a number of sites both large and small some excellent lengths may still be seen. Of houses with large precincts, Battle possesses a long portion of 700ft. (Midmer, 1979, p. 60). This is on the north side where it screened the post-Dissolution mansion, unlike the wall on the other side which was pulled down probably to permit views of the parkland from the house. There are also substantial sections of precinct wall at Bury St Edmunds to the north and east of the site, the wall at one place actually being carried over the River Lark on the thirteenth-century Abbot's Bridge.

Five further examples of a monastic house with long lengths of precinct wall still visible are the rural houses of Beauvale in Nottinghamshire, Fountains in Yorkshire, Maxstoke in Warwickshire, Penmon in Anglesey and Pluscarden in Morayshire where the wall in each case seems to have been retained mostly for fencing the fields. Boxley in Kent also possesses much of its boundary wall, though substantial portions are tumbled down. At Repton in Derbyshire, the precinct wall passes through much of the small town.

Several cathedral-priories converted to secular cathedral status immediately after the Dissolution also have kept much of their precinct walling, no doubt to protect their reorganised closes. Canterbury, Winchester and Worcester exemplify this continuing usage.

In what we must assume was a relatively small number of instances, the precinct wall was made considerably higher than normal, about 15–20 feet. One reason for this was seemingly to deter people not only from climbing over the wall but to stop them from looking into the monastery from high ground beyond the precinct. This is illustrated at Bruton in Somerset, where to the west of the parish church in the street called Plox is a short length of high and buttressed precinct wall placed in the valley between the abbey site to the south and the town to the north, both abbey and town standing on rising ground.

The extra-high precinct wall sometimes crowned with a wall-walk instead of a simple cope-stone, was more a feature of the monastery that was specially fortified. Such a wall would have been equipped with architectural features of a military type, installed not just for show but to deter potential aggressors in districts where law and order was weak. A rare surviving instance in the British Isles of a fortified monastery is provided by Ewenny Priory in South Wales where the precinct wall, as high and as strong as the curtain wall of a castle, runs between towers and gatehouses. Similarly a need to protect the Carmelite Friary of Hulne near Alnwick in Northumberland also resulted in a specially strong precinct wall. Today this wall, which still envelops the friary, is lower than formerly owing to the removal of the parapet which protected its wall-walk.

At Tynemouth the priory was constructed within the bailey of a castle and was protected by walls which it shared with its castle. Chester Abbey, reconstituted as a cathedral in 1541, was sited in the north-east quarter of the city. Its precinct is still partially surrounded by the massive city wall complete with wall-walk and parapet which in earlier days must have doubled as a precinct wall for the abbey.

Probably the best two surviving examples of a high-standing precinct wall are found at York St Mary's Abbey and St Andrews Cathedral-Priory. New (1985, p. 463) claims the St Mary's wall to be the most complete to survive in England, and he is probably correct in respect of the larger houses. Some portions of this precinct wall rise to a height of perhaps 20 feet. They are provided with loopholes and have a wall-walk and parapet. Unquestionably the wall at St Andrews, restored and probably heightened in the sixteenth century, offers a Scottish equivalent to that at York. The surviving wall is punctuated with 13 towers and 4 portals, these being embellished with coats of arms and niches for statues and equipped with loopholes.

FUNCTIONS OF THE MONASTIC PORTAL

Regulatory
The chief purpose of a portal was to act as a two-way regulatory device, namely to control the entry and exit of people, animals and vehicles. 'People' in this context refers to three main categories of individual: members of the religious community living in the abbey or priory, servants and tradesmen, and visitors and guests. 'Animals' includes draught and mounted horses, and other farm animals such as milking cows, hens and the like. The term 'vehicles' is restricted to farm-carts and litters.

In many gatehouses, often of the larger kind as at Battle, the ground-floor area was divided into two parallel sections or passages running through the building from the front to the rear. This arrangement filtered the traffic, facilitating the movement through one section of pedestrians, and through the other section vehicular or mounted travellers. In other gatehouses a common passage sufficed for all types of traffic, such as at Usk.

Symbolic
A secondary function of the gatehouse was to impress on all visitors and travellers an awareness of the power and authority of the monastery. A gatehouse normally stood on the boundary of the precinct where it afforded a first sighting of

the monastic buildings. Thus its front elevation was often of a striking architectural design, reinforced with appropriate embellishments such as ecclesiastical symbols and coats of arms (as at Kirkham) that would instantly convey a visual message both religious and secular signifying the importance and status of the house.

Defensive
Not infrequently the abbey or priory portal was equipped with military features such as battlements (e.g. Bristol, Pentney). Such features served several purposes: not only did they transmit even stronger visual messages (for instance messages conveying a sense of awe) to approaching visitors and travellers, thereby helping to deter potential attackers or rioters, but additionally they provided a practical defensive capability if or when a forced entry into the precinct were attempted. The Great Gate at Bury St Edmunds which was constructed in the mid-fourteenth century, was the direct outcome of a response of the abbot to a history of violence including rioting on the part of the townspeople. It was equipped with loopholes and a portcullis which could have been used in an emergency.

Accommodatory
The siting of a portal at the boundary of the precinct of an abbey or priory made such a location ideal for various types of accommodation (especially for the gatekeeper or porter), accommodation which could not suitably or conveniently be provided in the heart of the precinct or for that matter, at a location beyond the precinct boundary. Therefore accommodation placed at the side of a portal probably preceeded the traditional design of the monastic gatehouse, in which the gateway and associated accommodation were planned and constructed as a single entity.

TYPES OF PORTAL

At this point it is necessary to distinguish between several of the terms, we have been using or will use later. For convenience the word 'portal' is used *generically* to cover all the different types of entrance to a monastic precinct, namely 'gatehouse', 'gate-tower', 'gateway', 'porch-tower', 'water-gate', 'cemetery gate' and 'postern'. As we shall show, the first four types of portal listed above display differences in design (Figure 4), while the last three are defined in terms of their topographical location and may exist as gateways or gatehouses.

Numerically speaking the **gatehouse** is the most common surviving type of monastic portal. Apart from the porch-tower which rivals it closely in design, it is the most interesting type of portal to examine. Constructed as a single building, the gatehouse normally consisted of two to four storeys. In its simplest form, seen for instance at Usk (Photograph 4), it comprised a wide passageway constructed at ground-floor level above which was a first-floor chamber entered via a spiral stairway at the side. The gatehouse passageway, or gate-hall as we should properly call it, traversed it from front to back. In roomier gatehouses the gate-hall occupied some of the ground-floor area only, the remainder of this area being taken up by a wing or extension on one side (e.g. Blanchland, Wetheral) or on both sides (e.g. Bridlington, Thornton) of the gate-hall. The wing (or wings) of the gatehouse would normally be occupied at the level of each storey by accommodation which extended over the gate-hall too.

The gate-hall and its storeys directly overhead may be called the main section of the gatehouse, to distinguish it from its wing or wings. Architecturally, the main section and wing(s) comprise a single structural and visual entity.

Sometimes the gatehouse had ranges (as opposed to wings) placed on one or both sides. These ranges were long buildings, normally with distinctive architectural identities compared with those of the gatehouse proper (such as different-shaped roofs or windows, or constructed of different materials, and so on), such as at Abingdon and St Osyth. Occasionally, as at Cirencester and Glastonbury, the accommodation was restricted to one side of the gate-hall instead of being placed on one side and 'spread' over the gate-hall.

A variation of the gatehouse is the **gate-tower** which survives in its pure form at a number of Oxford and Cambridge secular colleges but at only one monastic college,

GATEWAY

One-storeyed portal joined to precinct-wall; no overhead accommodation; single (or double) archway, with no gate-hall.

GATEHOUSE

Normally free-standing, but joined to flanking precinct-wall; accommodation mostly overhead; front & rear archways separated by gate-hall.

GATE-TOWER

High, typically of three or four storeys; flanked by lower ranges to sides; gate-hall with front & rear archways.

PORCH-TOWER

Two-, three- or occasionally four-storeyed building joined to main range at rear, to which access is afforded via rear archway in porch-hall.

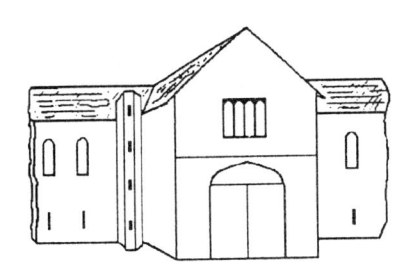

Figure 4   Types of Portal

the former Cistercian St Bernard's College, Oxford (now St John's College). The gate-tower (fifteenth century) which led from the street into a court, was essentially a portal with a tower constructed of several storeys over the gate-hall. Flanked on either side by lower buildings or ranges, the three-storeyed gate-tower at Oxford comprises the middle section of one of the four sets of buildings placed round a quadrangle or square court. Another instance of the gate-tower in its purest form is that built in the sixteenth century at Morwell, a monastic grange and out-of-town residence of the abbot of Tavistock.

Occasionally, the term gate-tower is used less precisely to describe a few of the gatehouses characterised by their height and bulk rather than their breadth, such as the St James' Tower (1120–48) at Bury St Edmunds, the Edgar Tower (early fourteenth century) at Worcester and the gatehouse (*c*.1395) at Michelham.

Besides being expensive to construct, gatehouses often took up much space, a difficulty that needed to be avoided in towns. Probably for these reasons the more utilitarian (though not necessarily unadorned) **gateway** was favoured by many houses. Such a structure normally consisted of an archway with flanking walls which were sometimes buttressed. This type of portal had the advantage of being sparing with the amount of land it occupied from front to back, as would not have been the case with a halled gatehouse.

Urban friaries, which were often poor and located on small or awkward sites on the edges of cities or towns, seem to have favoured such portals. King's Lynn, for example, retains two gateways: in design, the Augustinian Friary fifteenth-century gateway is the simpler of the two with a plain arch now bricked up, while the Whitefriars' gateway of the late fourteenth century possesses a more elaborate structure including three niches for statues. At Dunwich in Suffolk, where the town has long vanished, the Greyfriars possesses a third example of an urban gateway. What makes this last portal (late fourteenth/early fifteenth century) particularly interesting is that it has two entrances side by side, one for pedestrians and the other for vehicular or mounted traffic.

Further instances of gateways are found at Chester where two, the Little Abbey Gateway (fifteenth century) and the

Kaleyards Gate (of uncertain date), exist in addition to the main gatehouse, and at Dunster where there are two of late medieval date. The early sixteenth-century inner portal of the London Charterhouse, which consists of a brick arch only, may possibly have been part of a gatehouse later destroyed, as almost certainly happened at the entrance to Repton School where there is another archway (of late thirteenth-century date). Somewhat more elaborate are two gateways at Winchester and Peterborough. The fifteenth-century Prior's Gate at Winchester continues to provide an entrance to the cathedral precinct, and has the recent distinction of being decorated with the Royal arms of the present queen. At Peterborough is the richly decorated Prior's Gateway (1510) situated at the north-west corner of the cathedral.

All the above portals may be described as peripheral as they were inserted in a precinct wall or, occasionally, placed between other buildings in order to control movements between the exterior and a great court (e.g. Bromfield, Letheringham) or an outer and inner court (e.g. the fifteenth-century inner gatehouse at Aylesford, the fifteenth-century Inner Gate at Gloucester or the late thirteenth-century Abbot's Gatehouse at Peterborough). There is, however, another group of portals which are not peripheral and this group will now be identified.

As its name implies, the **porch-tower** was built as an entrance to a second building, this usually being the abbot's lodging. More commonly constructed in the later medieval period, the porch-tower consisted of two or more storeys of which the ground-floor storey provided a passage to the parent building which stood immediately behind it. Nearly always adorned with coats of arms, friezes and oriel-windows and so on, in general appearance it was like a gatehouse except for one important difference. Unlike a gatehouse which had free access to its front and rear, the porch-tower was joined at its rear to the parent building. Moreover, as it provided a main entrance for guests and other important visitors to the domestic accommodation which lay immediately beyond it, it did not afford vehicular access through its passageway or porch-hall.

The majority of surviving porch-towers are found in the south-west of England, with the most handsome of all,

Abbot Chard's Tower at Forde, built immediately before the Dissolution, in 1528. The slightly earlier porch-tower of $c.1500$ at Cerne is also handsome, though not quite as fine as that at Forde. The abbot's lodging which lay to the rear of the porch-tower at Cerne has been pulled down, and it is now possible to see the broken masonry at the rear of the porch-tower showing where it was joined to the lodging.

Three other towers, also in the south-west of England, fit into the porch-tower mould, though the evidence for their inclusion in our list is not clear cut in every case. These towers are at Torre, Exeter St Nicholas and Buckfast. Plainer than the Forde and Cerne towers, they are all sited on the west side of the west range to which they are (or were) joined. The fifteenth-century Torre tower with four storeys, an embattled parapet and west doorway, fits the general porch-tower pattern convincingly. At Exeter St Nicholas the three-storey tower (late fifteenth to early sixteenth century) was erected primarily to give additional access to the upper rooms of the west range of the priory. There is evidence at ground-floor level of an exterior doorway on the west side of the tower, evidence which would reinforce its claim to be a porch-tower. Whether the ground floor of the four-storeyed fourteenth-century Abbot's Tower at Buckfast ever served as a porch is uncertain.

Several other porch-towers deserve mention. A fine specimen survives in its entirety at Saighton Grange which belonged to Chester Abbey (now the cathedral). The three-storeyed porch of $c.1490$ is now attached to a Victorian building which probably replaced the medieval grange. The late fifteenth-century porch-tower which belonged to Leiston abbey in Suffolk was attached to the west range. Though ruined, it retains one of two flanking turrets. Much of Castle Acre priory in Norfolk was destroyed at the Dissolution, but part of the west range, which included the prior's lodging, was spared. In the usual position to the west of the range the porch-tower still stands. Built towards the beginning of the sixteenth century as a replacement for a smaller late twelfth-century inner porch which is hidden behind it, it consists of two storeys and is entered in the usual manner from the west.

The entrance to the abbot's lodging (erroneously called the Bishop's Lodging) at St Osyth in Essex has much in common with the above porch-towers. Although the building that stands behind it was rebuilt in the nineteenth century, the front façade is original and is dated 1527. At ground-floor level it possesses a great archway for vehicular entry which is flanked by two smaller archways for pedestrians. These archways, with a magnificent oriel above, form the central section of the front façade which, though not constituting the front of a semi-detached tower, may have originally led into a porch.

By no means were all portals fronted by dry land. As indicated earlier, the boundaries of a number of monastic precincts were defined by river banks, and these provided useful barriers against unauthorised entry. The **watergate**, therefore, was a type of peripheral portal which faced a river or estuary, and which in response to the security requirements of a monastic house could have been designed as a gatehouse or gateway. Several watergates have survived, including one at Waltham in Essex which displays a typically close relationship with its river. Built towards the latter end of the fourteenth century, this portal (which is incomplete and originally may have been provided with accompanying accommodation) is approached from its front over a fourteenth-century bridge. In effect, the latter serves as an apron immediately in front of the two archways leading into the building. Another instance of a watergate is provided at Pull's Ferry near Norwich, where there is a two-arched specimen of the fifteenth century. The gatehouse at Michelham commanded the entry to a moated priory. Though it is now approached over a bridge, there is evidence indicating that its apron was occupied in medieval times by a drawbridge. The remnant of a watergate may be seen at Cleeve where the jambs only of the front single archway of what constituted an outer portal may be seen in walling close to the river. Worcester possesses a watergate attributable to the fifteenth century. This consists of two storeys of which the upper has been rebuilt since the Dissolution. This watergate stands back from the river from which it is separated by a wharf which must have permitted docking in medieval times. The abbey of York St Mary possesses the remains of a late fifteenth-century watergate of which one wall only is standing.

The **cemetery gate**, also peripheral, was a portal that controlled the admission of lay people to the lay cemetery and was probably kept shut at night-time. It was normally situated on the north side of the conventual church, that is, on the side opposite to where the claustral buildings were placed. It sometimes also led to a church located in the monastic precinct reserved exclusively for worship by lay-people.

A few such gateways and gatehouses have survived the Dissolution. Ely possesses the Steeple Gate (mainly *c.*1500) which stands to the north of the nave of the cathedral and originally led to the now-demolished church of All Saints and its churchyard. A cemetery gate of more modest appearance stands to the south of the close and churchyard of Gloucester Cathedral. This fifteenth-century gatehouse formerly led to the lay cemetery on the south side of the abbey church, the claustral buildings being located less commonly to the north. This portal, known as St Michael's Gate, also afforded entry to the shrine of Edward II. A gatehouse of much earlier origin at Evesham leads from the north side of the precinct into a churchyard still occupied by two churches for lay people. These churches stand immediately to the north of the site of the conventual church which has long disappeared. The gatehouse is one of the oldest monastic portals to survive in the country, having a lower portion which dates from *c.*1139/1143.

Two other existing cemetery gates pose problems. At the west end of Tavistock Parish Church is the church tower, which unusually possesses large early fourteenth-century arches north and south at ground-floor level. It has been suggested that the lower stage of the tower was originally the cemetery gate which led from the north into the lay cemetery, which was situated between the abbey church to the south and the parish church further north. Whether or not the tower had ever been a cemetery gate must remain a matter of conjecture. The second is the early fourteenth-century cemetery gate at Furness, a Cistercian abbey. Now a ruin of medium height, it is located to the north-east of the conventual church which never, as far as is known, provided facilities for worship for the laity. As the cemetery gate led from inside the abbey precinct to the monks' cemetery rather than to a lay cemetery, the reason for its construction must remain obscure. Possibly, it enabled lay relatives to visit monks' graves.

A small gateway leading into or out of the rear or side of a monastic precinct is known as a **postern** or, sometimes, postern-gate. Normally inserted into the precinct wall, it would provide a short cut from a court to the exterior. A good example is found at Chester to the north-east of the abbey church (now the cathedral church) where, still in use, a postern placed in the city wall permitted the monks to tend their vegetable garden, the Kaleyards, situated beyond the wall. Two others exist, having fifteenth-century broken arches. One is at Bury St Edmunds at the south-east of the precinct and the other is at Coventry Charterhouse. Two small posterns (late thirteenth/early fourteenth century) may be seen at Battle in the precinct wall, one close to the parish church and the other nearer the gatehouse.

Other locations of monastic portals
The majority of peripheral portals were placed at the boundary of the monastic precinct, a boundary usually occupied by a wall, while a smaller number were placed between buildings, but isolated instances occur of portals placed elsewhere. At the priory of King's Lynn the main section of a two-storeyed fifteenth-century gatehouse forms part of a medieval south range now converted into a row of domestic dwellings. Possibly before the Dissolution, this gatehouse shared the south range with a refectory. A gatehouse at Caldey, probably dating from the thirteenth century, forms part of the west range of the small monastery established on that island.

Apart from the Saighton Grange porch-tower, further examples may be identified of portals constructed in outlying monastic property. Tisbury in Wiltshire is the location of Place Farm, formerly a grange which belonged to Shaftesbury Abbey. It possesses two gatehouses (Pevsner and Cherry, 1975, p. 523) of which at least one dates from the late fifteenth century. Leigh, near Churchstow in Devon, which was the grange of Buckfast Abbey, retains a remarkable two-storeyed gatehouse probably built in the fifteenth century.

False portals
One or two surviving gatehouses found on monastic sites are not genuine. The gatehouse which is located to the west of Smithfield St Bartholomew's Church in London is not a medieval structure. It was assembled after the Dissolution as a three-and-a-half-storey portal with picturesque half-timbering in the upper sections. The ground-level storey made use of the four-ordered south entrance to the west end of the medieval nave. Some of this stone fabric is *in situ*, dating from the thirteenth century.

Another building which may not be authentic is the outer portal at Wigmore. Placed at a distance to the west of the abbey church, the fourteenth-century portal now consists of two detached portions separated by a carriageway. However, New (1985, p. 451) suggests that the present structure may be the product of having broken the carriageway through a single building.

At least two gatehouses (at Merevale and Whitby) were built or totally reconstructed in the nineteenth century. That at Merevale, which was designed by Henry Clutton, is described as being 'so intensely medieval that it is at once recognised as Victorian' (Pevsner and Wedgwood, 1966, p. 353). Its position next to a *capella-ante-portas*, now a parish church, suggests that it may have been built on the site of a former gatehouse. At Whitby, however, the gatehouse, also built in the nineteenth century, almost certainly does stand on the site of the medieval portal.

THE MONASTIC VERSUS THE MILITARY PORTAL

We conclude this first chapter by briefly comparing the monastic portal with the military portal (including castle portals, and civic portals such as city and town gates), with particular reference to basic design and layout, defensive features and devices and ornamentation, and accommodation, topics that in respect of monastic portals will be subsequently dealt with in greater detail.

Basic design and layout
Superficially, portals placed at the entrances to monastic

properties tended to resemble those leading into castles or inserted into city and town walls, some architectural features being common to both types of portal (e.g. large, heavy gates hung within large arches, the latter flanked by tall walls or turrets, etc.). Such comparisons are, however, misleading as, apart from a relatively small number of instances located in militarily unstable areas such as Northumberland, the monastic portal generally served a somewhat different purpose from the military structure and almost always had a more refined design.

Gatehouses and gateways placed at the entrances to castles were primarily designed and operated to exercise control over entry, that is, to scrutinise the credentials of all those who sought admittance, to filter such applicants, and if necessary to repel with force those who tried to storm the gates. Only secondarily were such portals concerned with exit control. The portals of castles (and to a lesser extent the portals of cities and towns) were therefore designed as strongpoints. They had their main architectural features such as turrets, and key military devices such as loopholes and machicolations, normally placed at the front to discourage potential attackers or repel actual attackers.

In what respects did the monastic portal differ? The essential difference is that a monastery was a place of peace and tranquility where men or women had freely chosen to live their lives as members of a religious community. Having made this choice and taken their vows, they were no longer free to follow their private inclinations or whims. Only when granted permission were they able to enter or leave the abbey or priory precinct. Apart from a few exceptions, the religious portal did not possess military features and overtly defensive devices. More than the military portal, the typical monastic portal was designed to regulate traffic in both directions.

Defensive features and devices, and ornamentation
For protection military portals were always strengthened with major architectural features such as drum-towers, drawbridges and barbicans, and equipped with a panoply of defensive devices – battlements, loopholes, machicolations, murder-holes, portcullises and the like. Such architectural features and devices were normally arrayed facing outwards

in order to defend and protect the interior of the castle, city or town; they were not usually placed in a reverse position, that is to say, to prevent breakouts.

Intended to intimidate onlookers and to engender feelings of fear, awe and respect, the front façades of military and civic portals were often made to look grim. Hence the frequent placement of regal statues and symbols such as the crown and the portcullis emblem on the exterior, the use of iron studs on doors, and iron spikes on parapets from which the heads of executed criminals could be, and often were, displayed.

It was not customary to provide monastic portals with such architectural features and defensive devices. The twin drum-towers of the military portal displayed, for example, at Kidwelly in Carmarthenshire (Photograph 5) were a conspicuous feature of many castles; their absence from monasteries is total (unless the precinct wall drum-towers on either side of the Teinds Yett at St Andrews are counted as an exception). That some monastic gatehouses and gateways were crowned with battlements, a military device, is not significant any more than that many parapets on roofs of aisles, clerestories and towers of conventual churches were decorated with battlements. However, there were a few gatehouses that for local reasons were given additional protection: examples include the gatehouse at Alnwick, the Great Gate of Bury St Edmunds and the gatehouse of Michelham.

Monastic gatehouses generally were highly ornamented and well windowed. Many were emblazoned with the arms of the abbey or priory and of the founder, benefactors and other prominent individuals, and possessed exteriors enriched with the statues of saints and kings, the purpose of which was to engender awe, wonder and respect but not fear. Because of the two-way regulatory function, it is no coincidence that some gatehouses were emblazoned and ornamented as much on their rear as on their front façades (e.g. Bristol). Unlike military portals, many monastic gatehouses were given large front windows including oriels that enhanced their decorative appearance (but not, it must be noted, their defensive potential).

Accommodation
Manned by soldiers, the military gatehouse frequently possessed accommodation in the form of barrack-rooms, guardrooms and prison cells, and had a winch-room over the great gate from which the drawbridge and portcullis could be raised or lowered. In contrast, a monastic gatehouse was normally manned by a civilian porter or gatekeeper who would have an office next to the gate-hall at ground-floor level, and often living accommodation elsewhere in the building. Only exceptionally (as at Bridlington) was a prison or guardroom placed in a monastic gatehouse.

2

PRECINCT AND PORTAL LOCATION

THE STANDARD PRECINCT PLAN

The location of a chief portal (normally a gatehouse) and other portals of a monastery depended on the arrangement of the main buildings. With most abbeys and priories this arrangement, which had become standardised early in the history of the monastic movement, was determined mainly by the availability of water and, associated with this, the proximity of gently rising ground.

Water supply
Religious communities of all orders had learnt early in their history the importance to health of an abundant supply of clean water that could be channelled to enter the precinct and made available to the kitchen, lavatorium and reredorter. Spent or unclean water from these places had moreover to be collected and discharged from the monastic precinct, ideally the exit from the monastic premises being as far away as possible from the entry of the fresh water.

Rising ground
As water runs downhill, clearly the exit point was always lower than the entry, the fall of a few feet distributed across the precinct being taken into account and allowed for by planners.

There was another factor which also affected the arrangement of buildings, and this was the need to direct as much sunlight as possible into the cloister-walks, that is, the areas where the monks or nuns spent most of their waking hours.

For this important reason, the high-walled conventual church would normally be placed to the north of the cloister where it would not cast a shadow across the cloister-garth and walks, while the other main buildings – chapter-house, dormitory, refectory and cellarium – were sited round the other three sides. The chapter-house and dormitory were usually accommodated in the east range, the refectory in the south range, and the cellarium in the west range. To make the greatest use of the sunlight that could enter the claustral area and to facilitate ground drainage generally, a site was usually chosen where the surface of the precinct gently fell from north to south.

In summary, the standard site was therefore characterised by a fall from the upstream (entry) side of the monastery to the downstream (exit) side, coupled with a fall from north to south.

By placing the reredorter at the south-east corner of the claustral area next to the dormitory, and the kitchen at the south-west corner at the angle between the west range and the refectory, it became possible to maximise the use of fresh water entering the precinct. The normal practice therefore in selecting a site for a new monastery was to find a suitable area across which a river or stream ran from west to east and where a sizeable apron of land on the north bank rose gently to the north.

In keeping with this general arrangement, the great court of the monastery together with all the service facilities that lay around it such as stabling, workshops, brewery, granary and so on, was placed on the west side of the cloister, that is, away from the monks' domestic quarters which were placed on the east side.

PORTAL LOCATION

The great court determined the location of what in many monastic houses was the chief (or only) portal of the establishment, this entrance leading into the court on the west side of the precinct. Rarely was this portal positioned to the east. In the few cases where it was, the monastic layout did not conform to the standard model. At Worcester, for instance, where the River Severn bounds the west side, the great court lies to the south of the cloister and the main portal to the east of this court. The south-east siting of the chief portal at Durham is similar to that at Worcester, the River Wear passing by the cathedral site on its west side. A third example of the main portal placed to the east is provided by Tavistock where the river runs on the south side but from east to west, with the west and east claustral ranges in a reversed position.

An examination of some monastic sites to establish the most favoured locations and orientation of peripheral portals
In order to carry forward the present study, a number of monastic sites were investigated. Nearly all of them possess portals that survive in varying conditions ranging from 'complete and unaltered' to 'fragmentary' (see Chapter 6 for an explanation of these descriptions). Moreover, it has been possible to record the location of each of these portals in relation to that of their conventual churches, and their orientation.

In this study a total of 109 monastic sites were examined. These included 81 sites each with one known peripheral portal, and 28 where there were two or more known peripheral portals. Altogether 148 such portals were identified at these sites.

How was this sample selected? As many as possible portals of all kinds in England, Scotland and Wales were visited and their data evaluated. Some small groups of peripheral portals were discounted from the sample, as follows: all *cemetery gates* (e.g. at Barking, Furness) were excluded as this particular type of portal facilitating the entry of lay people into their own cemetery had a specialised function, the location not being necessarily linked to the typical monastic plan; *small gateways* (e.g. at Battle), seemingly unimportant, were also left out. Where *watergates* (as at Norwich and Worcester) were sited on or near the bank of a river or stream which determined their location, they were also excluded; but where they were placed in an artificial location such as fronting a moat (e.g. Michelham) they were included. A small number of other peripheral gatehouses (such as at Cerne, Kingswood and Wetheral) which otherwise would have met the requirements of the survey were not included because the precise location of the conventual church was not known or available. Lastly three portals (at Broomholm, Holyrood and Pluscarden) were not included because the appropriate data was not available at the time of writing.

Apart from these portals, at a small number of sites a well-documented portal has disappeared (e.g. the Reading outer and Bordesley gatehouses). As with the surviving portals, however, the location and orientation of this small group of destroyed portals is known, and such data has also been included in this study. Altogether, the sample includes approximately three-quarters of all the known peripheral portals.

By gathering evidence on the ground and to a lesser extent by relying on recorded information, it was possible to analyse these 148 peripheral portals and see whether there were any recurrent patterns in their location and orientation. This work involved:

a) identifying each portal by *name*;
b) placing each portal into one of three categories of *distance* as measured from the closest point of the conventual church, the categories being (1) 0–50 yards ('near'), (2) 51–100 yards ('middle'), and (3) 101 or more yards ('distant');
c) estimating the approximate *bearing* of each portal to the nearest 45° (namely, 'north-east', 'south', etc.) from the closest point of the conventual church;
d) calculating the approximate *orientation* of each portal, the product of an axis drawn through a portal from front to rear and given to the nearest 45° angle and expressed in terms of the points of the compass (e.g. 's–n' means that the orientation was along a south–north line with entry to the precinct through the portal in that direction; similarly, 'nw–se' indicates that the orientation was diagonal with entry from the north-west through the portal to the south-east).

The position of the cloister, south or north, in relation to the conventual church was an important consideration in the placing of portals. A total of 92 houses had their cloisters situated to the south of the conventual church. However, a small number (17) had their cloisters placed on the north side (Bury St Edmunds, Canterbury Christ Church, Canterbury St Augustine's, Chertsey, Chester, Cirencester, Dover, Gloucester, Lacock, Letheringham, London Charterhouse, Maxstoke, Minster-in-Sheppey, Mount Grace, Repton, St Osyth and Worksop). Arguably, Cartmel might have been added to this list as its claustral buildings, originally on the south side, were reconstructed on the north side in the early part of the fifteenth century.

The identity of the portals of these 'north' houses are shown in Figure 5 in boxes. In order to make their location and so on comparable with those of the houses with southerly cloisters, they have been allotted 'mirrored' positions and treated in the survey as if their parent houses were southerly ones. For example, at Cirencester there was a north cloister (now vanished) with a gatehouse (still standing) located beyond the site of the cloister further to the north, with entry to the precinct from north to south. This gatehouse is therefore shown in Figure 5 as a 'south' portal placed at the same distance from the conventual church as it actually is on the north side. Moreover, its entry is indicated as from south to north.

However not every portal of a 'north' house is necessarily affected as completely as the Cirencester gatehouse. Where a portal (e.g. Dover) is located to the west of its conventual church, that is, along the latter's west–east axis, its placement in the figure is unchanged though its entry is shown as being from north to south rather than from the actual south to north. At Chester, where there is a north cloister, its gatehouse, which is located to the north-west of the precinct, is placed in a south-west 'mirrored' position in the figure, but as entry is from west to east and thus unaffected by whether a cloister is on the north or south side of the conventual church, its orientation remains unchanged in the figure.

Summarised in Figure 6 the 148 portals looked at as a whole display a remarkably clear pattern. This is that the largest group (43) are located directly to the west of the conventual church, and somewhat smaller groups to the north-west and south-west (32 and 26 in each group

north   TOTAL=18

8	n-s 6; ne-sw 1; ni 1.
4	n-s 3; ne-sw 1.
6	n-s 4; w-e 1; s-n 1.

North-west   TOTAL=32

9	n-s 4; nw-se 2; w-e 1; ne-sw 1; ni 1.
13	n-s 8; nw-se 3; w-e 2;

North-east   TOTAL=1

NIL

NIL

10	n-s 7; w-e 1; ne-sw 2.

| | n-s 1. | 1 |

West   TOTAL=43

| 15 | nw-se 1; w-e 11; sw-ne 1; s-n 1; ni 1. | 12 | n-s 3; nw-se 1; w-e 8. | 16 | n-s 15; w-e 1. |

| | n-s 1. | 1 | NIL | NIL |

East   TOTAL=1

7	n-s 4; w-e 3;

| nw-se 1; w-e 1; s-n 2. | NIL |

| | ne-sw 1. | 1 |

8	n-s 1; w-e 4; sw-ne 1; s-n 1; e-w 1.

| | s-n 3; e-w 3; ne-sw 1. | 7 |

11	w-e 4; sw-ne 1; s-n 5; ni 1.

South-west   TOTAL=26

South-east   TOTAL=8

4	sw-ne 1; s-n 4; se-nw 1; e-w 1.
7	nw-se 1; w-e 2; sw-ne 2; s-n 3;
8	

south   TOTAL=19

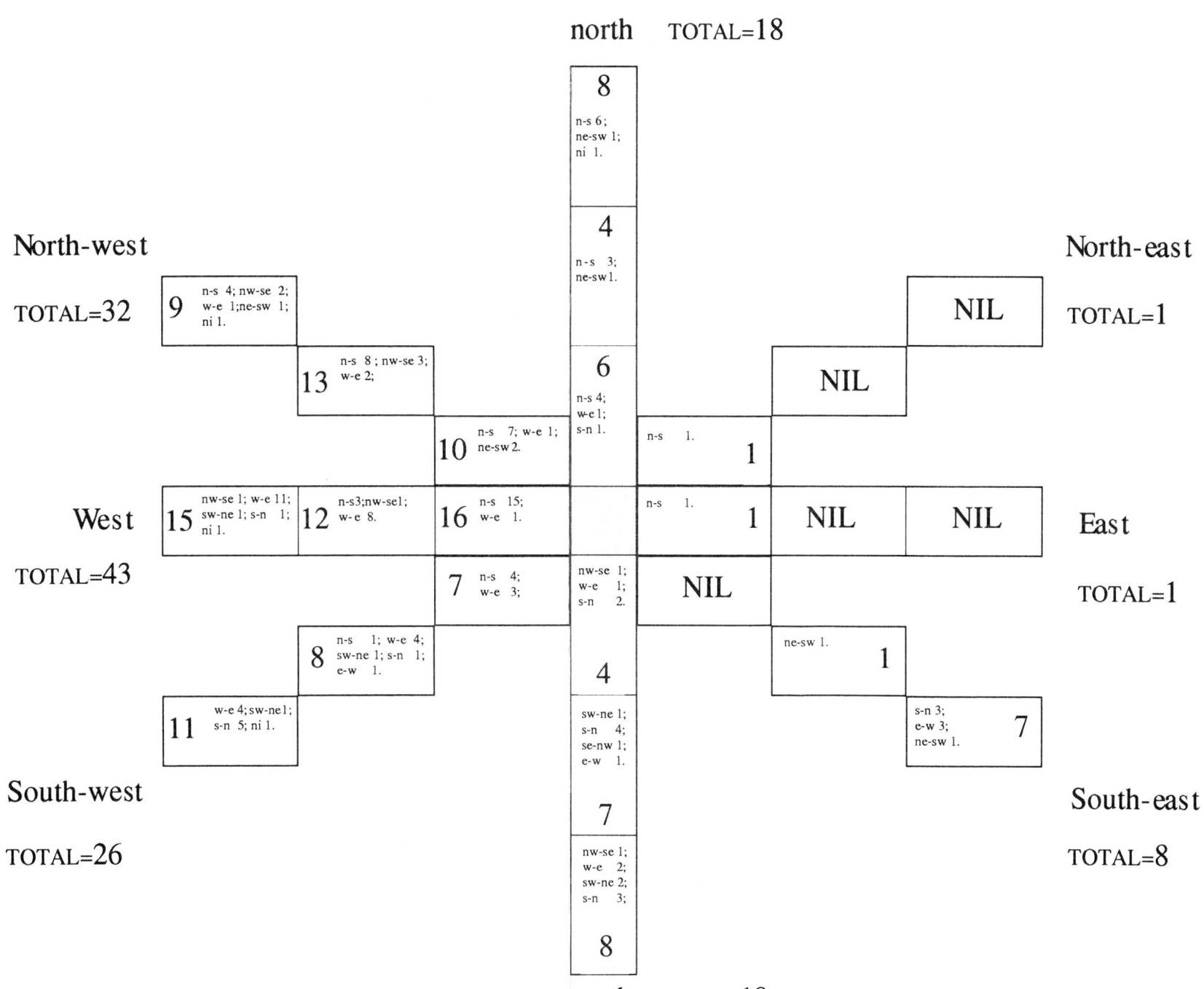

Figure 6   Summary of Locations of Portals

	North-east	North	North-west	West	South-west	South	South-east	East
NEAR < 51 yards	WHALLEY inr n-s	ALNWICK n-s AYLESFORD otr n-s ELY sacr n-s PETERBORO' prs s-n ROCHESTER sxy w-e st osyth grt n-s	ABBOTSBURY otr n-s FORDE n-s LEICESTER n-s letheringham n-s LEWES n-s london chse. inr ne-sw london chse. otr ne-sw MALLING w-e repton n-s WHITBY n-s	AYLESFORD inr n-s ARBROATH n-s BLANCHLAND n-s BURNHAM NTN. w-e BRECON n-s BRISTOL mn n-s dover n-s DUNSTABLE n-s KENILWORTH n-s LANGLEY n-s MALVERN n-s minster-in-shep. n-s PETERBORO' abts n-s READING inr n-s ST ALBANS grt n-s USK n-s	BRISTOL abts w-e chester abb w-e CROSSRAGUEL n-s ELY plce n-s LINDISFARNE w-e S.ANDREWS pds n-s WIGMORE inr n-s	D'NF'ML'NE pds nw-se K'G'S LYN. PRY s-n lacock w-e LINDORES s-n		TAVISTOCK crt n-s
MIDDLE 51 - 100 yards		BRADSOLE nth ne-sw gloucester k edw n-s WALSINGH'M kts n-s worksop n-s	BATTLE nw-se BAYHAM n-s BUCKFAST nth n-s cant'bury cccg nw-se CLEEVE inr n-s EWENNY nth n-s GLASTONB'RY w-e HEXHAM n-s KIRKHAM n-s MICHELHAM nw-se M'K BRETTON n-s mount grace w-e Y'K S. MRY. mg n-s	BROMFIELD w-e bury st ed st j n-s CARLISLE nw-se DUNKESWELL w-e EVESHAM grt w-e GUISBOROUGH n-s NORWICH erp w-e PETERBORO' mn w-e TEWKESBURY n-s TYNEMOUTH w-e WALSINGH'M mn w-e WENLOCK n-s	ABBOTSBURY inr e-w bury st ed sa fnd n-s EWENNY sth s-n gloucester inr n-s gloucester st m w-e HULNE sw sw-ne TAVISTOCK btsy w-e TORRE w-e	cant'bury cc ld s-n cant'bury cc pt se-nw DRYBURGH sw-ne HULNE mn s-n maxstoke inr s-n ROCHESTER prs s-n WORCESTER edg e-w	EASBY ne-sw	
DISTANT > 100 yards		CASTLE ACRE n-s FURNESS inr n-s FURNESS otr ne-sw NEATH ni NORWICH bsps n-s POLESWORTH n-s ST ALBANS wax n-s THETFORD n-s	CLEEVE otr w-e CULROSS n-s KIRKSTALL ne-sw LENTON ni RAMSEY n-s RIEVAULX n-s ROCHE nw-se ST BENET nw-se WEST ACRE n-s	ABINGDON w-e BINHAM sw-ne BORDESLEY w-e BYLAND w-e CALDER w-e CARTMEL s-n C'V'TRYW'FRS w-e COVERHAM w-e DALE ni FOUNTAINS w-e LANERCOST w-e READING otr w-e THORNTON w-e WHALLEY otr w-e WIGMORE otr nw-se	BIEULIEU inr s-n BIEULIEU otr s-n BOLTON w-e BR'DLINGT'N sw-ne BUCKFAST sth s-n bury st ed grt w-e chertsey s-n FURNESS wst w-e JERVAULX ni LLANTHONY s-n NORWICH s eth w-e	cant'bury cc fmn w-se cant'bury cc mg sw-ne cant'bury cc nth sw-ne cirencester s-n ELY prta w-e maxstoke otr s-n S.ANDREWS t yt s-n WINCHESTER w-e	BEAUVALE s-n BRADSOLE se s-n D'NF'ML'NE se s-n DURHAM e-w PETERBORO' se e-w S. ANDREWS s yt e-w Y'K S. MRY pst ne-sw	

N.B. The portals of monasteries with north cloisters are indicated above in lower-case type.

Figure 5 Table of Monastic Portals Showing for each its (a) approximate distance and bearing from the church, and (b) orientation

respectively). The scatter falls off sharply to the north and north-east, and to the south and south-east, while directly east of the church, that is, in line with the choir, only one portal (discussed below) is situated.

We may well ask why this pattern obtains of portals placed overwhelmingly on the west side of monastic precincts rather than the east.

Whalley's inner portal illustrates the disadvantage of placing a gatehouse on the remote (north-east) side of the church, access to the abbot's house to the south-east having to be made round the east end of the choir. Moreover, entry through portals located to the north of the great church meant, as in the cases of Alnwick, Aylesford and St Osyth to name but three, that the west front of the church had to be trekked across in order to get to the great court.

Sometimes a portal placed to the north, north-east, east, south-east or south was provided for a specific, and probably non-standard, purpose. Thus Norwich possesses a north gatehouse which led to the bishop's medieval palace (and which still provides access to his modern house) placed in a remote situation, well away from the area of the great court. Tavistock is the rare instance of a portal (the Town Gate) that stood immediately to the east of the conventual church. This portal gave access to the abbey's great court which, most unusually, occupied the area to the south-east of the east range. Easby and Durham, both with portals situated to the south-east of the conventual church and cloister, also exemplify a non-standard layout of claustral buildings. Yet however exceptional such instances were, the most prevalent pattern involved placing portals near the great court, that is, to the west, north-west and south-west of the conventual church.

The other general feature of the scatter is that there was a tendency as much to set portals well back from the west end of the conventual church and the west range of the claustral buildings, as to set them close to the church. Thus, not including the portals that lay directly to the north or south, 35 were placed in the 'distant' position, 33 in the 'middle' position, and 33 'near' to the church.

What considerations governed the placement of such portals?
The west front of a conventual church was almost always

regarded by its religious community as the chief external feature of the abbey or priory, the part of the monastic complex that was first seen by visitors and guests when approaching the buildings. Take, for example, the effect on viewers that the great west front of Byland or Peterborough must have had. However, placed close to the west front and facing it directly in line with the front's central east–west axis, a portal would have obscured the west front's façade, a situation that would have been made even worse had the portal been flanked by long and high lengths of precinct wall, or by high wings or ranges. There was therefore a good practical reason why, almost always, portals were not placed in line with the middle of the west front to face it closely. Of the portals examined in the sample, only the gatehouse at Burnham Norton is situated close to the west end of the church, with entry through the portal from west to east.

This problem of location was solved in two main ways. One was to set a portal well back from the west front, as in fact was done at nearly all the monasteries with 'middle' and 'distant' gatehouses, especially when made to occupy a central westerly position (e.g. Byland, Walsingham main); alternatively, it was placed some way off to the north-west (e.g. Glastonbury,Thetford) or south-west (e.g. Bridlington, Jervaulx). Another and perhaps more radical solution was to place a portal deliberately near the west front, not centrally but quite close to the north or south corner of the front (e.g. Malvern, Shrewsbury, Usk). In such an off-centre position it would not obtrude on the front's façade as undoubtedly it did at Burnham Norton, where a visitor having passed through the portal would not have had the opportunity of appreciating the visual appearance of the church before entering its west door.

This brings us to consider the orientation of portals. Our study revealed some definite preferences by the monastic planners. By far the greater number of portals were oriented either west–east or occasionally east–west ('facing'), or north–south or south–north ('cross-placed'). Of the 148 portals, 44 were oriented west–east/east–west, and 77, north–south/south–north. This leaves a disparate group of 23 that were diagonally oriented (i.e. north-west–south-east, etc.) or were unable to be categorised owing to a lack of information ('ni').

We also observed that of 45 portals placed in the 'near' location, 35 had north–south or south–north orientations compared with only 7 in the west–east orientation (and none in the east–west orientation); while of 45 in the 'middle' location, 20 were north–south or south–north compared with 16 that were west–east (including 2 that were east–west). When the 'distant' location is examined, the pattern of orientation is seen to be different again. Of 58 portals at this distance, 21 faced west–east (including 3 that were east–west), as opposed to 22 which were oriented north–south or south–north.

The diagonally oriented portals comprised 3 'near' the church, 9 in the 'middle' position and 11 in the 'distant' position, insignificant as far as the total pattern is concerned.

The evidence therefore seems to be quite compelling, namely that close to the conventual church and especially its west front, portals tended to be oriented north–south or south–north, while the further away portals were from the church the more likely they were to be oriented west–east.

The cross-placed portal

As already mentioned, portals of this type tended to be placed adjacent or fairly close to the west front but at right angles to it (Figure 7). Moreover, the south end of the west front was preferred where the entrance would lead directly and immediately into the great court normally placed to the south-west of the conventual church. The north end of the west front was almost never favoured as entrants on horseback or in wagons as well as on foot would have to cross the open ground which lay before the west front. At Whitby Abbey, however, is a nineteenth-century cross-placed gatehouse which is situated at the north-west corner of the church. If, as is likely, it stands on the site of a medieval portal, it may offer a unique example of a portal placed at the 'wrong' end of the west front. It does not, however, offend this principle as the ground drops sharply beyond the west front and the gatehouse is too low to obscure the façade of the church.

Given this placement and orientation of portals at the south end of the west front, to ensure complete privacy and security the precinct wall was made to run a short distance from the south-west corner of the church to the portal and

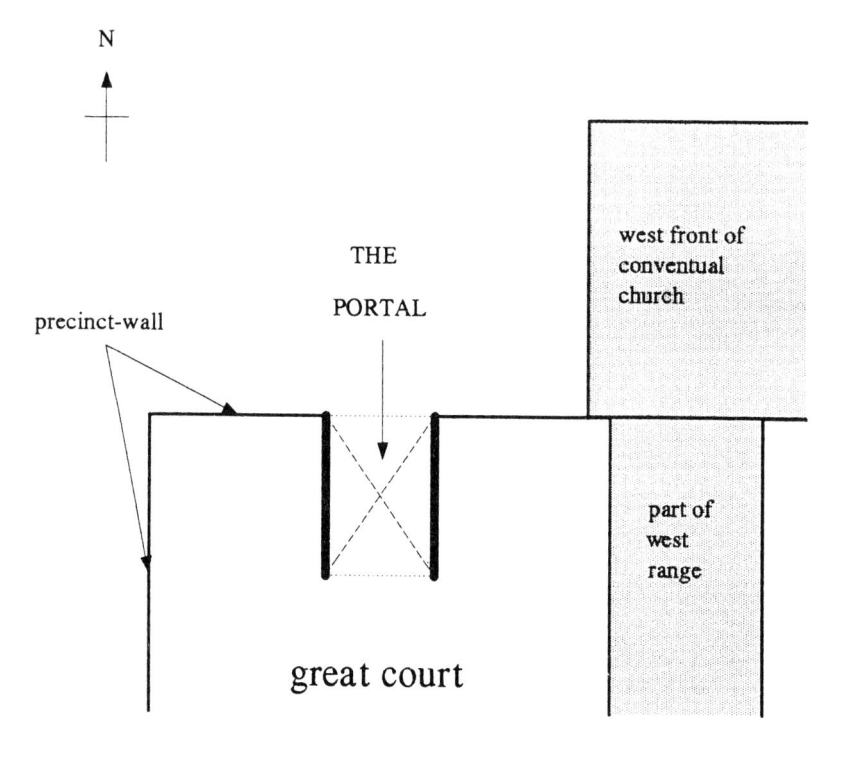

NB In this figure the portal selected for illustration was a gatehouse. It could have been, however, a gateway.

Figure 7 The Cross-placed Portal

then on around the great court. Rarely now is a portal seen to be joined by a short length of precinct wall to the conventual church. One possible instance exists at Usk, where the gatehouse is connected to the church by a length of churchyard wall. Worcester provides another, with some high precinct wall joining the Edgar Tower (main gatehouse) to the cathedral church. A less convincing example may occur at Coventry on the site of the cathedral-priory. Here the cloister was placed to the north of the great church now almost totally destroyed. Immediately to the north-west of the fragmentary west front a short section of walling runs to a jamb which may have belonged to a portal now vanished.

There are a number of examples of monastic sites which display cross-placed portals, nearly all of which we must assume originally led into the great court. Among them are Arbroath, Blanchland, Brecon, Bristol (Abbey Gatehouse), Kenilworth, Malvern, Minster-in-Sheppey and St Albans. Except for that at Brecon which is in the form of a double gateway, all the other portals are gatehouses.

Later in the medieval period the west range was sometimes developed or extended within the great court to form the abbot's or prior's lodging, the cross-placed portal thenceforth serving as an entrance to his quarters, as happened for instance at Gloucester and Peterborough. It is likely in some such cases that the great court's area was redefined with entry provided elsewhere.

The facing portal
In contrast to the cross-placed portal, the facing portal was placed further away from the conventual church, normally to the west or north-west in a 'middle' or 'distant' position. In such a location it would be oriented so that it faced the church, an imaginary straight line through the gate-hall from front to rear extending to the church (Figure 8). When a portal of this kind was placed at a distance on the west side and made to face the west front directly, it must have been quite an experience for travellers or visitors arriving at the gatehouse to see the monastic church before them, framed in the open archway of the gate-hall. As many conventual churches were not open to the public, the view from a facing portal may probably have been the only complete sighting

gatehouse in the
north-west position

or

gatehouse
in the
west position

N

conventual
church

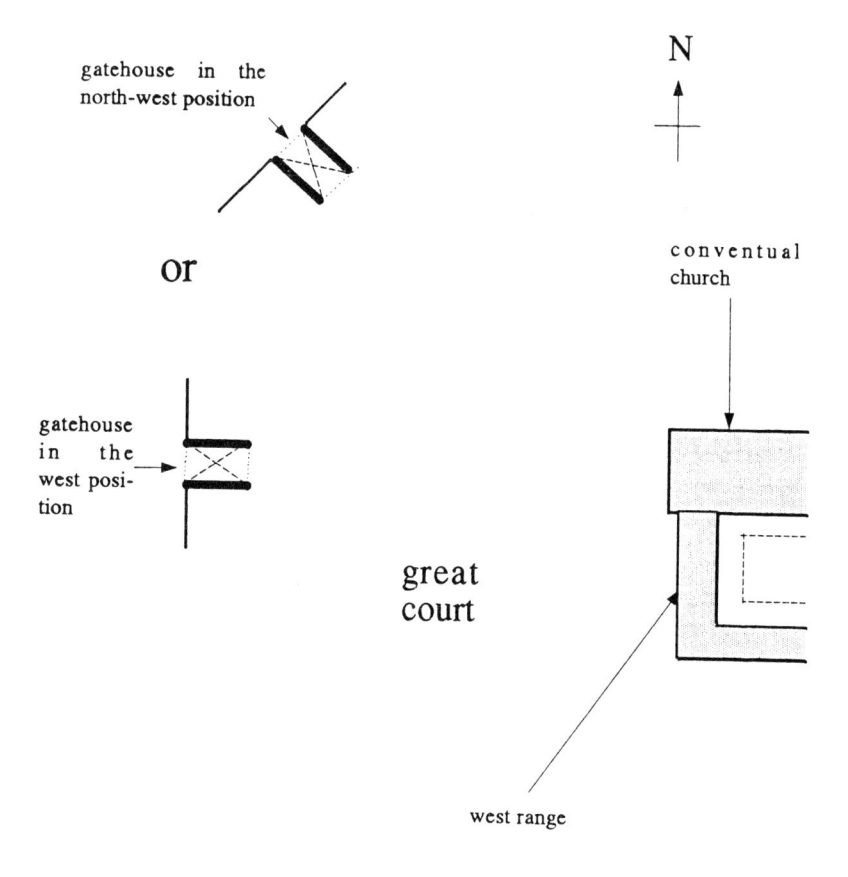

great
court

west range

Figure 8 The Facing Portal

that they could have had of the magnificent building displayed before them. Even when the facing portal was placed to the north-west or south-west, the view of the church through the gate-hall must have been almost as impressive.

It is possible to identify a number of abbeys and priories which still possess facing portals standing well to the west of the conventual church but normally in approximate line with its east–west axis. Here is a selection: Abingdon, Binham, Bromfield, Bury St Edmunds (St James' Tower), Evesham (Great Gate), Thornton and Walsingham. Instances of north-west portals of the facing type, oriented diagonally, include Battle (great gatehouse), Bayham, Buckfast (north gatehouse), Roche, and St Benet of Holme.

THE SITING OF PORTALS BY THE DIFFERENT ORDERS

The Benedictine arrangement

At this point it is necessary to distinguish between on the one hand the Benedictines (which may be loosely grouped with several other contemplative orders, mainly the Augustinians) and on the other the Cistercians (and Premonstratensians). The differences which affected the monastic layout of these orders was derived from the fact that the first of these two groups often permitted lay people to enter their conventual churches for worship while the second group almost never did.

The Benedictine requirement necessitated the 'open' side of the conventual church (i.e. the side of the church opposite to that bordering the cloister) to be placed beyond (i.e. outside) the main precinct wall which normally ran from the south-west corner of the nave round to the north-east of the choir (Figure 9). In keeping with this arrangement, lay people were enabled to enter the conventual church from the north, often by means of a porch that would be attached to the north aisle of the nave near its west end. Benedictine examples of this plan may be seen at Ewenny, Malvern and Usk, and Augustinian ones at Bridlington and Christchurch. Conversely, where the cloister was located to the north of the

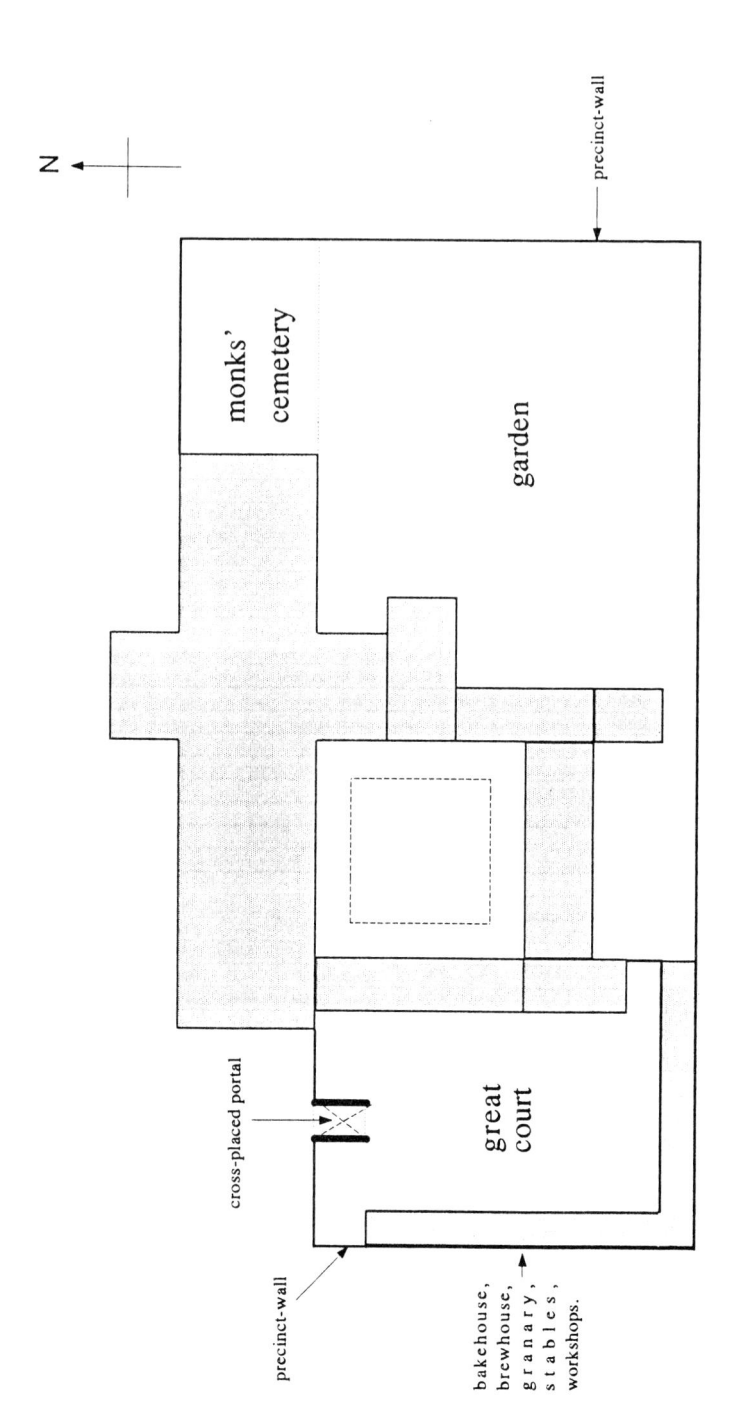

Figure 9 The Benedictine One-portal Plan

great church, the arrangement was reversed with the lay entrance to the south, as at Chester and Sherborne (both Benedictine), Dorchester (Augustinian), and Edington (Bonhommes).

In some churches of the same orders, lay people could enter the nave via a west doorway (where there was no north porch or, in the case of monasteries with a north cloister, no south porch). A number of instances may be cited, including Nun Monkton, Peterborough and St Albans (all Benedictine), and Dunstable and St Germans (Augustinian). Sometimes entry from the west had to be made through a mid-positioned west tower as at Bolton (Augustinian), or through a north-west or south-west tower as at Bourne (Augustinian) and Bromfield (Benedictine).

Clearly the cross-placed portal, usually a gatehouse, placed at the south-west corner of the conventual church sealed off the great court, stopping lay worshippers and casual visitors but not tradesmen or merchants from entering the domestic area to the west of the cloister. In many of the small houses and one or two of the great houses (such as Bristol and St Albans) a portal in this position could effectively regulate the traffic. In some of the other great houses, where the number of potential visitors may have anticipated problems of control, it must have been realised quite early on in the development of the planning of monastic sites that it would be necessary to have another, outer, portal. This second portal was normally placed at a distance to the west where it would face the conventual church, its purpose being to control entry to the outer court leading to the west front. At night, in particular, roisterers could be prevented from approaching the church and making a noise (Figure 10).

There are several monastic sites where this pattern of two portals prevails, with a facing portal placed well to the west of the church giving access to an open space or outer court in front of the great church, and a second, cross-placed portal standing at right angles to the east–west axis of the church and leading into the great court.

What instances of this double arrangement survive? The best examples are seen at Peterborough and Gloucester, where both portals in the form of gatehouses survive on each site. Peterborough, with its cloister on the south side of the

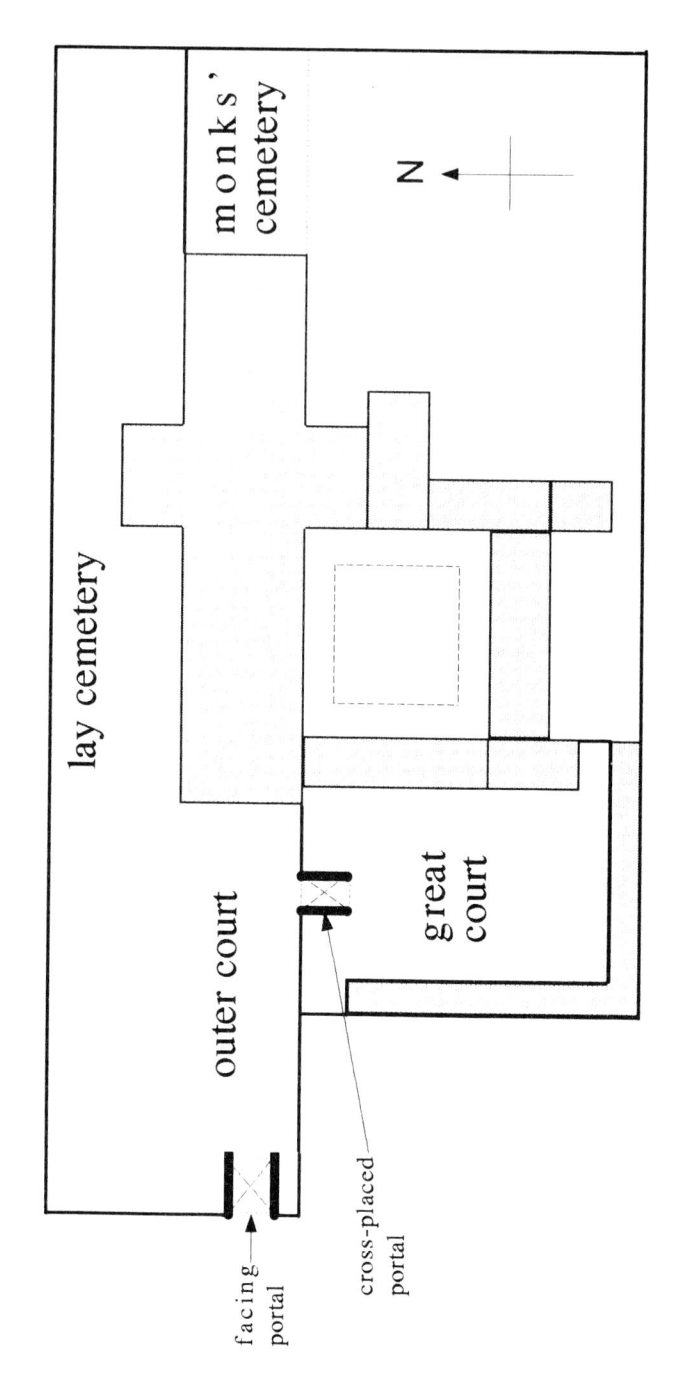

Figure 10 The Benedictine Two-portal Plan

conventual church, has its cross-placed portal located just to the south-east of the great church, and Gloucester, with the less common north cloister, has its cross-placed portal located to the north-west. Several incomplete examples may also be identified. At Reading the cross-placed portal in the form of a large and highly restored gatehouse survives on the south side almost due west of the destroyed nave, while the facing portal, now disappeared, occupied a known site adjacent to St Laurence's Church considerably further away to the west. Binham possesses the roofless ruin of a facing portal which stands some distance to the west of the nave of the conventual church. Fragmentary evidence suggests that a totally destroyed cross-placed portal may have stood immediately to the south-west of this church to give access to the great court nearby. At Bermondsey Abbey, which has almost completely vanished, examination of the ground plan (see New, 1985, p. 66) suggests that the double arrangement may have existed there too.

These instances of a precinct with a facing portal located at a distance to the west and a cross-placed portal located close to the conventual church come from great houses, and this is probably not coincidental. It is also true that, apart from one or two of the larger houses, nearly all the smaller monasteries such as Blanchland or Malvern appear to have managed with one portal, in all probability occupying the cross-placed position.

The Cistercian arrangement
Several Cistercian conventual churches have survived since the Dissolution, but they are all incomplete, having lost much of their fabric. They include the fine choir and crossing of Abbey Dore, and portions of the naves of Margam and Holmcultram. Besides these abbey churches, there are also survivals of portions of some Cistercian nunnery churches, for example Heynings, Swine and possibly Llanlugan. However, the Cistercians never normally permitted laypeople to use their churches for worship and with the exception of Swine, there is little evidence that parochial rights of access of the above or any other Cistercian churches were granted or conceded until after monastic worship had ceased.

Thus a situation existed at almost all Cistercian (and probably nearly all Premonstratensian) houses where the precinct remained permanently out of bounds to lay persons (with the exception of the conversi or lay brothers who had part of the conventual church nave set aside for their worship, tradesmen who were permitted to enter the abbey or priory premises in connection with the execution of their work, and visitors).

This denial of entry of lay people to the conventual church meant that a typical Cistercian or Premonstratensian precinct could be made more secure by enclosing the conventual church within the precinct wall which was thrown around its north as well as its south side (Figure 11). The great court was thus made contiguous with the space that lay to the west and north, all being enclosed within the wall. This layout also influenced the location of and probably the number of portals.

Quite a number of Cistercian houses still display what we may now call an extended great court, typical examples including Byland, Cleeve, Furness and Kirkstall. Even allowing for post-Dissolution removal of many of the ancillary buildings such as stables, workshops and storehouses, the spaciousness that characterises the west and north sides of these abbey sites is quite remarkable. This feature is possibly less evident at Kirkstall where a modern road has been driven through the monastic site to the north of the conventual church, cutting off the gatehouse which is located further away to the north-west.

Entry to Cistercian great courts tended to be effected through a portal that was placed in one of several locations ranging from due west of the conventual church (as at Bordesley, Boxley, Dunkeswell or Fountains), to the north-west (as at Culross, Roche or Stoneleigh) and less frequently to the north (as at Neath). Occasionally, as at Jervaulx, Cistercian portals were placed to the south-west. This is not to say that the Cistercians favoured the west position as much as did the Benedictines but, because their great courts were extended to the north, they could (and often did) tend to choose an entry point to the precinct further to the north-west than was common with other orders. The chief difference between the Cistercian and Benedictine allocation of

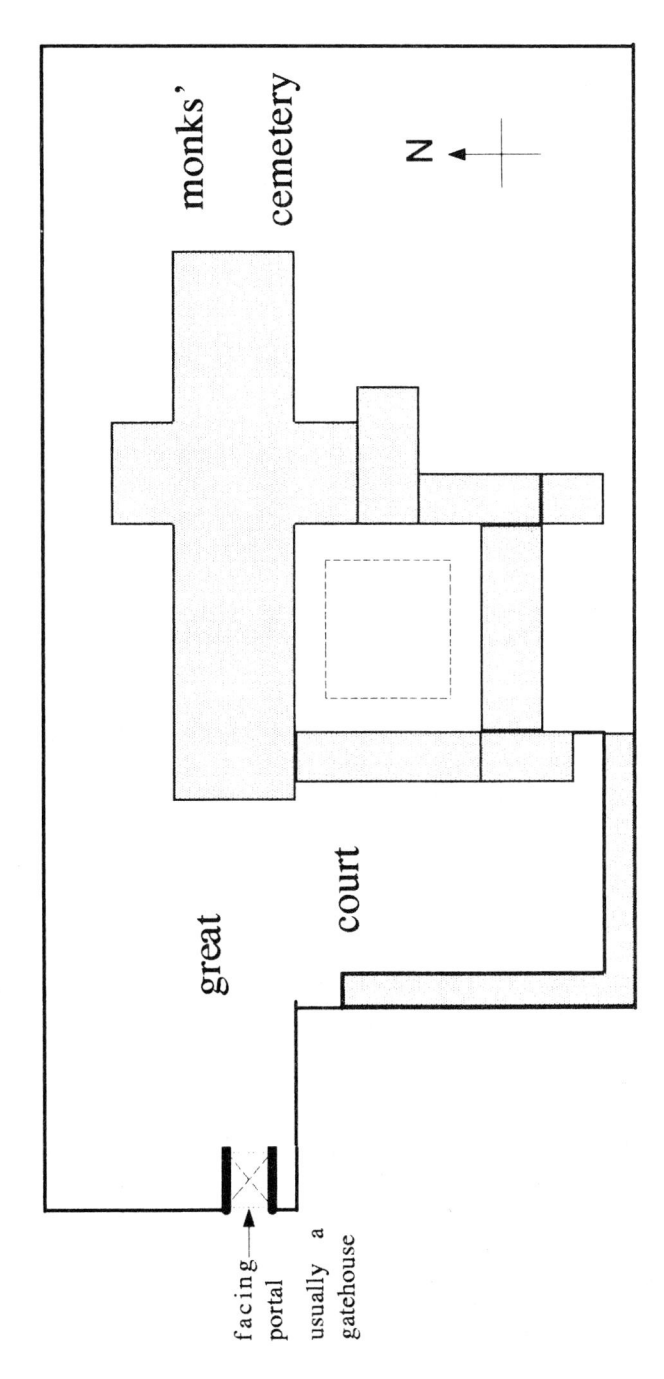

Figure 11   The Cistercian One-portal Plan

space was that the white monks tended to bring into one great court all the space within the precinct wall to the south-west, west and north of the great church, whereas the black monks seem to have preferred dividing the same space into great and outer courts of roughly equal size.

There is evidence, however, that some Cistercian houses had a self-contained small outer court (Figure 12). The most revealing example of this arrangement is to be found at Cleeve. At this abbey, the great court, which may alternatively be called an inner court, occupies a large area to the west of the cloister and to the west, north-west and north of the conventual church. Further to the north-west beyond the inner gatehouse (as we should now call it) is a small area, the outer court, that was originally completely bounded by a wall, while at the extremity of the latter court is a fragment of an outer portal.

Another instance probably existed at Fountains where the partly dismantled surviving gatehouse served as an inner portal, separated from a long-vanished outer portal by a narrow outer court. What the Cistercian purpose was in having a small outer court beyond a large inner court is conjectural. It is likely that the monastic stables and some of the noisy or smelly workshops were consigned to this distant part of the abbey premises. Indications of similar arrangements are suggested at Byland, Rievaulx and Roche.

This Cistercian plan of inner and outer court was sometimes adopted by other orders, for instance by the Augustinians at Maxstoke where two gatehouses are placed about one hundred yards apart, the outer a high-standing ruin flanked by good sections of the precinct wall and the inner converted into a post-Dissolution farmhouse.

Friary portals
The friars mendicant arrived on the medieval scene somewhat later than the main contemplative orders. Their mission was to preach the Gospel to the poor and needy and to help people by good works. Thus by far the greater number of friaries were located in towns and cities. Coming later, they often had to establish their friaries on plots of land that nobody else wanted, frequently on the fringes of urban areas (e.g. immediately outside the city walls or on marshy land near rivers).

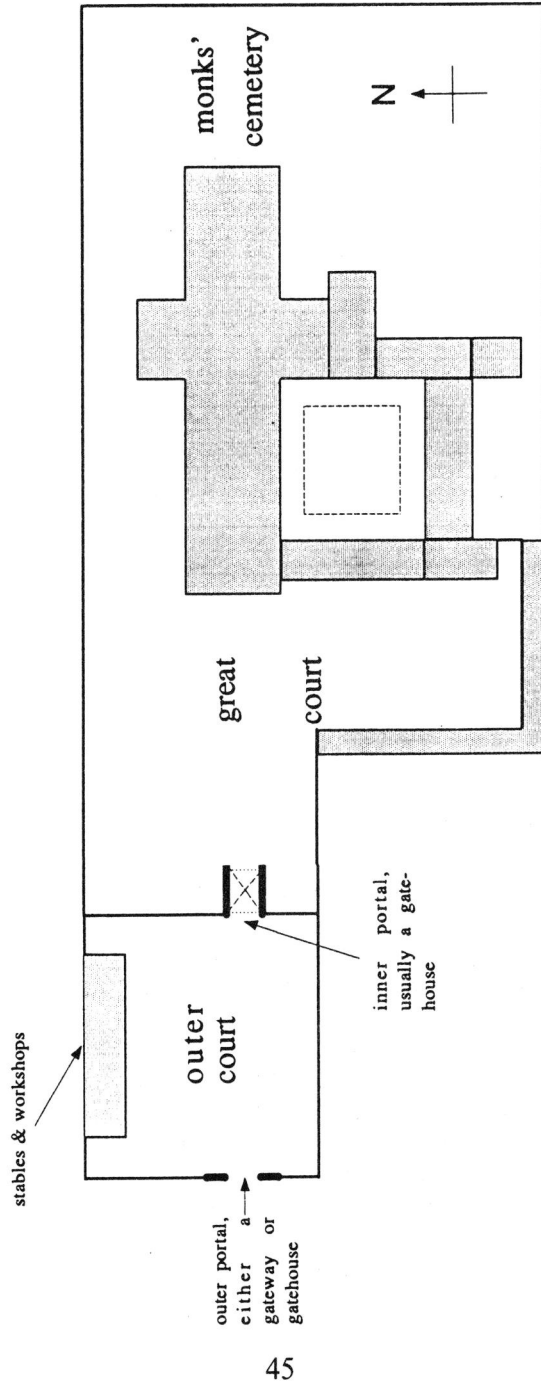

Figure 12 The Cistercian Two-portal Plan

This shortage of land resulted in the buildings of a friary having to be planned in order to make the best use of the available space. Moreover, a perpetual lack of money among the mendicant orders meant that, with the possible exception of a friary church, claustral and other buildings erected within a precinct were necessarily small and placed close together.

Such considerations also applied to the siting and size of friary portals. Unlike portals of the contemplative orders, friary portals tended to be placed on the north side, and sometimes beyond the west end of the conventual church, to facilitate entry of lay people to the church (Figure 13). Only a few examples of such portals exist, nearly all being swept away in the post-Dissolution expropriation of urban land for commercial and industrial development. Instances of friary gatehouses are found at Stamford Greyfriars and Coventry Whitefriars. Designed to occupy a small area of land, some portals may have been preferably constructed in the form of gateways, as at King's Lynn Austin Friars and King's Lynn Whitefriars (Photograph 6).

NAMED PORTALS

A number of surviving portals have names, most of which probably originated in the monastic period. Some of these portals have titles referring to their pre-eminent size or location and so on, suggesting that they were the chief or only entrance to an abbey or priory. This importance is recognised, for instance, at Evesham where the Great Gatehouse forms the core of a post-Dissolution mansion, at Lewes where the Great Gate survives as a gatehouse remnant next to the parish church of Southover, at Bury St Edmunds where a splendid and complete gatehouse continues to be called the Great Gate of the abbey, and at St Albans where the large gatehouse still standing to the west of the abbey (now cathedral) enjoys the description, Great Gateway. In a few cases such as Canterbury St Augustine's, Norwich and Worcester, the main portal is known both as the Great Gate and by an alternative name: Fyndon Gate for the first of these, St Ethelbert's Gate for the second and Edgar Tower for the third.

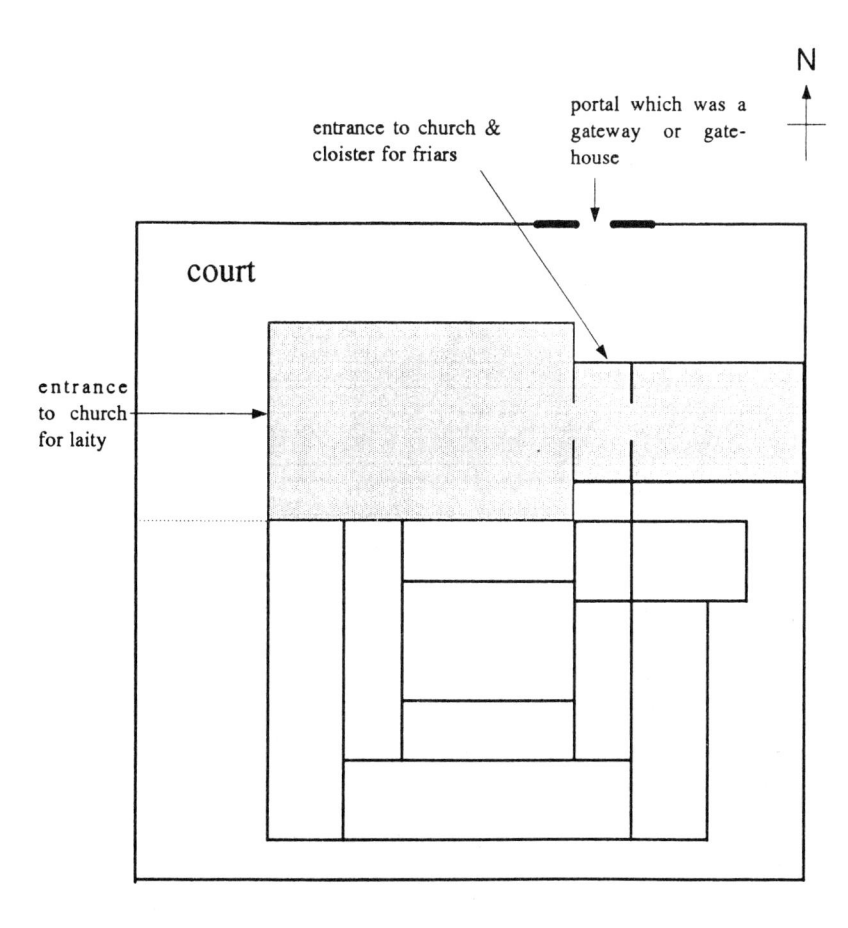

Figure 13   The Friary Portal Plan

Sometimes the superior status of a gatehouse is marked by calling it the Abbey Gate (as at Abingdon and Reading), Priory Gate (as at Hexham) or Porta Monachorum (as was the case at Ely). Other marks of esteem were to name the portal after a patron saint (for example, St John's Gate at Clerkenwell, St Mary's Gate at Gloucester, or St Swithun's Gate at Winchester) or shrine (King Edward's Gate at Gloucester). At Canterbury the importance of the portal was recognised by naming it after the dedication of the cathedral (Christ Church Gate). In all these instances it may reasonably be assumed that the portal in question was at some time in its monastic existence the chief entrance to the religious house or its conventual church.

Conversely, less important portals were awarded other names, sometimes to denote their proximity to a senior official's personal quarters. The Abbot's Gatehouse at Tewkesbury, Sacrist's Gate at Ely, Bishop's Gate at Norwich, Abbot's Gatehouse and Prior's Gateway at Peterborough, and Sextry (sacrist's) Gate at Rochester all come into this category.

Sometimes builders' names were linked with portals, a practice more often, though not always, associated with the later medieval period. Thus, apart from the twelfth-century north gatehouse at Evesham which is occasionally called Abbot Reginald's Gateway, the following instances all derive from the fourteenth century or later: at Forde the porch-tower is named Abbot Chard's Tower; at Norwich, the Bishop's Gate (mentioned above) is alternatively known as Bishop Alnwick's Gateway; and at Canterbury Christ Church, a porch-tower is called Prior Selling's Porch.

Geographical or topographical considerations almost certainly led to the naming of some portals, such as the Kentish Gate at Bayham, the Town, Court or Higher Abbey Gate at Tavistock, the North and South Gates at Buckfast, and the North Gate (otherwise known as the Court Gate) at Canterbury. Sometimes the relative unimportance of an entrance was reflected in a name, the Little Abbey Gateway at Chester so-named to distinguish it from the main entrance. The Pentise Gate at Canterbury, and The Pends at Arbroath, Dunfermline (Photograph 7) and

St Andrews suggest that even an architectural feature nearby may have been responsible for the name given to a portal.

Occasionally, as at Norwich where the watergate is now named Pull's Ferry after a nineteenth-century ferryman, portals received post-Dissolution names. Betsy Grimbal's Tower, by which name the part-ruined west gatehouse at Tavistock is now known, may also come into this last group. It has been suggested (Finberg, 1951, p. 287) that Betsy Grimbal is a corruption of a ninth-century scholar–saint called Blessed Grimbald with whose name the Tower was associated in the medieval period.

GREATER AND LESSER PORTALS

Which portals were designated or recognised by their abbey or priory owners as being the chief or main gatehouse of their establishment?

This question is not a simple one to answer as it does not always follow that a portal standing in a particular position (for instance, an outer gatehouse) would have been designated as the chief entrance any more than a portal situated in another position would have been so designated. On the other hand, as we have just seen, portals possessing names of long standing have enabled us to identify some greater (and lesser) portals.

Quite clearly, some portals were awarded recognition because of their size and location, and may have been erected to fulfil such a role. The Great Gateway at St Albans is a case in point. Erected in the cross-placed position near the west end of the great conventual church, anything smaller would have looked out of proportion compared with the huge expanse of the church. No other medieval portals have survived at St Albans except for the Waxhouse Gate substantially rebuilt in the eighteenth century. This lesser portal may have co-existed with other now-vanished smaller portals all giving access to the wide precinct of the abbey. The Great Gate or Edgar Tower at Worcester which continues to guard the entrance to the great court (now the cathedral close) fulfils a similar role. With the small watergate at the opposite end of the close, it may also be the last survivor of several portals round the precinct.

At a few monasteries the outer portal, constructed as a gatehouse rather than a gateway, was the chief or main one. Gloucester's St Mary's Gate and Peterborough's main or outer gatehouse provide examples of this, as possibly does Maxstoke where the outer gatehouse appears to be bigger than the inner one. In rather more houses such as Reading, where Abbey Gate was the chief one, it would seem that the inner portal took precedence over the outer portal. Other instances are located at Beaulieu, Cleeve, Furness and Leez. Where this occurred, the outer portal normally consisted of a smaller gatehouse (e.g. Beaulieu, Leez) or a gateway (e.g. Furness and possibly Cleeve). Not every chief portal was constructed on the grand scale, however: Tavistock, for instance, retains its main portal, the Town Gate. In contrast to other main portals, its size and appearance do not draw particular attention, and it must have been awarded this status because it was in a dominant location where it led into the great court from the town.

Occasionally the status of a main gatehouse appears to have been transferred from an earlier-built portal to a newer one constructed elsewhere. Thus at Gloucester the thirteenth-century St Mary's Gate which stands to the north-west of the abbey church was replaced by the fourteenth-century King Edward's Gate which stands now half-dismantled on the south side of the church. It is quite possible that the massive twelfth-century North or Court Gate at Canterbury gave way in status to the Christ Church Gate erected 1507–17 on the opposite side of the cathedral-priory church. A third instance may well be provided at Bury St Edmunds where the Great Gate (Photograph 8) built 1327–c.1384 in response to rioting, was given precedence over the immense Norman gatehouse (St James' Tower). Still standing to the west of the site of the abbey church where it faces the west front, it must surely have served as the main gatehouse before the Great Gate was erected.

THE NUMBER OF PERIPHERAL PORTALS TO A SITE

For reasons already discussed in Chapter 1, portals were needed to control the flow of traffic into as well as out of a precinct. Thus, it is improbable that any monasteries would have existed without at least one manned gateway. The likelihood is that small abbeys and priories (and most were small) would have possessed one portal through which all communication with the outside world could have been controlled, and this a gatehouse or even a simple gateway.

As well as the smaller but, at the same time, more affluent ones which could afford to build additional peripheral portals, the larger houses obviously needed several entrances: a main gate for the use of visiting dignitories, a tradesmen's entrance, a gatehouse leading to the abbot's lodging, and so on. It was therefore quite common for an abbey or priory to possess two or more portals, with several of the very large houses, especially the cathedral-priories, having as many as four, five or even more peripheral entrances.

When we attempt to identify those monasteries which had specific numbers of portals at the time of the Dissolution, we are faced with a practical difficulty. When a grantee took over a site, he often destroyed some or all of his newly-acquired portals. By far the majority of such portals have disappeared, leaving little or no trace of their former existence.

At a number of monastic sites where whole abbeys or priories have been obliterated, comprehensive archaeological investigations have been carried out. These digs have revealed the locations of former portals, for instance at Bardney (Pevsner and Harris, 1989, p. 113), Bordesley (Rahtz and Hirst, 1976), and Thornholme (Coppack, 1990, pp. 120, 121). Valuable as such findings are, an identification of one or more portals at a site does not necessarily provide a definitive answer as to how many portals a monastery possessed. Much of the archaeological evidence must therefore be treated as inconclusive.

Only in the few instances where information was recorded soon after the Dissolution can we be reasonably certain as to how many portals a particular monastery actually had. Reading, where the layout of the abbey in the sixteenth century was documented, is one such instance. It possessed five portals (North, East, South and West Gates – now all destroyed – besides the Abbey or Inner Gate, fortunately preserved). Bury St Edmunds is another. This also had five portals, two of which, the Abbot's Gate to the north and the South Gate, have vanished, leaving two more, the Great Gate and the St James' Tower, unscathed, and a small gate or postern surviving in a mutilated form.

Such recorded examples are quite exceptional, and all we can really do in the absence of firm evidence is to identify the number and structural condition of peripheral portals that survive at individual monastic sites today.

Examples of small-to-medium-sized houses, each with a single surviving portal, include Alnwick, Beauvale, Blanchland, Bromfield, Broomholm, Burnham Norton, Calder, Cartmel, Cornworthy, Coverham, Dover, Hyde, Kenilworth, Kingswood, Kirkham, Letheringham, Lindores, Llanthony, Michelham, Minster-in-Sheppey, Montacute, Pentney, Polesworth, Stamford Greyfriars, Usk, West Acre and Wetheral. It is probable that most if not all of these instances had only a single portal in the monastic period.

The larger monastic houses with single surviving peripheral portals include Abingdon, Arbroath, Barking, Bermondsey, Byland, Carlisle, Castle Acre, Cerne, Cirencester, Clerkenwell, Colchester St John's, Dryburgh, Durham, Easby, Forde, Fountains, Glastonbury, Guisborough, Hexham, Holyrood, Jervaulx, Kirkstall, Leicester (St Mary's), Lewes, Malling, Mount Grace, Neath, Osney, Ramsey, Reading, Rievaulx, Roche, St Benet of Holme, Tewkesbury, Thetford, Thornton, Tintern, Torre, Waltham, Wenlock, Winchester and Worksop. The majority of these houses almost certainly must have each possessed two or more portals in medieval times.

The abbeys and priories with two surviving portals are:

Beaulieu two complete gatehouses, one converted into a mansion
Bradsole two fragmentary gatehouses
Bristol two complete gatehouses
Buckfast one recently reconstructed gatehouse and one partially dismantled gatehouse

Cleeve	one high-standing ruined gatehouse and one fragmentary portal
Dunfermline	one complete gatehouse and one fragmentary gatehouse
Dunster	two complete gateways
Ewenny	one complete gatehouse and one high-standing ruined gatehouse
Hulne	one almost complete gatehouse and a remodelled gateway
Leez	two complete gatehouses
London Charterhouse	one complete and rebuilt gatehouse and the other a complete gateway
Maxstoke	one gatehouse converted into a house and the other a high-standing ruined gatehouse
St Albans	one complete gatehouse and another gatehouse substantially reconstructed
St Osyth	one complete gatehouse and the second portal, a gateway
Tisbury (Shaftesbury)	two complete gatehouses
Walsingham	one gatehouse and one gateway, both complete
Whalley	one complete gatehouse and the other gatehouse a high-standing ruin
Wigmore	one complete gatehouse and one partially dismantled
Worcester	two complete gatehouses.

The survival of three peripheral portals surviving on a single site is somewhat less common than two. The full list is:

Abbotsbury	one complete gateway, one gatehouse converted into a house, and another gatehouse now fragmentary
Aylesford	three gatehouses of which two are complete and one has been adapted as part of an office block
Battle	one complete gatehouse and two small and complete gateways
Bury St Edmunds	two complete gatehouses and one part-ruined gateway

Canterbury St Augustine's	one complete gatehouse, one gatehouse converted into a house, and a complete gateway
Chester	one complete and partly rebuilt gatehouse, and two gateways
Rochester	one complete, and two complete and partly rebuilt gatehouses
Tavistock	Of three gatehouses, one is complete, a second has been adapted as a church tower and the third is partially demolished
York St Mary's	One gateway is complete, one gatehouse is ruined and another gatehouse is partly demolished.

Four surviving peripheral portals are found at three abbeys and three cathedral-priories. Of the first group, Evesham has a gatehouse and gate-tower both in good order, together with a gatehouse turned into a house, and the fragment of a gateway or gatehouse. Furness possesses three gatehouses all in a state of severe disrepair and one gateway which, though complete has been partly reconstructed. At Gloucester (now cathedral) two gatehouses survive in a complete state of repair, one gatehouse is partially dismantled and the fourth gatehouse is complete but partly rebuilt. Of the three cathedral-priories, Ely possesses four gatehouses. Of these, three are complete and another has been adapted as domestic accommodation. Norwich also has four gatehouses, of which three are complete and the fourth complete but partly rebuilt. Lastly, St Andrews has two derelict gatehouses and two complete gateways.

Peterborough Abbey (now cathedral) displays evidence of five portals. Of these, two gatehouses and two gateways are complete, and another gatehouse is fragmentary.

Appropriately enough, the monastic site with the largest number of portals, far outnumbering any of those already identified, is the cathedral-priory of Canterbury. On this site there are eight peripheral portals of which three are gateways and five gatehouses. Of the gateways, one is complete though blocked, while of the other gateways, both are complete though one of them has been moved to a new site. Three of the five gatehouses are complete and original, while two have been substantially rebuilt.

3

STRUCTURE (1)

HISTORICAL DEVELOPMENT AND DESIGN

How did the portal evolve in design and appearance during the medieval period and then in the intervening centuries down to the present day?

If 1066 is taken as a starting date, an examination of the surviving complete and ruined portals indicates that there appears to have been relatively little change in the basic design throughout the period to the Dissolution affecting the main passageway and the provision of an upper chamber or chambers. The only exception to this general picture of minor change (and this is conjectural) is that some gatehouses may have been erected in place of earlier gateways, a development which may explain the origin of the extant and mainly fourteenth-century gatehouse at Battle.

In adhering to the basic design of main passageway and upper chamber (or chambers), many early gatehouses were taken down and rebuilt or remodelled in the later medieval period. With some gatehouses it is evident that the remodelling retained a considerable portion of the earlier fabric. Canterbury Christ Church and Peterborough provide examples of portals altered but not excessively so. Canterbury's North Gate continues to display parts of its twelfth-century Norman external façades though its front and rear archways were strengthened in the fifteenth century by the insertion of additional arches and the replacement of most of the upper storey. The remodelling at Peterborough seems to have been effected in an opposite way, with the twelfth-century main gatehouse having received a new front façade in the early fourteenth century behind which the original fabric including the twelfth-century Norman arch, still stands. Another instance is the Abbey (or main) Gatehouse at Bristol, where much of the original Norman work has been overlaid by a fifteenth-century Perpendicular exterior and, posssibly, by the addition of a third storey (see below).

The gatehouse at Kingswood originally dates from the fourteenth century, and most of what survives there may be attributed to that period. However, its external ornamentation as illustrated by its one surviving façade at the front was given an uplift in the sixteenth century, while on both sides of the building ranges were added about the same time that the façade was being remodelled. This portal is illustrative of the changes that affected a number of rebuilt or remodelled gatehouses in the later medieval period, that is, in the provision of additional wings and extended ranges, and an application of more ornamentation or newer windows to exteriors. The two-storeyed inner gatehouse at Cleeve, which substantially dates from the thirteenth and fourteenth centuries, also displays alterations involving ornamentation and windowing which were carried out in the fifteenth century.

In other gatehouses the rebuilding was more drastic. At Monk Bretton, for example, the whole of the original fourteenth-century building (or perhaps thirteenth-century), identified by blocks of small masonry, appears to have had its walls taken down to perhaps eight feet before being rebuilt and extended to the rear in the early fifteenth century. The fifteenth-century gatehouse at Minster-in-Sheppey supplies us with another instance of severe rebuilding, all that is left of the original structure being its thirteenth-century rear turret which still displays lancet windows. Tavistock's Town Gate is a third example of a gatehouse which has been drastically rebuilt. Its cross-wall arches appear to be all that survives of the original twelfth-century building, converted in the fifteenth century into a virtually new building.

Then there are a number of gatehouses which date in their entirety in their present form from the fourteenth, fifteenth or sixteenth centuries but which may have been replacements for earlier gatehouses, now totally vanished but whose location may well have been used and general ground plan or shape copied. Though the origins of such conjectural replacements are now impossible to verify, instances may occur at one or two sites. Usk possesses a small gatehouse with architectural features (square-headed windowing and plain semicircular arches) of the late medieval period, even sixteenth century. It is, however, sited to the west of the conventual church in a standard position where it possesses an earlier, 'long' shape, and its semicircular arches may hark back to a twelfth-century origin. The Carlisle gatehouse, which has an inscribed date of 1527 on it, fits into a similar mould, that of occupying the right type of location, of having an earlier shape, and of possessing architectural features (such as semicircular arches) that are an echo of an earlier period of construction.

Since the Dissolution, which was completed in England and Wales in 1540 when all the remaining monastic houses were closed, and in Scotland in 1587 when all the surviving monasteries were formally annexed to the Scottish Crown, the changes made to the fabric of portals which had not been quickly demolished tended to be minimal. Alterations often affected the external appearance of portals. Many religious statues were swept away from façades, especially if they could be easily reached, leaving empty niches such as at Battle. Occasionally such statues were immediately replaced by secular figures, as at Hinchinbrooke where part of the Ramsey gatehouse was taken and reassembled.

For perhaps two-and-a-half centuries many buildings gradually deteriorated, some of them falling into a permanent state of disrepair as the Marygate at York St Mary's and the Priory Gate at Hexham.

From the middle of the nineteenth century, however, the tide began to turn and monastic gatehouses started to be properly restored. One outcome was that after a delay of several centuries empty niches began to be renovated and refilled with religious figures (e.g. the Edgar Tower at Worcester) or have coats of arms regilded (e.g. Clerkenwell). At other gatehouses, recent restorations have sometimes made good the main fabric but not always renewed or replaced the external ornamentation (e.g. the Abbey Gate at Reading).

Before we can identify the main changes that took place in the design of gatehouses during the medieval period, it is necessary to describe the layout that was common to nearly all of them.

Number of storeys
Of 73 complete and largely unaltered peripheral gatehouses in England, Wales and Scotland, the number of main storeys including the ground floor as well as those above the chief archway is as follows:

One-storeyed gatehouses   5
Cirencester (1+), Glastonbury (1+), Hyde (1+) (Photograph 9), Norwich Erpingham Gate (1+), Wigmore inner (1+).

Two-storeyed gatehouses   54
Abingdon, Alnwick (2+), Aylesford outer, Barking, Beaulieu outer (2+), Blanchland, Bridlington (2+), Bromfield, Burnham Norton, Bury St Edmunds Great Gate, Canterbury Christ Church North Gate, Canterbury Christ Church Forrens Gate, Canterbury St Augustine's Fyndon Gate, Carlisle, Cartmel, Clerkenwell, Colchester St John's, Coventry Whitefriars, Dover (2+), Durham, Ely Sacrist's Gate, Evesham North Gate (2+), Ewenny south, Forde west, Gloucester St Mary's Gate (2+), Gloucester Inner Gate, Hulne main, Kingswood, Kirkstall, Leez outer, Leigh (Buckfast), Malling, Malvern, Norwich St Ethelbert's Gate, Norwich Bishop's Gate, Peterborough main, Peterborough Abbot's Gatehouse (2+), Polesworth, Quenington, Reading, Rochester Prior's Gate, St Osyth Great Gatehouse (2+), Stamford Greyfriars, Stoneleigh, Tavistock Town Gate (2+), Tewkesbury, Tisbury inner (Shaftesbury), Tisbury outer (Shaftesbury),Torre, Usk (2+), Walsingham main, Whalley inner, Worcester Edgar Tower (2+), Worksop (2+).

Three-storeyed gatehouses   13
Battle, Bristol Abbey Gatehouse, Canterbury Christ Church Christ Church Gate, Crossraguel (3+), Dunfermline The Pends, Ely Porta Gate, Ely Steeple Gate, Leez inner, Michelham, Minster-in-Sheppey, St Albans Great Gateway, Thornton, Wetheral.

Four-storeyed gatehouses   1
Bury St Edmunds St James' Tower.

The plus signs which are given with numbers after some of the above gatehouses, indicate the presence of accommodation in a roof, or an additional storey in a wing. For instance, Usk has two main storeys plus additional room-space in the gabled roof. At Glastonbury, the additional accommodation is in an upper storey in the wing at the side of the gate-hall.

Thus most gatehouses were two-storeyed buildings, examples coming from all periods: twelfth century – Canterbury North Gate, Evesham North Gate, Tavistock Town Gate; thirteenth century – Gloucester St Mary's Gate, Peterborough Abbot's Gatehouse; fourteenth century – Burnham Norton, Dunfermline The Pends, Stamford Greyfriars, Stoneleigh; fifteenth century – Barking, Colchester St John's, Whalley inner; sixteenth century – Carlisle, Clerkenwell, Crossraguel.

It is reasonable to assume that when gatehouses were rebuilt in the later medieval period, some were made taller by adding a storey. This may have happened in a few cases of which the Bristol Abbey Gatehouse may be one. Substantially reconstructed about 1500, this portal retains a considerable portion of its twelfth-century Norman fabric at the ground-floor level. Though now a three-storeyed building, there is a possibility (and it is no more than this) that the Norman gatehouse was two-storeyed before being reconstructed and added to in the later medieval period.

However, there is no evidence to support this type of development taking place generally. Of surviving gatehouses that are three- or four-storeyed, it is clear that gatehouses with these numbers of storeys were popular in every medieval century after the Norman Conquest. Including the one four-storeyed gatehouse in a group of 14 otherwise entirely composed of three-storeyed gatehouses, there is a spread of earliest known construction dates for each of them as follows: Bury St Edmunds St James' Tower (twelfth century), Bristol Abbey Gatehouse (twelfth century), Minster-in-Sheppey (thirteenth century), Battle (twelfth century), Dunfermline The Pends (fourteenth century), Ely Porta (fourteenth century), St Albans (fourteenth century), Thornton (fourteenth century), Michelham (fifteenth century), Wetheral (fifteenth century), Ely Steeple Gate (fourteenth century crypt), Crossraguel (sixteenth century),

Leez inner (sixteenth century), Canterbury Christ Church Christ Church Gate (sixteenth century).

To describe a gatehouse as one-storeyed is almost a contradiction in terms, as one would expect by definition a gatehouse to have an upper storey. Yet a few one-storeyed buildings do exist which appear to be gatehouses rather than simple gateways, five examples being listed above. Their common feature is that the porter's accommodation is provided in a one- or two-storeyed lodge at the side of the entrance. The gatehouses of this small group have immediately over the main passage-way a raised roof into which an attic or other room-space may have been inserted. This provision of additional room-space is particularly noticeable in the Saxon Arch at Cirencester, but is not so obvious at the other one-storeyed gatehouses.

Development of the portal
The simplest and plainest type of gateway was essentially two-dimensional in form, that is, it had breadth and height but negligible depth as measured from front to rear (apart, that is, from the thickness of the gateway wall). This contrasts with more substantial or later types of gateway and especially the gatehouse, all of which, having some depth as well as breadth and height, were three-dimensional (Figure 14).

A plain gateway would normally have consisted of little more than a stone archway in which were hung inwardly opening timber gates or a single door (Figure 15). In some cases the gateway may have been protected by a drawbridge which could be lowered over a dry ditch or river, though there is no firm evidence to support this probability. The responds or half-piers of the archway would have been reinforced by precinct walls forming abutments at the sides, an arrangement to be seen at the Little Abbey Gate at Chester, and at Battle and at Dunster (at both of which there are two examples).

It would seem that several developments were made to the plan of this plain gateway, each of which contributed towards its being altered spatially from a two- to a three-dimensional building, possibly anticipating the development of the gatehouse proper. One of these changes involved introducing a

2-D

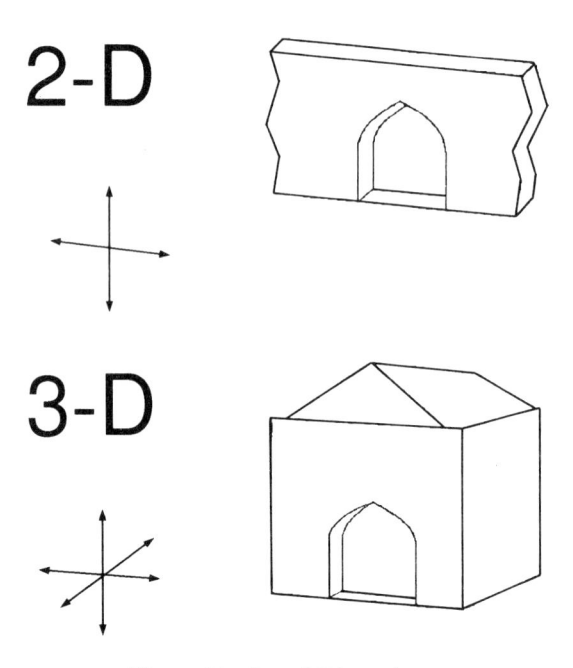

3-D

Figure 14 Portal Dimensions

wall-walk that in some monasteries was made to run behind the parapet of the precinct wall and, as demonstrated at Hulne, to descend to ground level by a flight of steps when it met a portal. The improvement involved continuing the wall-walk over the gateway, itself strengthened by being made broader from front to back, thus enabling watchmen to patrol the walls without having to descend to the ground when arriving at the portal. Several instances of gateways displaying the vestige of an overhead wall-walk include Brecon, the Knight's Gate at Walsingham and the Prior's Gateway at Peterborough. Another development may have been to set back the gateway a few feet behind the boundary line along which ran the precinct wall, to provide a forecourt giving off-street space for visitors awaiting permission to pass through the gates (as tentatively suggested by the watergate at Tintern or the Prior's Gate at Winchester).

However, what this 'improved' gateway still lacked was, first, a covered area or porch rather than just an open space, where visitors could await entry to the monastery, and

1. THE PLAIN GATEWAY

2. THE EMBATTLED AND BUTTRESSED GATEWAY

3. THE RECESSED GATEWAY WITH FORECOURT

4. THE VAULTED GATEWAY

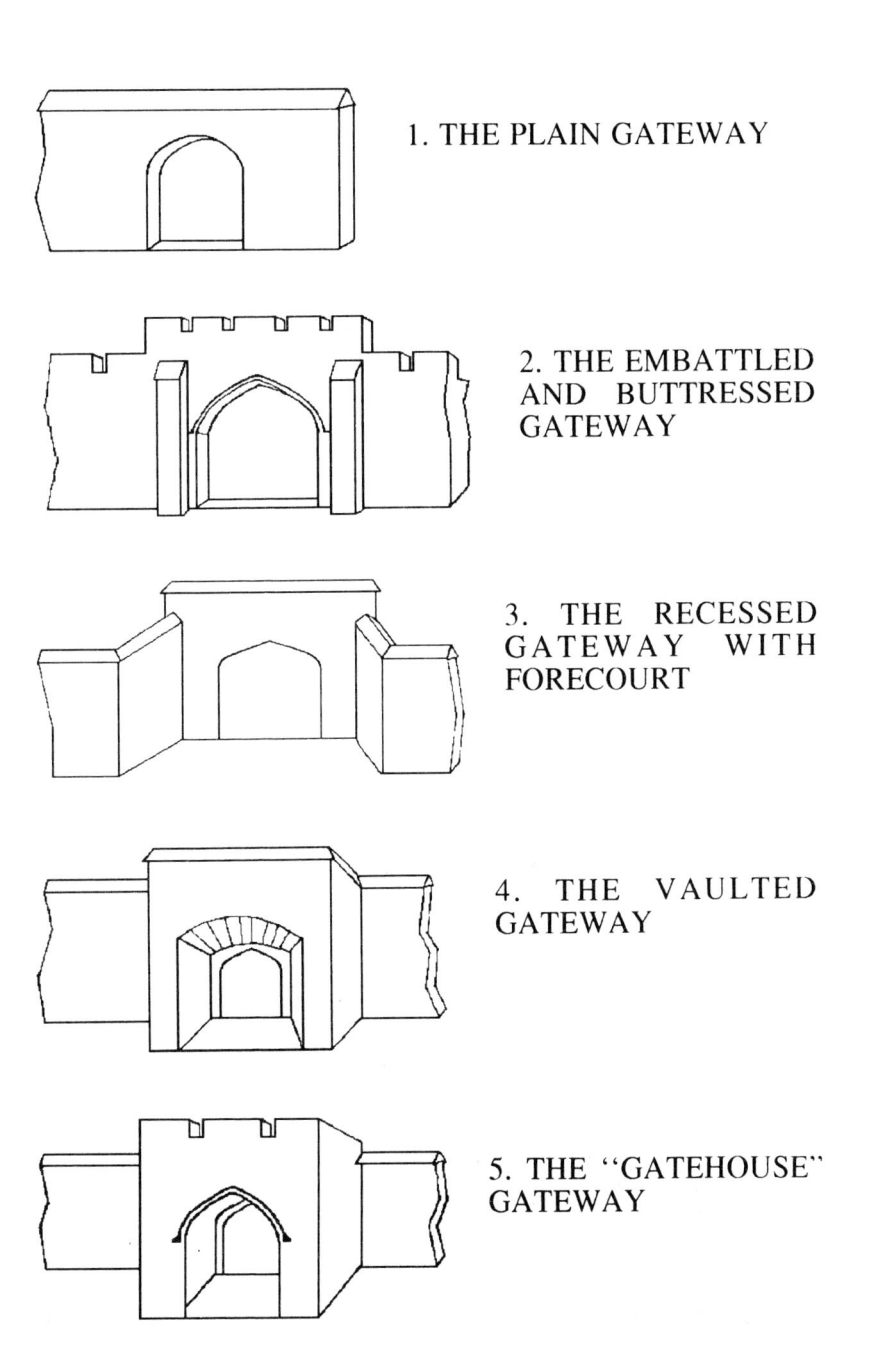

5. THE "GATEHOUSE" GATEWAY

Figure 15 Gateways: Conjectural Development

second, suitable on-site accommodation for the porter or gatekeeper.

With regard to a covered area in front of the gate, two gateways survive, each with a porch of sorts. The first and possibly the more primitive instance is the north gateway at Pluscarden. This possesses the remnant of an open-ended high vault having a depth of approximately four feet from front to back, the vault being placed in front of a gated archway to provide a shallow porch. The second instance of a porched gateway is the gateway of the Whitefriars at King's Lynn. This building which has the superficial appearance of a small gatehouse, is approximately six feet deep from front to back and has over the small arched entrance a fascia containing three empty niches suggestive of a rudimentary upper stage. Its short passageway which was probably gated at its rear end, provided a small porch at the entrance to the friary. Both portals therefore appear to be intermediary in design between the simple gateway and gatehouse.

With regard to accommodation, at York St Mary's there is a gateway (Postern Gate) near Botham Bar which has a separate (i.e. unconnected) porter's lodge placed at its side. Though the postern was constructed, at least in its present form, as late as $c.1503$, it may represent the last surviving example of an unknown number of gateways which included on-site accommodation.

It would seem that the gatehouse proper developed in two ways. In both, the gatehouse was provided with a square or rectangular gate-hall which occupied an area from the front wall of the gatehouse to the rear wall. The hall was characterised by having a high vault or ceiling (about ten to twelve feet from the ground) in order to accommodate carts piled high with hay and the like, and in possessing a tall archway at each end through which the traffic could pass. One or both of these archways would have been fitted with timber doors. The gate-hall floor was usually covered with a layer of cobblestones or, less frequently, slabs of stone.

In other respects the two types of gatehouse were different. In the first and probably earlier Type 1 (Figure 16), the porter's accommodation or lodging was placed on one side of the gate-hall where it was not unlike that of the postern at

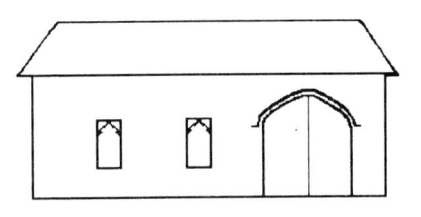

with the accommodation
in a single storey

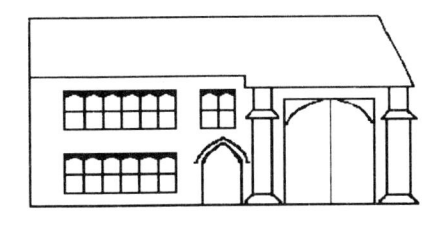

with the accommodation in a
double storey

Figure 16   Gatehouses, Type 1

York St Mary's. Sometimes the accommodation consisted of one storey (e.g. Hyde) or two (e.g. Glastonbury), this accommodation often being continued into the raised roof over the gate-hall. In the Type 2 gatehouse which was far more common, most of the accommodation was placed over the gate-hall in one, two or three storeys. In high gatehouses with two or three upper storeys, such buildings resembled a tower-house.

To conclude, one practical advantage of gateways over gatehouses, whether of the simplest design or having the improvements described above, was that they tended to occupy relatively little space. This must have been an important consideration at some monastic sites (e.g. urban friaries) where to construct a gatehouse may have been seen as an uneconomic if not wasteful use of land.

DESIGN FEATURES

Building materials
By far the majority of all existing gatehouses and other portals, whether complete, ruined or altered in some manner since the Dissolution, are constructed of stone. Apart from being a building material which was abundantly available in most parts of the country, its use satisfied two important criteria. The first was that it reduced the risk from fire, even more so if it had internal stone vaulting. The second was that for precinct walls and portals, stone gave an extra measure of security especially in helping to prevent unauthorised entry into monastic premises.

Stone was used throughout the medieval period, and there are many examples of complete gatehouses made of finely dressed stone from Norman times onwards:

Twelfth century	Bury St Edmunds St James' Tower
	Canterbury Christ Church North Gate
Thirteenth century	Gloucester St Mary's Gate
	Peterborough Abbot's Gatehouse
Fourteenth century	Alnwick
	Dunfermline The Pends
Fifteenth century	Michelham
	Wetheral
Sixteenth century	Canterbury Christ Church Christ Church Gate
	Carlisle.

In districts where ashlar was not available or was in short supply, alternative materials were often employed. This applied particularly to East Anglia and south-east England where flint could be readily obtained. Sometimes the unknapped flint was used as a coarse building material set in mortar, as may be seen for instance in sections of the gatehouse walling at Walsingham. More often, knapped flint was applied to the outside faces of buildings, as at Castle Acre and West Acre. Permanently resistant to weathering, external surfaces made of flint are as good now as when first constructed.

A common material used in eastern counties as an alternative to stone (including flint) was brick. This material, though employed centuries earlier by the Romans, did not come back into use until the twelfth century when builders, for instance at St Albans and Colchester St Botolph's, removed it from ancient Roman sites to construct conventual churches. It is believed that the art of medieval brickmaking was rediscovered early in the thirteenth century, and from this period brick was often used as a building material in abbeys and priories. The use of the material is demonstrated in a number of gatehouses in East Anglia, notably Castle Acre and Letheringham. In the first of these, the brick is used in conjunction with flint; in the second, the whole building is made of brick.

Were any portals (other than their doors) built of timber? It is possible that immediately following the foundation of a monastery, timber gateways were erected as a temporary measure prior to the construction of permanent buildings of stone. As far as is known, no timber gateway (if ever it existed) has left any trace. Timber, however, was a cheap substitute or replacement for stone in the upper storey of a gatehouse where it could be inserted with less risk from fire or damage. There are several complete gatehouses in existence which display stone below and timber above. Examples include Bromfield, the North Gate at Evesham, the Steeple Gate at Ely, Polesworth and the inner gatehouse at Wigmore. None of the timberwork is older than the fourteenth century, and all these gatehouses have an attractive appearance with their timbered patterning and jettied upper storeys.

Buttresses, turrets and windows
Simplest and often smallest of all gatehouses was the box-shaped free-standing gatehouse unadorned by buttresses or corner turrets, and with a low-pitched roof partially hidden behind a horizontal parapet usually embattled. Possibly Michelham and Minster-in-Sheppey come closest to this design.

More often than not, buttresses of one kind or another were needed to support free-standing gatehouses. Diagonal buttresses, introduced and more frequently used in the later medieval period, are employed at Coupar Angus, Tewkesbury, West Acre and Whalley (inner), and octagonals, a rarity, at Letheringham. Such buttresses were less commonly used than the earlier-introduced angle or square buttresses which meet the wall at 90° and which may be seen at a number of sites such as Bridlington, Bromfield, Kenilworth, Llanthony and Stamford Greyfriars. One or two of the older gatehouses (Bury St Edmunds twelfth-century St James' Tower and Peterborough thirteenth-century Abbot's Gatehouse for example) display an even earlier type of buttress, the flat clasping buttress or pilaster which sometimes encases the corner.

In several of the older and lengthier gatehouses, square buttresses and sometimes pilasters were placed along the sides to reinforce the walls and to withstand the thrust of internal stone vaulting. Easby (*c*.1300) displays several such pilasters. This building consists of three bays, the pilasters marking externally the division of the bays of the gatehouse.

Gatehouses were often sandwiched between neighbouring buildings which provided reinforcement at the sides instead of buttresses, but not of course at the front or rear where there may have been angle buttresses, as at Carlisle, Ely (Sacrist's Gate), Norwich (Bishop's Gate), where they climb up the corner of the building and terminate in pinnacles or become part of the parapet.

The more refined or elaborate kind of free-standing gatehouse would employ turrets instead of buttresses which could provide not only support but internal circular stairways leading from the ground to the upper storeys. Normally placed at the corners, turrets could number between four and one. Examples of four exist at Alnwick, Colchester St John's, Leez (inner) and Reading. Three turrets are found at Torre, and two at Thetford (placed at the rear). Occasionally, as at Barking and Wetheral, there is one turret only, in both cases placed at the rear to avoid spoiling the visual appearance of the front.

When a gatehouse was placed between other buildings, the arrangement did not seem to inhibit the placement of turrets. Thus Battle and Canterbury St Augustine's Fyndon Gate (both with two at the front and two at the rear), Canterbury St Augustine's Cemetery Gate (two at the front), Clerkenwell (two at the front and two at the rear), and Montacute and St Osyth (both with two at the rear) are all illustrative of this kind of layout. Very infrequently, a gatehouse was planned on such a grand scale as to warrant more than four turrets (e.g. Thornton, where there are four at the front and four at the rear).

The surviving gatehouses with turrets indicate that the majority of the latter were octagonal or semi-octagonal in cross-section, as at Battle, Canterbury Christ Church (Christ Church Gate), Pentney, Tavistock (Betsy Grimbal's Tower) and Worcester (Edgar Tower). A few, such as Ely (Porta Gate) and Clerkenwell, were rectangular or square. At Colchester may be seen a turret which starts below as square and converts half-way up to octagonal. A few of the earlier gatehouses, such as the two gatehouses at Peterborough, have octagonal turrets (main gatehouse), or square turrets (Abbot's Gatehouse) that are placed on pilasters below.

Did monastic gatehouses generally have more and larger windows at the rear than at the front? Two reasons spring to mind as to why this would have been desirable. One involves the need for security which dictated that it would have been safer for windows, especially at ground-floor level, to be made to face inward where they could overlook the monastic precinct; the second suggests that less windowing at the front would have permitted more space for friezes, niches, panelling and other types of external decoration, the fronts of gatehouses tending as we shall see to be more embellished than their rear walls.

As with rooms in other monastic buildings, the rooms of a gatehouse whether above the gate-hall or at the sides of the building needed to receive sunlight, and windows were commonly provided. We must therefore examine what this provision was.

Though some gatehouses do have more and/or larger windows at their rear, such as Blanchland ($c.1500$), Bridlington (1388), Bury St Edmunds (Great Gate, 1327–46, 1353–$c.$1384), and Norwich (St Ethelbert's Gate, $c.$1328), the case is not conclusively proven as there are a number of portals which have as many windows at the front as at the back. Instances of such windows, all of which are large (i.e. with three lights), include Barking (fifteenth century),

Clerkenwell (1504), Durham (c.1500), Ely (Porta Gate, 1396–97), Leez (inner, sixteenth century) and Thetford (fourteenth century). Burnham Norton even has a three-light window (fourteenth century) at its front but no window at its rear. Probably the gatehouse with the biggest windows of all is at Worksop where there is a six-light window (fourteenth century) divided by a transom into sub-lights at the front balanced at the rear by a four-light window (fourteenth century) also divided into sub-lights.

It will be noticed that all the above examples of gatehouses with large windows come from later medieval times, a period when larger windows were regularly being constructed. This is neatly demonstrated at Cleeve where the inner gatehouse which dates substantially from the thirteenth century, would be expected to have small windows. However, at the front and back are square-headed four-light windows, undoubtedly insertions of a late fifteenth-century reconstruction of the upper storey.

Though gatehouses built or reconstructed in the later medieval period were often given large windows, many of them also received small windows (i.e. of two and sometimes one light). The earlier gatehouses (unless reconstructed, as at Cleeve) tended to retain their older windows that were almost always small. A few instances are still in existence. The early twelfth-century St James' Tower of Bury St Edmunds possesses Norman windows of one and two lights with semicircular heads. Lancet windows, typical of the Early English style, illuminate the upper storey of Beaulieu's thirteenth-century outer gatehouse, while small windows of the same period as at Beaulieu may be seen at Ewenny (both gatehouses) and Minster-in-Sheppey.

Ground-floor windows of medieval date at the front of gatehouses are a rarity, with examples only to be seen at a few gatehouses such as Castle Acre (late fifteenth/early sixteenth century) and Kenilworth (fourteenth century). The Worksop gatehouse possesses a ground-floor chapel-porch which is attached to the front of the building. It too has a large fourteenth-century window of three lights facing the front.

The oriel or projecting window appears to have been introduced into the upper stage (or stages) of gatehouses during the fifteenth century. Apart from its aesthetic value, it enabled officials apart from the porter, such as an abbot, prior or senior obedientary to observe visitors' comings and goings. A few have avoided destruction: Bristol possesses oriels (*c*.1500) at the front and rear of its main gatehouse, oriels which project at both the middle- and upper-storey levels. Montacute also has oriels (fifteenth century) at the front and rear, both projecting from the upper storey only. The single fifteenth-century oriel at Malvern extends from the front of the upper storey, while another oriel (1382) at Thornton projects from the rear of the middle storey. Shallow oriels survive at first-floor level, front and rear, at Ramsey where part of the great gatehouse (*c*.1500) has been left standing.

The porch-towers of Cerne (*c*.1500) and Forde (1528) each display a fine oriel which has been placed in front of both the middle and top storeys of their respective buildings, while at St Osyth at first-floor level there is a splendid high six-light oriel divided by a transom into twelve sub-lights which illuminates the Bishop's Lodging hall of 1527 (Photograph 10). Saighton Grange porch-tower (probably constructed towards the end of the fifteenth century) possesses a small but refined oriel. This window, which is of three lights and stands on a crested corbel, is located on the side wall of the building. Undoubtedly, these instances show that in the late medieval period the builders of porch-towers regarded oriels as a popular ornamental feature and regularly included them in the design of such buildings.

Shapes, parapets and roofs
It will be recalled that the simplest gatehouses were of a rectangular boxlike appearance. They tended to be provided with a horizontal parapet which was often embattled, as at Michelham and Minster-in-Sheppey. Occasionally the parapet was not embattled, for example at Reading where, however, the present work may the product of the nineteenth-century restoration of the gatehouse and not be a faithful copy of the medieval structure. Behind the parapet would be a low roof frequently hidden when viewed from the ground as at Battle, Bridlington and Minster, or a roof standing high as at Aylesford (outer), Michelham and Ely (Porta

Gate). Sometimes a parapeted roof was gabled on both sides (e.g. Abingdon) or hipped on all four sides behind the parapet (e.g. Ely Porta Gate).

In a number of these rectangular gatehouses, there was no roof parapet. Instead, a common practice was to place tall gable-ends over the front and rear walls of a rectangular gatehouse and join them by an overhanging high-sloping roof. There are many instances of this kind: Calder, Easby, Kingswood, Llanthony, Maxstoke (outer), Stoneleigh and Usk. Infrequently as at Bromfield and Cartmel, the gable-ends of the roof were at the sides, with the roof overhanging the front and rear walls.

Sometimes, as at Arbroath and the Sacrist's Gate at Ely, the inverted 'V' of the front gable-end was given a stepped parapet as a decorative feature.

The inner gatehouse at Beaulieu (now Palace House) is probably unique in possessing a roof which, viewed from the front, consists of two gabled sections placed side by side with a deep valley in between.

Very occasionally the four sides of an overhanging roof were hipped, as at Ely (Steeple Gate).

Lean-tos, wings and ranges
Viewed from the front, early gatehouses were generally long and narrow rather than short and wide. Often they had ancillary buildings joined to their sides(s). Such attached buildings, which provided office or living accommodation for the porter, almonries, hospitia and the like, were quite small and often only one storey high. Their roofs, which were quite separate from those of the gatehouse proper, were of the lean-to type with rafters (Figure 17). Instances are displayed at Beaulieu (outer) and Cirencester, and are suggested by remnants at Llanthony.

From the fourteenth century onwards, gatehouses generally became broader, incorporating such additional accommodation as they needed within large wings placed either on one side or both sides of the gate-hall and under the same roof. These wings were thus an integral part of the main structure of the gatehouse, rather than attached buildings. Besides the four examples of winged gatehouses mentioned in Chapter 1 (Blanchland, Bridlington, Thornton and

Wetheral), other examples include Bromfield, Crossraguel, Ely (Porta Gate), Minster-in-Sheppey, Monk Bretton, Polesworth, St Albans (Great Gateway) and Worksop.

The gatehouses of the above group have the following ground plans:

Blanchland Asymmetrical with gate-hall to left, and what may have been the hospitium to the right.
Bridlington Symmetrical with gate-hall in middle, prison to left, and porter's lodge to right (Figure 18).
Bromfield Symmetrical with gate-hall in middle between accommodation of porter to right and stairs to left.
Crossraguel Asymmetrical with gate-hall to left and porter's narrow office on ground floor to right.
Ely (Porta Gate) Symmetrical with gate-hall in middle between chambers of uncertain purpose.
Minster-in-Sheppey Asymmetrical with gate-hall to left and porter's office to right on ground floor.
Monk Bretton Asymmetrical with gate-hall between wider almonry (?) to left and narrower porter's lodge to right.
Polesworth Asymmetrical with gate-hall to right and porter's lodge to left.
St. Albans Symmetrical with gate-hall in middle between chambers of uncertain purpose.
Thornton Symmetrical with gate-hall in middle, porter's lodge to right and accommodation of uncertain purpose to left (possibly part of abbot's lodging).
Wetheral Asymmetrical with gate-hall on left and porter's office to right.
Worksop Symmetrical with gate-hall between guestmaster's chamber and porter's room to left, and chapel with porch to right.

There are also a number of later gatehouses where the middle or gate-hall section is flanked by one or two substantial ranges or attached buildings, each with its distinct architectural identity (such as type of roof, division into bays, style of windowing, use of decorative features, etc.) Good examples of gatehouses with attendant ranges exist at Arbroath, Battle, Ely (Sacrist's Gate), Kingswood, Montacute, Norwich (Bishop's Gate), Polesworth, St Osyth and Stoneleigh.

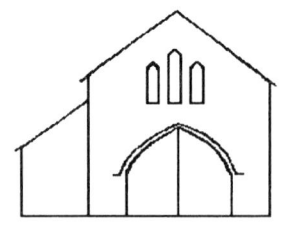

a gatehouse with one lean-to

a gatehouse with two lean-tos

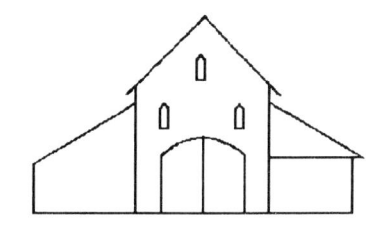

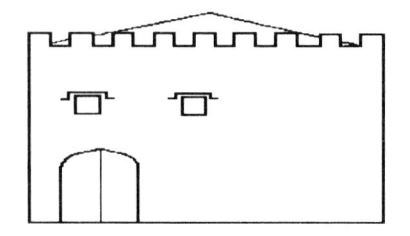

a gatehouse with one wing

a gatehouse with two wings

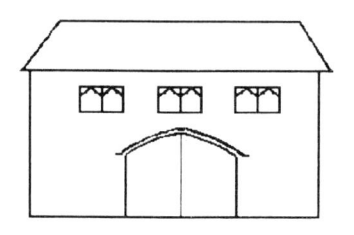

Figure 17 Gatehouses: Lean-tos, Wings and Ranges

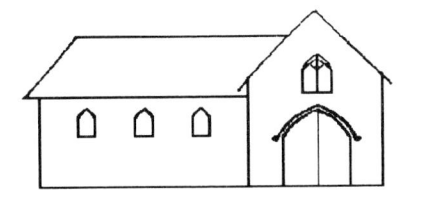

a gatehouse with one range

a gatehouse with two ranges

a gatehouse with one wing and one range

a gatehouse with two wings and two ranges

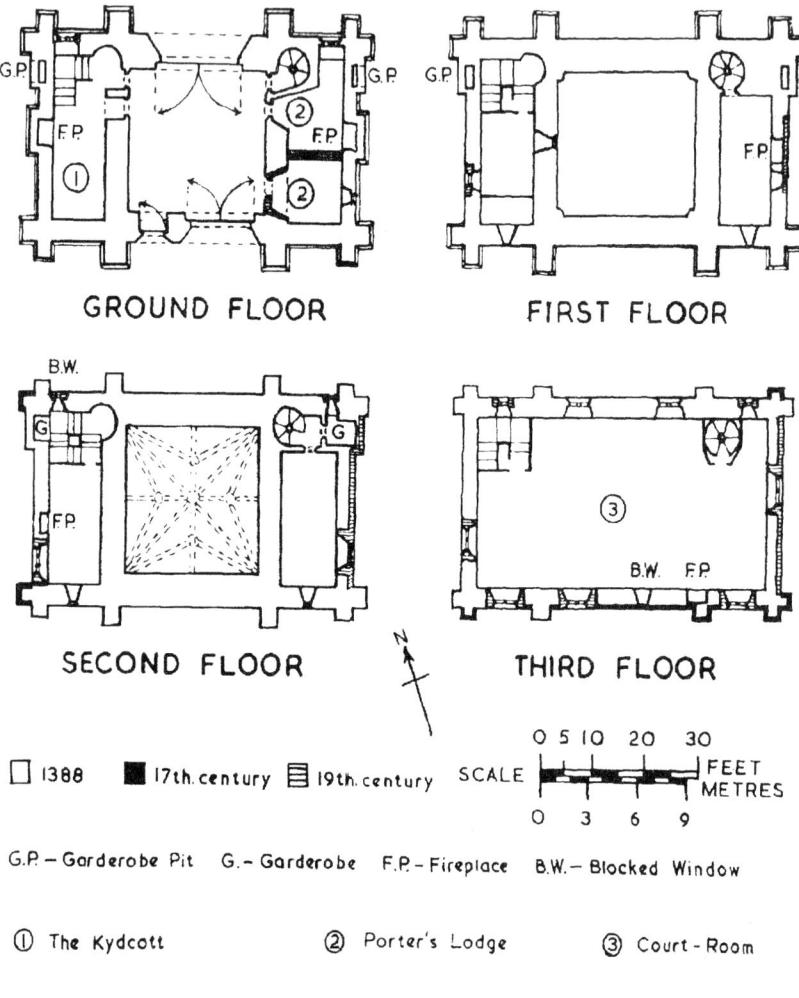

[From Earnshaw, J.R. "A reconstruction of Bridlington Priory", p.5.]

Figure 18   Bridlington Priory, Ground-plan of Gatehouse

Arbroath To the right was the Regality Courthouse (partly destroyed) and Tower, and to the left is the guest-house.
Battle To the right is an early Norman porter's lodge and to the left an almonry (?) converted after the Dissolution into a courthouse (Photograph 11).
Ely (Sacrist's Gate) Almonry (?) to right, sacristry (?) to left.
Kingswood Almonry (?) or porter's lodging to right (partly destroyed) and a complete range (guest-house?) to left.
Montacute Big range, possibly prior's apartments, to left, and shorter range, possibly porter's lodging, to right.
Norwich (Bishop's Gate) Prison (later, porter's lodging) to right, granary to left.
Polesworth In addition to details noted above, almonry to right.
St Osyth (Great Gatehouse) Ranges of unidentified use to left and right.
Stoneleigh Hospitium to left.

Some gatehouses possess (or possessed) wings and ranges. Polesworth, for instance, has a wing to the left of the middle or gate-hall section and a range (almonry) to the right. Wetheral displays the porter's accommodation in a wing to the right of the middle section and the roofline of a former range (possibly indicating a barn or stables) beyond that.

Military devices
The few gatehouses that were built as proper military portals, as at Tynemouth and Portchester where the priory was sited within the bailey of an existing castle or fortress, were equipped with a full complement of architectural paraphernalia for defence. The Tynemouth gatehouse, for example, is partly ruined but it still displays its machicolations. It is fronted by the remnant of a barbican and, most unusually, possesses another barbican to its rear. At Ewenny, where the priory was built and then fortified, the two gatehouses display murder-holes, the north also retaining the grooves of a portcullis. Another instance of a fortified priory is that of Lindisfarne, where the porch-tower is protected by a barbican. Characteristically, such military portals were not necessarily given the types of ornamenta-

tion (niches with statues, religious symbols, etc.) that were employed on the façades of many ordinary monastic portals.

Some ordinary portals, however, were fitted with military devices mainly for show, the most common being embattled parapets. Until the fourteenth century these parapets tended to be plain in appearance, as at Michelham (*c*.1395) which lacks panelling and mouldings. Increasingly, however, later battlements were ornamented as at Bristol Abbey Gatehouse (panelling and pinnacles of *c*.1500), Canterbury Christ Church Christ Church Gate (trefoiled panelling of 1507–17), Montecute (strong fifteenth-century mouldings) and St Osyth Great Gatehouse (flushwork ornamentation of *c*.1475).

An absence of battlements on a gatehouse today, as at the St James' Tower at Bury St Edmunds or at Reading, does not necessarily mean that they were never constructed, merely that they may have fallen down or been removed. At some gatehouses which were photographed in the mid-nineteenth century, such as Clerkenwell, missing battlements have been replaced within recent times.

Several portals have loopholes (e.g. Battle, Bury St Edmunds Great Gate, St Andrews, Thornton), these probably being more for observation than for shooting arrows from. Other devices include machicolations at Alnwick and Canterbury St Augustine's Cemetery Gate, a murder-hole at Crossraguel, an original portcullis at Bury St Edmunds Great Gate, and portcullises at Thornton and the Worcester watergate. Remnants of the drawbridge structure exist at Michelham.

4

STRUCTURE (2)

EXTERNAL ORNAMENTATION

The outside faces of the front and rear walls of gatehouses (and sometimes the fronts of gateways) were often embellished with a variety of architectural features and devices.

Niches, statues and vesicas
Most gatehouses whether large or small possessed at least one niche filled with a statue of its patron saint or a representation of the Godhead such as the Holy Trinity or Christ in Glory. Indeed, many gatehouses displayed a panoply of niches housing, besides those subjects, other saints, doctors of the Church, kings and wealthy founders and the like.

A niche of the simplest kind consisted of nothing more than a shallow recess in the wall: rectangular and framed with plain mouldings (as at Cartmel); a plain round-arched recess (Letheringham); an ogee-arched recess (Chester); or trefoil-headed recess (Canterbury Christ Church Christ Church Gate, Kirkham) (Figure 19). The niche was frequently canopied above the recess, shafted at the sides and provided with a platform below on which the statue could stand. Many façades still exhibit canopied niches, of which instances at St Osyth, Thornton (Photograph 12) and Worcester have survived in reasonably good condition.

Most niches had their statues pulled down and destroyed, especially if they could be reached from below without too much difficulty. A few original statues, however, outlasted the immediate aftermath of the Dissolution and later religious bigotry, and some still occupy their niches. Abingdon,

trefoil-headed

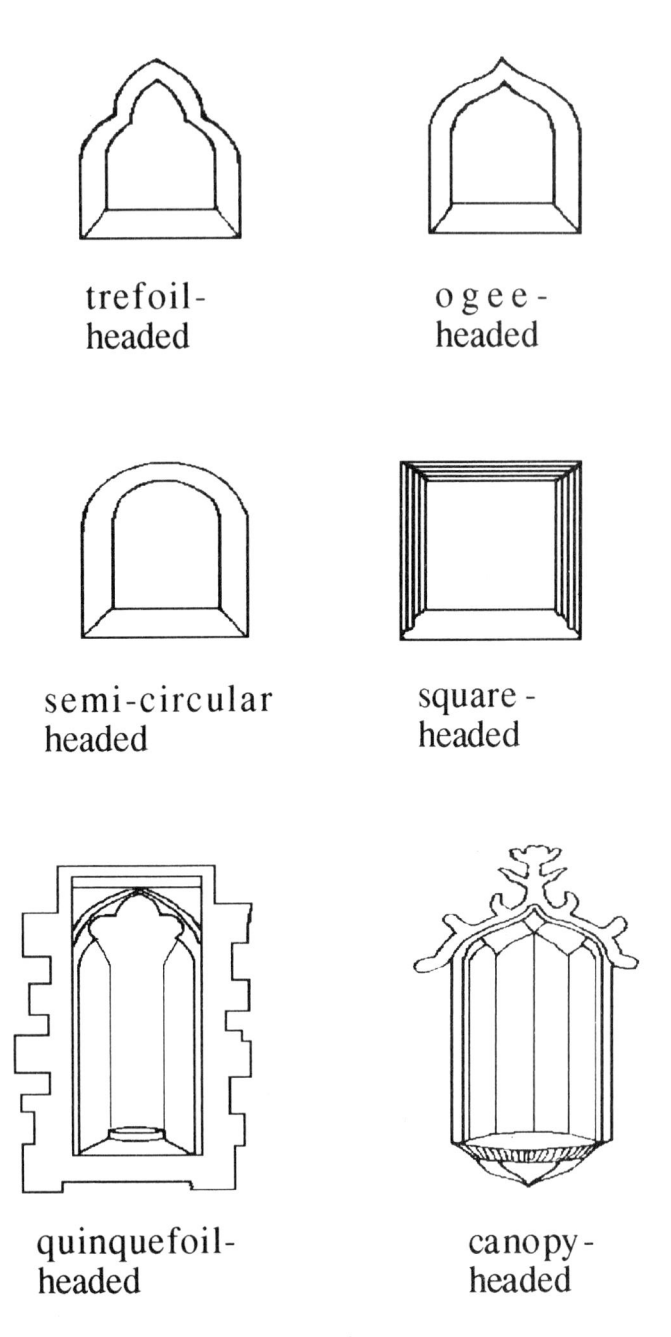

ogee-headed

semi-circular headed

square-headed

quinquefoil-headed

canopy-headed

Figure 19 Niche Types

for instance, claims to possess an original statue of the Blessed Virgin Mary (Pevsner, 1966, p. 55). Worksop has several medieval statues including a figure of St Cuthbert, patron saint of the priory, and a representation of the Holy Trinity. Other ancient statues may be seen at Kirkham (for instance, the figures of SS Phillip and Bartholomew) and at the Abbot's Gatehouse at Peterborough where there are three on each façade. The identities of these figures, according to Mee (1945, p. 259), are King Edward II between an abbot and a prior at the front, and apostles at the rear.

A collection of ancient figures survives at Thornton, remarkable (given the zeal of the destroyers) in that the main central niches still contain statues of the Blessed Virgin Mary (patroness of the abbey) in the middle, St John the Baptist to the left and a bishop (possibly St Augustine) to the right. Other smaller niches also are filled with statues, including one seated figure believed to be Christ.

A less common type of recess than a niche for the display of a figure was the vesica or pointed oval. The seated figure of Christ exists at the gatehouse of Kirkham where the vesica is placed high above the main archway leading into the gate-hall.

Sometimes, instead of a statue-occupied niche or vesica, a recess was provided in which would be placed a panel containing a Biblical or other religious scene in shallow or high relief. The inner gatehouse at Cleeve still possesses two panels of this type, on the front façade a portrayal of the Virgin with the Child on her left arm and a lily in her right hand, and on the rear façade a scene of the Crucifixion.

Shields and coats of arms

From the thirteenth century onwards, the display of heraldic symbols usually in the form of coats of arms mounted on shields became a common form of adornment of gatehouses on their front and rear faces. Probably the earliest display is at Kirkham (late thirteenth century, Photograph 13) where there are ten shields. These are arranged in a row of four immediately below the parapet of the building and as two groups of three on either side of the main archway. The coats of arms displayed are chiefly those of the founders and patrons of the priory, the lords of Helmsley, but the arms of England are also shown there.

Sometimes a single coat of arms was displayed in a prominent position, as at Bridlington, Bristol (Abbey Gatehouse), Leez (both gatehouses) and St Osyth (Great Gatehouse rear façade). However, it was probably more usual to place a row of shields on a façade: thus at West Acre there is a row of three on the front wall, and at Castle Acre a row of four. At Clerkenwell the original five shields on the front wall and the three on the rear wall had become badly eroded. They were replaced in 1893 by the present ones. The Prior's Gateway (c.1510) at Peterborough (Photograph 14), possibly the most ornate surviving gateway in the country, has a row of nine coats of arms.

The gatehouse which exhibits an ostentatious array of coats of arms on its front face is Butley, where there are 35 shields in five rows (the display dating from c.1325). The shields are placed, seven to a row, in a chequerboard pattern over the vehicular and pedestrian archways. Pevsner (1961, p. 139) supplies the identity of the coats of arms which include those of England, France and the Holy Roman Empire, Christ's Passion, and many East Anglian baronial families.

Occasionally, as at Stamford Greyfriars, shields may be seen that do not have (nor ever seem to have had) coats of arms incised on their surfaces and thus serve a purely ornamental purpose on the gatehouse façade. The gatehouse at Malvern also possesses plain shields, five being placed at the front in a row on either side of the main archway.

At the gatehouse of Kingswood (fourteenth century, reconstructed in the sixteenth century), over the front main archway there is a carving of an angel holding a shield, possibly originally bearing the arms of the abbey, while at Monk Bretton in a similar position is a figure which may also be an angel, holding a shield on which are incised the arms of the priory. These are single instances of a popular device used towards the end of the medieval period, namely to display coats of arms by means of angels or demi-angels. Probably the best example of this method of displaying arms is found on the front façade of the Christ Church Gate at Canterbury where there is a rank of five demi-angels on either side of the principal niche, each figure bearing a coat of arms. Clearly, such a use of angelic figures softened the military/civic symbolism conveyed by a shield bearing arms, while at the same time adding religious significance to it.

Panelling, blind arcading and friezes
Quite a number of the larger or more important gatehouses and gateways were decorated with a variety of architectural devices, such as blind arcading, which were built into the external faces of front and sometimes rear walls. These devices, which were characterised by utilising greater or lesser degrees of relief, were in addition to other types of decoration such as flushwork and ornamental brickwork which contrasted with the plain surface of a wall.

Panelling, frequently produced by constructing blind or blank mini-arcades, was applied by builders in all centuries between the Norman Conquest and the Dissolution. An early example (c.1120–48) of work of this kind is evident at Bury St Edmunds on the St James' Tower, where there are six blind arches with semicircular heads arranged in three pairs across the front façade at the level of the third storey, while at the fourth- or top-storey level the panelling is in the form of shallow roundels. Exceptionally for gatehouses, this work is repeated not only on the rear face of the tower but on the two sides as well.

The thirteenth century is represented typically by pointed arcading on the front of the upper storey of St Mary's Gate at Gloucester. Here there are four prominent arches of which the two inner ones are taller than the two outer or flanking ones. The lower portions of these archways (of which the two inner ones are subdivided) are occupied by small windows. In the gable overhead is more blind arcading, this consisting of a set of three arches of which the middle is taller than the two flanking ones. A simple or rudimentary type of panelling may be observed on the front and rear façades of the Abbot's Gatehouse at Peterborough. This remarkably fine thirteenth-century gatehouse (Photograph 15) has the corners of its pilastered buttresses ornamented with triple-round shafts which descend from the level of the roof parapet to the ground. Large 'panels' are produced as a result of the meeting of these shafts with string-courses running horizontally across the walls.

The finest examples of external panelling come from the fourteenth century. The main gatehouse at Peterborough, the gatehouse at Battle, The Pends at St Andrews, the St Ethelbert's Gate at Norwich, the Fyndon Gate at Canterbury St Augustine's and the Great Gate at Bury St. Edmunds all offer good examples of panelling and arcading of that century. The work at Peterborough was probably constructed at the beginning of the century. It consists of a series of panelled arches which have been placed across the front wall of the gatehouse at the upper-storey level and continued on to the octagonal turrets at the sides. Two of the arches on the main wall are pierced by small windows; the others have shallow recesses which formerly may have housed statues.

The Battle gatehouse which was almost certainly constructed in the middle of the fourteenth century (on the site of an earlier portal), has a rich array of panelling on its front face at the level of the first-floor storey, panelling which is repeated in identical form at the rear of the building. This panelling consists of a set of twelve arches stretching across the face of the gatehouse. Like the gatehouse at Peterborough, the arcading is continued across the lateral octagonal turrets. The arches have well-cusped ogee heads, these heads being interposed by a series of quatrefoils, the whole assembly of heads and quatrefoils giving the appearance of a long frieze. Ten of the arches across the main wall are blind, the middle two being windowed.

The ruined west front of St Andrews Cathedral-Priory, which was rebuilt soon after the disastrous fire of 1378, displays a set of blind arcading over the great west doorway. The Pends gatehouse located nearby exhibits similar arcading of the same approximate date over its front archway. The gatehouse arcading consists of seven shallow, shafted arches all of the same size under trefoiled heads, probably deep enough to have originally held statues.

At Norwich the St Ethelbert's Gate exhibits across its front face a spread of niches of varying sizes. These recesses possess pointed and cusped heads with steep gables. The display effectively constitutes panelling which, with the attendant flushwork (see below) and a narrow frieze of quatrefoils immediately underneath, is visually striking.

Of these six gatehouses, the Fyndon Gate at Canterbury St. Augustine's probably has the most luxuriant display of blind arcading. This portal, extensively restored after being severely damaged in the Second World War, was first built in a mature Decorated style during the first ten years of the century, that is, about the time of the remodelling of the Peterborough gatehouse. The panelling, like that at Peterborough and Battle, stretches from the lateral octagonal turrets on which it is also applied, to the middle of the main wall over the super-arch of the gatehouse. The panelling, which is rhythmically irregular, consists of a series of gabled trefoiled niches and two-light windows. Over the panelling there is a band or frieze of cusped triangles occupying the wall-space between the panelling below and the roof parapet above. Additional panelling is provided on the turrets by long shafts of stone which are carried down from the mullions of high windows.

The Great Gate of Bury St Edmunds exhibits fourteenth-century decorative work at its maturest phase (1327–48). Besides having a variety of long niches some of which are gabled, the whole front façade is divided by long shafts and string courses creating and emphasising the effect of panelling and, incidentally, anticipating the impending Perpendicular style. There are also on this face four roundels or circular panels, of which the lower two are filled with quatrefoils and the upper two with six-pointed stars.

In the fifteenth and sixteenth centuries, shallow panelling was frequently placed on the walls of English churches, cloisters, and so on, but there are few surviving gatehouses or gateways of this period displaying such Perpendicular panelling. The Christ Church Gate at Canterbury Christ Church, which dates from the early sixteenth century, is probably the most ornately panelled example of all. All the surfaces of the exterior of the front wall are panelled, as are the turrets. The levels of the three storeys of the gatehouse are marked visually by two broad bands. The lower band dividing the ground floor from the first-floor storey consists of a frieze of shields on quatrefoils; the upper band marking the division between the upper two storeys has half-length angels carrying shields. Another instance is the fifteenth-century gatehouse at Malvern where the lower and upper storeys of the front façade (but not the rear façade) are covered with cinquefoiled and trefoiled panels respectively. A late example of panelling is displayed by the Evesham gate-tower (detached bell tower) of 1529–39 where the exterior walls and buttresses of this elegant building are profusely adorned. Ramsey's gatehouse remnant ($c.1500$) also retains several tall cinquefoiled panels.

The Prior's Gate at Peterborough, though single-storeyed, carries a frieze below the row of nine shields referred to earlier. This frieze consists of a row of fourteen quatrefoils. There are other friezes at Montacute where there are quatrefoils over the fifteenth-century oriel, at the fifteenth-century Bishop's Gate at Norwich, and at Ramsey. At the last of these, the friezes are adjacent to windows and consist of fleurons and quatrefoils.

It may have been thought that some of the porch-towers, especially if built later, would have exhibited external wall panelling. As it happens only the fragment of the late fifteenth-century west range porch at Leiston has such decorative work. Constructed of red brick, its north turret (Photograph 16) displays a few cinquefoiled panels typical of the period in East Anglia.

Flushwork, mosaics and brickwork

Flat surface forms of ornamentation were also popular in medieval times, especially in the east of England. Flushwork notably was employed on many different buildings, particularly churches, and quite a number of portals survive which are decorated in this manner.

Nine portals display flushwork and three of them – Broomholm, Dunwich and St. Benet at Holme – have small portions only. St Benet's (early fourteenth century) has flushwork in the form of a laddered pattern on the buttresses; Broomholm (fifteenth century) exhibits on a spandrel of a rear arch a small amount of flushwork adjacent to a shield; Dunwich (late fourteenth/early fifteenth century) has a few quatrefoiled panels over its smaller, pedestrians' archway.

The other six portals, all complete, comprising five gatehouses [Burnham Norton, Butley, Colchester St John's, Norwich (St Ethelbert's Gate) and St Osyth (Great Gatehouse)] and one porch-tower at Castle Acre, have much more ornamentation of this type. Burnham Norton (early fourteenth century) vies with Butley in possessing the earliest flush-work displayed in these portals. The Burnham gatehouse (Photograph 17) exhibits flushwork on the front and rear walls in the form of sham windows which have cusped and trefoiled tracery at the front and cusped and intersecting tracery at the rear. Butley (c.1320–25) shares with Burnham Norton in using sham windows which possess cusped and trefoiled 'lights', but Butley's employment of flushwork compared with Burnham Norton is more luxuriant if not extravagent, for its gatehouse is adorned with chequerboard and several shapes (such as mouchette, cinquefoil, quatrefoil, flowing tracery, etc.).

The St Ethelbert's Gate at Norwich (c.1328) is memorable for the three large rose windows executed in flushwork which appear immediately below the gabled parapet. Though much restored in the nineteenth century, there is evidence (Pevsner, 1962, p. 232) that the original design of the front of this gatehouse was adhered to.

When we come to the gatehouses at Colchester St John's and St Osyth, both of which probably date from the second half of the fifteenth century, we find flushwork applied to every available space on the front wall exteriors. This is chiefly in the form of long sham panels separated by plain shafts, but whereas the Colchester panels mainly have cinquefoiled head and terminate in sham pinnacles, the St Osyth panels have trefoiled heads only. At Colchester the panelling takes in the parapet as well, while at St Osyth the parapet carries chequerboard and diamond-work designs instead. The rear façades of both gatehouses are toned down in their use of flushwork, this being restricted chiefly to the parapets, with panelling at Colchester and diamond-work at St Osyth. Compared with these two gatehouses, the prior's house porch of the sixteenth century at Castle Acre is limited in its employment of flushwork designs. It has a broad spread of flushwork over the main archway, the pattern being chequerboard-work only.

Other forms of surface decoration were also used on façades. The St James' Tower at Bury St Edmunds displays within the gable over the great archway fishscale, a reticulated type of twelfth-century ornament giving the impression of a mosaic. The Leez inner gatehouse has on its façade and turrets diaper-work (brickwork patterned in two colours) of the late fifteenth century. These are isolated instances of surface decoration, and today we have no means of knowing how prevalent or widespread was the use of such ornamentation on portals generally.

Main arches, super-arches and spandrel infills
Great arches, through which visitors entered or left a gatehouse or passed through a gateway, were often considered important enough to be subjects of ornamentation, a practice that was adhered to throughout the medieval period. The plainest of arches had no mouldings whatsoever [e.g. the rear arch at Blanchland (c.1500)]. Sometimes there was a continuous moulding, often in the form of a single chamfer [e.g. flat at Crossraguel and Usk (both sixteenth century), hollow at front of Blanchland] or sometimes as a three-quarters roll, as at Bromfield (fourteenth century). The front archway at Calder (fourteenth century) exhibits slightly more ornamentation in having a small capital on each respond allied above to a double-chamfered moulding divided by a quirk.

A number of the larger portals have archways possessing highly ornamented mouldings. The twelfth-century Norman gatehouse at Hexham, for instance, has a front arch with plain capitals. Below each capital is a half-round bordered by a flat chamfer, and above, a triple-round of which the middle one is smaller than the outer ones. The main gatehouse at Peterborough also possesses a twelfth-century Norman front archway, more elaborate than the Hexham arch, having stepped capitals decorated with chevrons and cones. On each side of the archway below the capitals are two round shafts which descend to the floor. Above the capitals is a set of three-quarter rounds. The rear archway of this gatehouse is typical of several in having a simpler design than the front, namely one shaft only per side descending to the floor.

Ornamentation of thirteenth-century archways tended to be akin to those of the previous century with shafting set below capitals, Gloucester (St Mary's Gate) providing a basic example of the period. Its front arch, though eroded, displays stiff-leaf foliage on the right-hand surviving capital. Below this capital a single round shaft descends to the ground, while above, the arch has a triple-round design, the central round being larger than its two flanking partners. As an instance of a more elaborate thirteenth-century archway, the Abbot's Gatehouse at Peterborough cannot be bettered. Its outer archway has four engaged round shafts which are separated from each other by small steps. Above round capitals, the arch is continued to its apex with four flat chamfers separated by three quirks.

Probably the double flat chamfer separated by a quirk was the most frequently employed moulding-set on arches in the fourteenth century. This is exemplified on the front vehicular and pedestrians' archways at Chester where the mouldings are continuous. Less commonly, however, the rear archway of the same gatehouse has triple flat chamfers divided by two quirks. Stamford Greyfriars illustrates another commonly used ornament of the fourteenth century, a front arch with two continuous hollow-chamfered mouldings separated by a quirk.

The fourteenth century also provides us with some more ornate examples, typical of the Decorated style. The obtuse-pointed archway for vehicles at the front of the gatehouse at Battle exhibits a variety of mouldings arranged in three sets, above which is a prominent hoodmould. Similar mouldings are repeated round the pedestrians' entrance and round the single rear archway of this portal. Other ornate examples of archway mouldings (e.g. fleurons) may be seen at Canterbury St Augustine's Fyndon Gate.

As an example of fifteenth- and sixteenth-century decorative work on archways, Montacute has mouldings both at the front and rear of the gatehouse that are alike. They are continuous except for being interrupted at the shoulders by small, nominal capitals. The mouldings themselves comprise a hollow chamfer which divides a half-round on the inner side from an ogee on the outer side. Surviving embellished gateways (as opposed to gatehouses) are extremely rare, and we must look (again) to the Prior's Gate at Peterborough to find an ornate example. The larger (vehicular) archway of the early sixteenth century has rich continuous mouldings which house seven small empty niches on each side.

A few gatehouses have been equipped with super-arches that envelop the front archway, as at Bury St Edmunds (Great Gate), Canterbury St Augustine's (Fyndon), Chester (Abbey Gateway), Easby, Peterborough (main) and Thornton. It is quite possible that in one or two of these cases the erection of a super-arch, for instance at Peterborough, was part of a general reconstruction of the gatehouse and may have been intended to strengthen the existing fabric. Whatever the reason may have been for providing a super-arch, the opportunity was often grasped to embellish the arch and/or the area between it and the lower arch. The Bury St Edmunds (early fourteenth century) super-arch, which is embellished with a foliated hoodmould, is in the form of a great ogee. Underneath it are three empty niches and below them a segmental functional arch. The fourteenth-century super-arch at Canterbury St Augustine's is so wide that it spans the whole distance between the flanking turrets. Like the functional arch below, it is decorated with fleurons. Chester, too, has a wide super-arch of the fourteenth century. Double-chamfered, it encompasses the two functional archways (vehicular and pedestrians) as well as two arched but otherwise plain niches.

Easby is slightly different as its super-arch (*c.*1300), which is two-centred, envelops a semicircular functional arch. Somewhat more decorated than the latter, the super-arch, which displays a well-formed hoodmould, possesses two orders of shafting below its capitals, and flat chamfers divided by a quirk above the capitals. The Peterborough super-arch (fourteenth century) has no capitals. However the mouldings above its springing, which include a hoodmould, are different and more complex than those of the respond below and include rounds, hollows and a quirk. The functional arch underneath is twelfth century, semi-circular and quite plain, with a series of three-quarter rounds. At Thornton is a super-arch (*c.*1382) which is different again. It is segmental and springs from buttresses or turret-bases at its flanks. It is richly cusped and sub-cusped, and supports a walkway in front of the second storey. Recessed below it is the great functional archway leading into the gate-hall.

The spandrel or area of walling immediately to the left or right of a main archway, approximately triangular in shape, was frequently used for decorative purposes, especially in the middle and towards the end of the medieval period. The variety of spandrel infill carvings is quite extraordinary. The spandrels of the super-arch (early fourteenth century) of the front of the Fyndon Gate at Canterbury St Augustine's have quatrefoils enriched with ballflower, while within these shapes are seated figures now sadly mutilated. Butley's main archway (early fourteenth century) has pointed trefoils in its spandrels, and at St Benet's the left spandrel of the early fourteenth-century archway displays a man holding a spear, and the right, a lion (?). At Norwich the archway of the Erpingham Gate is possibly the tallest in the country. Dating from 1420, it possesses spandrels which are bounded externally by handsome half-octagonal buttresses, panelled and niched. The spandrels themselves are enriched with shields and tracery-figures.

Both the spandrels as well as the fifteenth/sixteenth-century main archway at Sudbury Blackfriars are carved in wood, the spandrels having floral designs. At St Osyth Great Gatehouse of *c*.1475 there is a dragon on one spandrel and a figure of St George or St Michael on the other. The royal arms and the arms of the abbey are displayed at Abingdon (late fifteenth century), while the inner gatehouse at Leez (sixteenth century) has its spandrels ornamented with the fleur-de-lis (left) and Tudor rose (right).

Inscriptions
The gatehouses of Bristol, Canterbury Christ Church (Christ Church Gate), Carlisle and Cleeve are possibly the only surviving ones to display lettering cut in the stonework. These inscriptions are written in Latin, the universal language of the Western medieval world. The inscription at Bristol appears on the front vehicular archway, and that at Canterbury immediately over the two front archways. On the rear face at Carlisle an inscription records the name of the builder, Prior Slee, and the date of construction, 1527. A rectangular stone tablet (probably dating from the sixteenth century) over the front archway of the inner gatehouse at Cleeve has an inscription which translated into English reads, 'Gate be open, shut to no honest person'. Another tablet in a similar position on the rear wall gives the name of

the abbot, 'Dovell', who was responsible for reconstructing the gatehouse at this time.

One porch-tower has an inscription on it, this being at Forde. The lettering is placed below the roof parapet and records in Latin the name of the builder of the tower (Abbot Chard) and date of construction (1528).

Comparisons and contrasts between portals

Having identified the chief architectural features (mainly of a decorative kind) which are visible when looking at the exteriors of gatehouses and other portals, our final task in this chapter is to examine the material as a whole, and to draw comparisons and contrasts between the different buildings.

Some gatehouses such as Blanchland, Calder and Carlisle were devoid of ornamentation at the front and rear except in minor respects (e.g. battlements at Blanchland, responds and simple mouldings on the arches at Calder and chamfered arches at Carlisle etc.). Were the location of the conventual church and claustral buildings at these three sites not already known, it might have been uncertain as to which façade of the portal was at the front and which was at the rear.

As a general rule, however, the front façade of a gatehouse was ornamented in order to present its abbey or priory to the world in the best possible light. This did not mean that the rear façade was denuded of embellishment. On the contrary, it was often decorated though usually to a lesser degree than the front, for instance in the employment of fewer niches (e.g. Worcester Edgar Tower), fewer coats of arms (e.g. Clerkenwell) or less complex mouldings of main archway (e.g. Malvern). Sometimes, however, the rear wall would match the front wall architectural feature by architectural feature, as at Barking (e.g. three-light window), Battle (e.g. wall-arcading), and Montacute (e.g. archway mouldings).

Curiously enough, at Bristol (Abbey Gatehouse) the twelfth-century rear archway for vehicular traffic is moulded more elaborately than the corresponding twelfth-century front archway, the former consisting of three orders and the latter one order. Such a disposition of ornamentation is quite exceptional, and rarely did the rear façade of a gatehouse outdo the front façade.

There were, of course, enormous differences in the amount and quality of ornamentation applied to the front and rear of gatehouses and, to a lesser extent, to gateways. Many of the smaller gatehouses, and some of the larger ones too, such as Bridlington, Crossraguel and St Albans, were quite plain.

Typically, the front façade of a small gatehouse would have had one architectural feature to provide the focus of attention. Normally this feature was placed in the area of walling immediately over the great archway at the front of the gatehouse where it would attract the eyes of a viewer. Often this feature would have been a niche filled with the statue of the saint or Godhead to whom the abbey or priory was dedicated. Among a numerically larger group, Cartmel, Letheringham and Tewkesbury still display their central niches but in each case the statue has been removed. At Letheringham, where the cloister and its attendant buildings have completely vanished from the one or other side of the conventual church, the niche is inserted into the south-facing façade of the gatehouse. As the north-facing façade has no niche (or other ornamentation), the inference may be drawn that the cloister lay to the north of the church.

Alternatively, the focal point of the front façade could have been a delicately traceried central window. One instance of this is at Stoneleigh, where the fourteenth-century window possesses flowing tracery; a second is at Kingswood, where the sixteenth-century window has a mullion of Renaissance character in the form of a lily-plant representing the Annunciation to the Virgin, the saint to whom the abbey was dedicated. Other central devices used to draw the attention of visitors include a shield on which would have appeared the arms of the monastery (e.g. Bridlington), or a frieze always used in combination with other forms of ornament such as windows or blind arcading (as at the Fyndon Gate of Canterbury St Augustine's and the main gatehouse at Peterborough).

In some gatehouses their front façades would display not one device but several of the same kind, often repeated in association with other devices. Probably the most common plan was to combine the use of windows and niches in two ways: Durham, Burnham Norton and Maxstoke have a central window (Durham and Burnham Norton three-light,

Maxstoke two-light) flanked by one niche on each side. In contrast, Norwich (Bishop's Gate) and Tewkesbury have a central niche flanked by two windows. A variation of this occurs at Whalley (inner) where the central niche has shields with coats of arms on each side, with the two windows just above.

Beyond such 'double' combinations, the use of ornamental devices does not seem to have followed any set pattern. To take three differing instances of the employment of such features, the main gatehouse at Bristol displays on both its façades an oriel at two levels in association with shields and niches. Cleeve's inner gatehouse combines a four-light window with inscription panel and two niches at the front, and a nearly identical arrangement at the rear with three niches instead of two. The Porta Gate at Ely has four niches plus windows of three, two and one light at the front and a similar design from which niches are absent at the rear.

The gatehouses with elaborate and possibly the most luxuriant (if not in every case the most handsome) forms of exterior decoration are those at Bury St Edmunds (Great Gate), Butley, Canterbury Christ Church (Christ Church Gate), Canterbury St Augustine's (Fyndon Gate), Colchester St John's, Kirkham, Norwich (St Ethelbert's Gate), St Osyth (Great Gatehouse), Thornton, Worcester (Edgar Tower) and Worksop. A cursory examination of these eleven portals suggests that, as façades became more complex in design in the later middle ages, the design of each portal was developed along singular lines without much reference to the emerging designs of the others.

The Bury gatehouse is to be remembered for its severe square façade on which has been grafted a series of niches and roundels at several levels, all leading the viewer's eye towards the big ogeed super-arch. Butley's, in contrast, has a façade the outline of which is disseminated in a gabled roof and flanking proto-turrets reinforced with prominent angled buttresses. Given the abundance of ornamental detail which competes for the attention of onlookers, the clean lines of Bury's Great Gate are missing at Butley. However, a profusion of ornamental detail does not always cause distraction, and the Kirkham gatehouse shows how a façade generously covered with niches, shields, well-traceried windows, panelling and arch-gables may still display a unity of design which is satisfying to the observer.

The Benedictine abbey of Canterbury St Augustine housed the important shrine of St Augustine, who revived Christianity in the south of England. Its great gatehouse, Fyndon Gate, built at the beginning of the fourteenth century, served as a signpost for pilgrims intending to visit the church in which the shrine was located. It was therefore given several striking features. These included the two great octagonal turrets between which are friezes, rows of niches, and a large super-arch.

A few hundred yards away at Canterbury Christ Church, the cathedral-priory, was the newer shrine of Thomas à Becket, a shrine which undoubtedly diverted pilgrims in that direction in the middle and later medieval period rather than to the older shrine of St Augustine's. It is surprising that the monks of the cathedral-priory apparently permitted two centuries to elapse before constructing a gatehouse of even grander design than the Fyndon Gate down the road, to channel their stream of pilgrims. The Christ Church Gate at Canterbury is a sophisticated product of applied early sixteenth-century ornamentation where Renaissance influences are apparent on the Gothic work. The dignified gatehouse serves as a fitting entrance to England's chief cathedral. Though taller than wider, it is perfectly proportioned for a three-storey building. The horizontal rows of shields, demi-angels, small niches and so on collectively focus attention on the large central niche that surely must have once contained a medieval figure of Christ in Glory (and which now has a modern figure of Christ).

The gatehouse of Colchester St John's and the Great Gatehouse of St Osyth may be geographically in close proximity and alike in their lavish use of flushwork on their façades but, apart from these, comparisons are not easy to make. The St Osyth building has wide ranges beyond its two wings, collectively giving an expansive horizontal profile. Colchester's has a ruined narrow range (probably the porter's accommodation) to the left of the middle section and a wing to the right. Together with the tall turrets with conical caps, these characteristics emphasise the building's verticality. Though both buildings display façades of the finest appearance, the symmetry of the front elevation of St Osyth puts it slightly ahead of the asymmetrical gatehouse at Colchester.

The mighty Thornton gatehouse is an architectural and ornamental *tour de force*. Its façade reveals that there is a main division into three cross-bays, with additional lateral walls beyond the outer bays. This laterally extended façade is suggestive of a palace rather than a gatehouse. Its decorative features are applied chiefly to the two upper storeys, and the most prominent of these features consist of richly canopied niches occupying the central bay over the great archway in two rows of three. There are more niches in the adjacent bays. Other decorative devices include brackets carried on caryatids, cusping and panelling. The striking thing about this façade is the sparing manner in which the ornamentation has been applied. Indeed the whole exterior of the front, which includes projecting half-octagonal turrets, exhibits a consistent and restrained use of ornament which lends dignity to the building as a whole.

The St Ethelbert's Gate at Norwich and the Edgar Tower at Worcester were both severely restored in the nineteenth century, and what we now see may not be entirely in accordance with the medieval intention for these buildings. Nevertheless, the Norwich gatehouse is memorable for the exciting and possibly original way in which the geometrically designed flushwork above complements the lines of niches, chequerboard-work and quatrefoils below. The Edgar Tower, characterised by its strength and solidity perhaps has less to commend it aesthetically apart from the canopies of the niches which may well be Victorian but of high quality.

This leaves the gatehouse at Worksop, a handsome building three bays wide. Its main decorative feature is its six-light front window, flanked by niches and smaller windows and accompanied by other niches and buttressing. None of these clutter the façade, and even the well-decorated chapel porch which is asymmetrically attached to the right side of the front wall does not spoil the general effect.

1   Great Gate, Staffordshire

2   Lenton, the White Hart Hotel

3   Maxstoke Priory, example of precinct wall

4   Usk Priory, gatehouse to front

5   Kidwelly Castle, main gatehouse to front

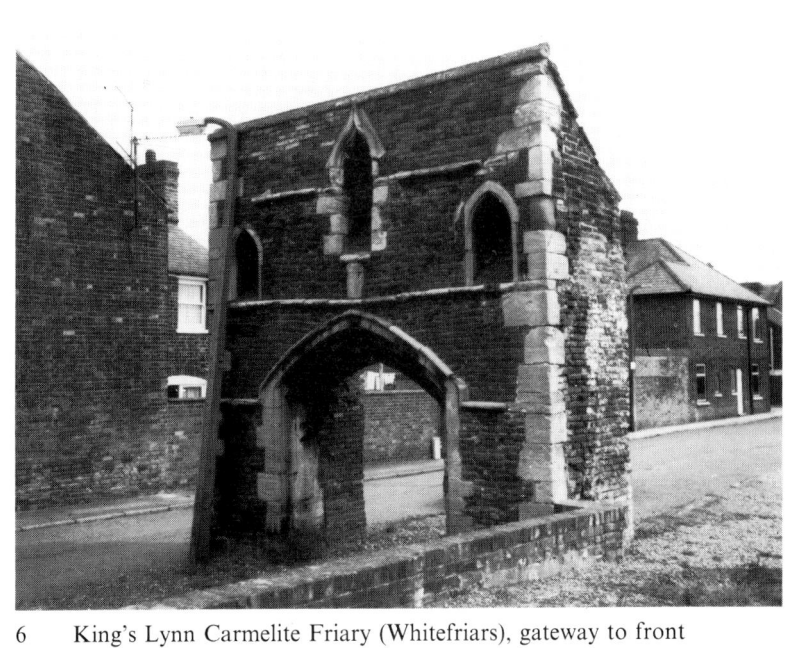

6   King's Lynn Carmelite Friary (Whitefriars), gateway to front

7   Dunfermline Abbey, gatehouse (The Pends) to rear

8   Bury St Edmunds Abbey, gatehouse (Great Gate) to front

9   Hyde Abbey, one-storeyed gatehouse to front

10 St Osyth Abbey, Bishop's Lodging hall to front

11   Battle Abbey, three-storeyed gatehouse to front

12   Thornton Abbey, front façade of gatehouse showing principal niches and original statues

13   Kirkham Priory, gatehouse to front

14   Peterborough Abbey (now cathedral), Prior's Gateway to front

15   Peterborough Abbey (now cathedral), Abbot's Gatehouse to front

16   Leiston Abbey, west range porch north turret fragment

17   Burnham Norton Friary, gatehouse to rear flushwork

18   Monk Bretton Priory, gatehouse gate-hall interior showing chase where main gates were fitted

19   St Albans Abbey (now cathedral), gatehouse to front

20   St Albans Abbey (now cathedral), gatehouse to rear

21   Bristol Abbey (now cathedral), Abbey Gatehouse showing interior wall arcading of vehicular gate-hall

22   Wetheral Priory, gatehouse to front

23 Evesham Abbey, North Gate to front

24 Alnwick Abbey, gatehouse to front

25   Ely Cathedral-priory, Palace gatehouse to front

26   Letheringham Priory, gatehouse to front

27   Forde Abbey, Abbot Chard's Tower to front

28   Oxford, St Bernard's College (now St John's College), gate-tower to front

29 Wigmore Abbey, inner gatehouse to front

30 Chester Abbey (now cathedral), Abbey Gateway to front

31 Norwich Cathedral-priory, watergate (Pull's Ferry) to front

32 Coventry Charterhouse, postern to front

5

THE GATE-HALL

Much of the following data is based on a survey of surviving gatehouses, the results of which are provided in the four sections of Appendix 2.

In its basic form, displayed in 56 out of 148 gatehouses examined (i.e. the gatehouses listed in Section 1 of Appendix 2, each having the following configuration of data: '1 n/a no no 1 n/a'), the gate-hall consisted of a high, rectangular chamber with a single large archway at each end enabling traffic of all types to proceed through in either direction (Figure 20). Moreover, in one or both side walls of the gate-hall there would have been one or more small doorways connecting with the porter's office or with other ground-floor accommodation. Clearly this general gate-hall arrangement was favoured in many smaller gatehouses (e.g. Calder, Letheringham, Usk), but also in some of the larger ones (e.g. the St James' Tower at Bury St Edmunds, Thetford). No other group of gatehouses identified in the survey equalled or surpassed this total of 58, and it is reasonable to conclude that gatehouses with one undivided gate-hall and two archways were a common if not the most common type.

The hall was frequently divided into a lobby or outer section, and a gate-passage or inner section by a stone cross-wall or transverse septum pierced by one or sometimes two archways (Figure 21). Thirty-four gatehouses with a single archway at the front and rear may be positively identified as having a cross-wall (each configured as '1 n/a yes no 1 n/a' in Appendix 2, Section 1), and clearly the insertion of such a feature was popular among designers.

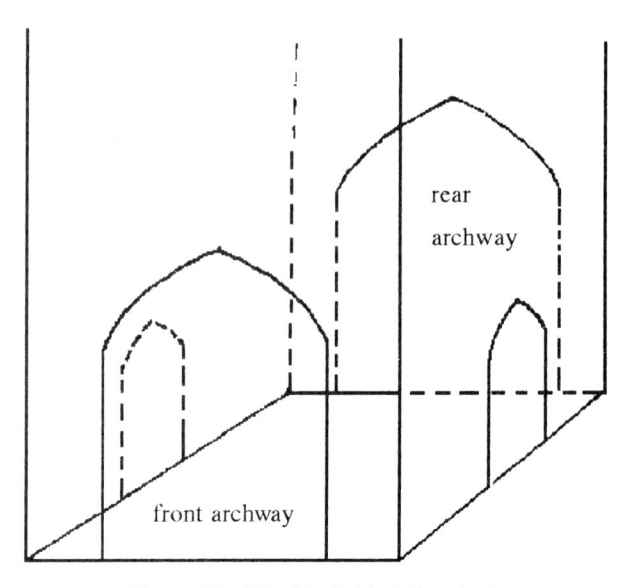

Figure 20   The Undivided Gate-hall

Structurally, the significance of the precise placement of a cross-wall along a gate-hall was that usually it was made to coincide with one of the interior bay intervals as defined in some gatehouses by the vaulting over the gate-hall (a subject to which we shall return later).

Of 51 gatehouses with cross-walls, 14 have (or display evidence of having had) a single archway (Appendix 2, Section 2, column b) which usually occupied nearly all the area of the cross-wall. Instances of these exist at St Mary's Gate at Gloucester, Mount Grace, Reading and Stoneleigh. Normally this intermediate and internal archway was fitted with doors which took the place of doors fitted to the outer archway, the arrangement permitting travellers to wait under cover in the lobby or porch, and to converse with the porter (who would also remain in the dry) before being admitted through the rear gate-passage to the precinct of the abbey or priory.

Less frequently the cross-wall was a timber structure, as at Malvern and Monk Bretton where, instead of being attached to an arch the gates were hung on two massive posts attached to the side walls reinforced by an overhead beam

cross-wall with one archway

lobby

cross-wall

vehicular archway

ped's arch.

cross-wall with two archways

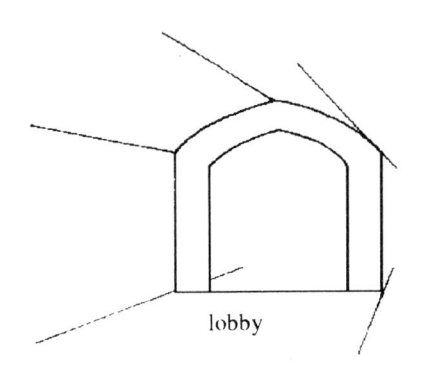

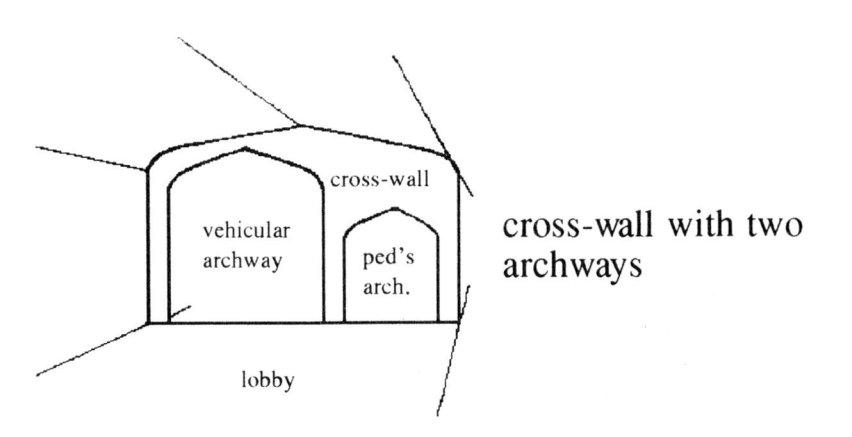

lobby

Figure 21   The Divided Gate-hall

holding the posts apart. The gates have disappeared at Malvern but the timber framework is extant. Though the timber framework at Monk Bretton has been removed, a vertical chase in the flanking wall of the gate-hall shows where the main gates were hung (Photograph 18).

Ideally, the porter's office would be equipped with a slit-window. This window (e.g. Monk Bretton) pierced the side wall of the gate-hall to the front of the cross-wall, enabling the porter to peruse an applicant for admission standing in the lobby. When satisfied as to the nature of the business of the visitor, the porter would then walk through the doorway leading from his office to the gate-passage and open the door in the cross-wall, thus permitting the visitor to enter.

The 51 gatehouses also include 27 where the cross-wall is pierced (or displays evidence of having been pierced) by two arches (Appendix 2, Section 2, column b). These 27 and the group of 14 gatehouses with single-arched cross-walls comprise quite small groups, and we should perhaps be wary of concluding that it was more common for a cross-wall to be pierced, not by one large archway, but by two archways of dissimilar size, the smaller for visitors on foot and the larger for carts, horses, and so on. Nevertheless, by installing a smaller as well as a larger archway, the need was obviated for having to draw back the big gate(s) of a single-arched cross-wall, unless of course the gate possessed a wicket. Hence visitors arriving on foot at the gatehouse with the double-arched cross-wall could be let in or out more conveniently. Some late medieval gatehouses (e.g. Carlisle, Tewkesbury, Whalley inner) had two-arched cross-walls, and we may be sure that this 'double' arrangement continued to be popular in some monastic houses until the eve of the Dissolution.

A unique arrangement is observable at Beaulieu where the inner gatehouse has been converted into a mansion. The gate-hall possesses a cross-wall with three archways, a large central archway (now blocked) flanked by two smaller, pedestrians' archways.

Was the pedestrians' archway normally on the left or right of the vehicular archway in the cross-wall?

Of the above 27 gatehouses examined (excluding one, Rievaulx, where the evidence is too imprecise to reveal which side the smaller archway was on) 13 had the pedestrians' archway on the left and 13 on the right (Appendix 2, Section 2, columns b and c). The small number of cross-walls which display two archways precludes drawing any firm conclusion as to left or right preferences for pedestrians' and vehicular archways. Designers of gatehouses probably tended to place the pedestrians' archway on the side of the gatehouse where the porter's office was to be located. In most cases the position of the office depended in turn on site considerations, such as availability of land, contours, drainage and the like.

Examples of gatehouse cross-walls with double archways having the pedestrians' archway on the left include Arbroath, Byland, Guisborough, Kirkstall and Roche; examples with the pedestrians' archway on the right include Easby, Kenilworth, Tavistock Town Gate and both the gatehouses at Whalley.

A variation of the normal cross-wall arrangement may be seen at Thornton, where a single large archway pierces the stone septum in the usual manner. However a doorway in the side wall on the right-hand side immediately before the cross-wall enables pedestrians to enter the precinct via a separate and angled passage leading to the rear, rather than through the main gate-passage.

The location of the cross-wall in the gate-hall was not the same in all gatehouses. Undoubtedly it tended to be placed either halfway along from the front archway or one-third of the distance along. This is borne out (Appendix 2, Section 2, column a) by 50 of the 51 gatehouses which still possess cross-walls (or evidence of cross-walls). Of these, 20 have (or had) the cross-wall located halfway along (e.g. Durham, Ewenny south, Kenilworth, Roche, Walsingham) and 16 one-third along (e.g. Broomholm, Guisborough, Hexham, Llanthony, York St Mary's Marygate). Of the remaining 14, 4 had their cross-wall placed two-thirds of the distance from the front archway (e.g. Byland). This left 10 at varying other distances from the front (four-fifths: e.g. Thornton; three-fifths: e.g. Furness inner; two-fifths: e.g. Kirkham; and one-quarter: e.g. St Andrews Pends).

These placements of the cross-wall suggest that the gatehouse lobby tended to be shorter or the same length as the gate-passage. Only infrequently was the former longer than the latter.

A gatehouse with a single-arched cross-wall included in the group of 16 placed one-third from the front archway is the Great Gate at Bury St Edmunds. What makes the ground-plan of this gate-hall unusual is that the lobby has been narrowed to accommodate small rooms or stairwells on either side of the forward part of the gate-hall. To the rear, the gate-passage occupies the full width of the cross-wall.

In a number of other gatehouses, the vehicular and pedestrians' archways were inserted not in an intermediate cross-wall but in the front wall, as at Binham and Butley, an arrangement less convenient for travellers or visitors who would have had to receive permission to enter while waiting outside the front of the gatehouse. Thirty-six of the 148 gatehouses display two archways (or evidence of two archways), that is, a large or vehicular entrance and a small or pedestrians' entrance (Appendix 2, Section 1, column a). Included in this total are the gatehouse at Abingdon and the Ramsey part-gatehouse at Hinchingbrooke, each of which actually possesses three archways of which the right-hand one in each was inserted after the Dissolution. In the case of two others (Coventry Whitefriars and St Osyth Great Gatehouse) there are three genuinely medieval archways in the front wall, a large (vehicular) entrance flanked by two small (pedestrians') entrances.

The placement of separate archways in the front wall of a gatehouse affected the interior design of the gate-hall in two ways. In some such gatehouses the vehicular and pedestrians' archways led into a large common gate-hall at the rear of which was a single archway, sometimes as wide as the front archways added together. There are a number of gatehouses that display these features, notably the Bayle Gate at Bridlington, Colchester St John's, the Bishop's Gate at Norwich, and the Great Gateway at St Albans (Photographs 19 and 20). In one or two gatehouses (Canterbury Christ Church North Gate, Hyde, Tisbury outer), at the back of the common gate-hall were two separate archways for vehicles and pedestrians. Unusually at Tisbury, the rear – but not the front – arches are of approximately equal size.

The other procedure was to insert a longitudinal wall or septum between the vehicular and pedestrians' archways so that it ran from the front to the rear of the building, thereby dividing the gate-hall into two passageways, a narrower one for pedestrians and a wider one for vehicles and horsemen. Only 13 gatehouses with two front arches (or evidence of two arches) may be identified (Appendix 2, Section 1, column d) as having this type of division, suggesting that it was not particularly prevalent.

The design may be seen in its simplest form at Bristol where there are two quite separate gate-hall passageways, each with their own arches at either end, the passageways divided from each other by a solid longitudinal wall running the length of the gatehouse. Polesworth also displays this plan with a pedestrians' passageway arched at its ends and a vehicular passageway timber-beamed at the ends. Moreover halfway along these two passages at Polesworth are traces of a cross-wall. An arrangement at Cornworthy is remarkably like that at Polesworth with two quite separate passageways, each of the latter divided into two equal lengths by a cross-wall. Unlike Polesworth, however, the passageways at Cornworthy are vaulted throughout. The presence of cross-walls at these two gatehouses indicates that the passageways were fitted with intermediate doors. Canonsleigh also has a gate-hall divided by a longitudinal wall into two passageways of which the vehicular only also possesses a cross-wall.

Sometimes, as at Castle Acre, the longitudinal wall was not continuous, but broached by an archway inserted so that the porter could walk from the pedestrians' passageway to the vehicular passageway (or vice versa). A variant of this is found at Battle where the gate-hall's stone vaulting has been designed to mark the division between the two passageways. A large pier supporting the vaulting is sited halfway along the septum with an archway in front and another behind it. This gatehouse, like that at Castle Acre, also has two archways at the front and two at the rear.

At Torre the division of the gate-hall is carried to the ultimate in design. It has a longitudinal wall in which are two semicircular arches, the wall dividing the gate-hall into two passageways both with arches at the front and rear. However the gate-hall is also divided halfway along by a cross-wall (with two arches) into two parts. Since doors or gates were fitted to the cross-wall (indicated by the surviving hinge-crooks), the divided portion of the gate-hall in front of the cross-wall must have consisted of both a vehicular porch and pedestrians' porch. To the rear of the cross-wall the divided portion of the gate-hall must have consisted of both a vehicular gate-passage and a pedestrians' gate-passage.

In the few instances where a gatehouse had its front wall pierced by a central vehicular archway and two smaller flanking archways for pedestrians, what was the arrangement behind the wall in the gate-hall?

At St Osyth these triple entrances lead into a common gate-hall behind which is a single rear archway leading out of the gatehouse. At Coventry Whitefriars the gate-hall is divided into three by two longitudinal walls. Thus at this gatehouse there are two narrow passageways for pedestrians which flank the vehicular section of the gate-hall. Though not all have survived to the present time, the three archways which led into these passageways were matched by three at the rear. The inner gatehouse at Beaulieu also used to have three front archways. Though we must treat with caution what we see there because of the alterations and additions carried out in 1872, it seems that these archways, a large central one flanked by two smaller ones, led into a lobby behind which were the three cross-wall arches mentioned earlier. In turn, these led into the gate-passage behind which was (and is) a single archway, now glazed, at the rear of the building.

Though porch-towers were almost always entered through a single archway, the hall of the Bishop's Lodging at St Osyth is unique within this group in displaying a triple entrance of one large archway flanked by two small archways.

Although most gateways appear to have consisted of single entrances, a few had separate archways for vehicular and pedestrian traffic. Seven may be identified, listed in the Addendum concluding Section 1 of Appendix 2). In addition to these, the watergate at Waltham, now surviving as a gateway, also has a double entrance. Its flanking turrets or watch-towers, of which the lower portion of the right-hand one survives, suggest that this gateway had almost certainly been a gatehouse before being partially dismantled.

Is there any stronger evidence than for the arches piercing cross-walls to show that the pedestrians' outer archway of gatehouses and gateways tended to be placed on one particular side?

Of the 36 gatehouses where there are two external archways at the front, 18 had the smaller archway on the left-hand side and 18 on the right-hand side (Appendix 2, Section 1, column b); of the seven gateways with two arches, four have the smaller archway on the left-hand side and three on the right-hand side (Appendix 2, Section 1, Addendum). We therefore conclude that as with internal cross-walls and their archways, it is unlikely that any general preference was exercised by monastic planners. The siting of external archways probably also depended on factors associated with the placement of the porter's office.

Number of bays
Gatehouse halls were often divided lengthwise into two or more bays. The bay divisions were sometimes indicated externally by a repetitive array of buttresses or pilasters placed along the sides of the middle section of the building. However, with the placement of gatehouses between other buildings and with the addition of wings and ranges, this external manifestation of bay structure was probably evident only in a small number of cases. Today the three-bay gatehouse (*c*.1300) of Easby, mentioned earlier, seems to be the only portal that reveals the arrangement of its bays externally.

Bay divisions were also indicated internally, that is within the gate-hall, by roof-vaulting frequently combined with wall-shafting, blind or blank wall-arcading, cross-walls and so on. Nearly all the existing evidence showing the layout of bays comes from this source, and is thus almost exclusively internal to gatehouses.

If earlier gatehouses, and especially their gate-halls, were generally longer and narrower, while later gatehouses and their gate-halls were shorter and broader, what effect did such a development have on bay design? As a rule we should expect earlier gate-halls to have had more bays than the later gate-halls. Does the existing evidence support this proposition?

All those gatehouses were included in our survey (Appendix 2, Section 4), in which by examining their gate-halls internally it was possible to determine with reasonable exactitude the number of bay divisions for each. The resulting total of 114 portals was grouped under three headings:

Gatehouses surviving from the twelfth and thirteenth centuries, the 'early period';
Gatehouses surviving from fourteenth century, the 'middle period'; and
Gatehouses surviving from the fifteenth and sixteenth-centuries, the 'late period'.

By averaging for each period the number of bays per gate-hall:

Early period   2.2 bays per gate-hall;
Middle period   2.0 bays per gate-hall;
Late Period   1.3 bays per gate-hall,

it was possible to show that as the medieval period progressed, the average number of bays in a gatehouse became fewer. This reduction was probably related to the inference that later-built gatehouses and their gate-halls appear to have been shorter and broader, though this relationship has not been proven beyond reasonable doubt.

Which bay designs deserve special mention?

Though the sample of early gatehouses with known numbers of bays (24) is rather small, the spread appears to favour those with two and three bays. The latter include, among others, Bristol Abbey Gatehouse ($c.1165$, two bays), Gloucester St Mary's Gate (thirteenth century, three bays), Hexham ($c.1160$, three bays), Kirkstall (twelfth and thirteenth centuries, three bays), and Llanthony (thirteenth century, two bays). Two gatehouses, Arbroath ($c.1300$, remodelled in the fifteenth century) and Fountains (early thirteenth century) each have four bays. A few early gatehouses with a single bay survive too, notably the St James' Tower of 1120–48 at Bury St Edmunds, the North Gate of $c.1139/43$ (remodelled in the fifteenth century) at Evesham, and the main gatehouse of the twelfth century (remodelled 1302–07) at Peterborough, all with approximately square-shaped gate-halls.

The survey's findings confirm the middle period, the fourteenth century, as being transitional in the medieval choice of bay numbers for gate-halls. In that century the layout of the 'long' gatehouse with three or more bays to its gate-hall seems to have been favoured by some houses as late as the end of the century, for by that time when probably many gatehouses had been remodelled or rebuilt, seven of the surviving ones display an internal design involving three or more bays in their gate-halls. Instances of these include Bury St Edmunds Great Gate (1327/46 and 1353–*c*.1384, three bays), St Andrews Pends (late fourteenth century, four bays), Thornton gatehouse (1382 and sixteenth century, five bays), and Whalley outer gatehouse (early fourteenth century, eight bays).

Notwithstanding this apparent lingering-on of a tradition of building 'long' gatehouses with several bays, one- and two-bay gatehouses were far more common, probably more so in the fourteenth century than in the earlier period. Of the 38 gatehouses looked at, 16 possess one bay, such as Alnwick (mid-fourteenth century), Bridlington (1388), Dover (1320) and the Great Gateway at St Albans (1360+); of the 15 two-bay gatehouses, eminent examples include Battle (1338), Norwich St Ethelbert's Gate (*c*.1328), Pentney (late fourteenth/early fifteenth century) and Worcester Edgar Tower (early fourteenth century).

During the late period, the fifteenth and sixteenth centuries, most of the rebuilt or new gatehouses had square or squarish gate-halls. Thus, of the 52 gatehouses surveyed, 39 possess one bay and 13 have only two bays. No surviving gatehouses of this period have more than two bays. Some of the best extant examples of gatehouses with single bays are Abbotsbury inner (fifteenth century), Aylesford outer (fifteenth century), Barking (*c*.1460), Clerkenwell (1504), Colchester St John's (fifteenth century), Crossraguel (sixteenth century), Forde (fifteenth century), Gloucester inner (fifteenth century), King's Lynn Priory (fifteenth century), Leez inner and outer (sixteenth century) and Wetheral (fifteenth century). Of the two-bay kind, mention should be made of Abingdon (late fifteenth century), Cornworthy (early fifteenth century), Durham (*c*.1500), Morwell (sixteenth century), St Osyth Great Gatehouse (*c*.1475), Tewkesbury (fifteenth/sixteenth century) and Whalley inner (1480).

In a few gatehouses built or rebuilt in the fourteenth or fifteenth century, the vaulting inside their gate-halls was divided into transverse bays as well as longitudinal bays, sometimes to accommodate the greater breadth. This is evident both at Battle and Torre where in addition to the two bays resulting from longitudinal divisions, there are two transverse bays, making four (2 × 2) vaulting units in all. Beaulieu's inner gate-hall has three transverse bays both in front of the cross-wall as well as to its rear, making six (2 × 3) vaulting units in all. Abingdon has one longitudinal bay but three transverse bays, and this gives it three (1 × 3) vaulting units in its gate-hall. The gate-hall at Tewkesbury has a longitudinal bay both to the front and rear of its cross-wall. At the front its lobby displays three small transverse bays giving three (1 × 3) vaulting units. However, the gate-passage has one central transverse bay flanked on either side by half a bay, making two [1 × (½ + 1 + ½)] vaulting units, or five in all. The longitudinally five-bayed gate-hall at Thornton is divided into two transverse bays, making ten (5 × 2) vaulting units altogether, with eight in front of the cross-wall and two to its rear.

Vaulting styles
It is not known how many medieval gatehouses had stone vaults over their gate-halls. Quite clearly, not every surviving gate-hall was originally vaulted in stone, and there are a number of instances where a plastered ceiling (often with exposed cross-beams) was installed. Among others, the group includes gatehouses at Aylesford (outer, and watergate), Barking, Bromfield, Bury St Edmunds (St James' Tower), Canterbury Christ Church (Forrens Gate), Leez (both portals), Rochester (Sextry Gate), Tisbury (both portals) and Worksop. It is of course possible that in some of these cases the stone vaulting was replaced by plasterwork after the Dissolution. Indeed several gate-halls may be identified (by the survival of vaulting springers, shafting etc.) where the vaulting was lost, never to be replaced by later vaulting, such as Bury St Edmunds Great Gate, Ely Porta Gate, Pentney and Walsingham.

Specimens of early vaulting in stone are rare. One or two twelfth-century gate-halls have a tunnel vault, for instance the North Gate at Canterbury Christ Church which has a vault 36ft long (Newman, 1969, p. 219) divided by a semicircular stone band or arch. The lobby of the gate-hall at Tavistock (Town Gate) possesses a rendered tunnel vault, and this may also belong to the same century. The fourteenth-century gatehouse of Polesworth has an ancient tunnel vault over its pedestrians' passageway and this may also be twelfth century in origin. When we come to the thirteenth century tunnel vaulting is equally uncommon with possible instances at Ewenny (both gate-halls) and Reading (the lobby of the gate-hall only).

Tunnel vaulting nevertheless continued to be used throughout the medieval period. Of three gate-halls of the fourteenth century [Alnwick, Ely (Sacrist's Gate) and Stamford Greyfriars] the latter two have cross-ribs. Indeed, the tunnel design seems to have had a resurgence in the fifteenth and sixteenth centuries with surviving instances at Blanchland (*c*.1500), Crossraguel (sixteenth century), Carlisle (1527), Hulne (main gatehouse, fifteenth century), Norwich (Erpingham Gate, 1420), Tavistock (Betsy Grimbal's Tower, fifteenth century), Wetheral (fifteenth century), Worcester (watergate, fifteenth century). Three other gatehouses [Bolton (early fourteenth century), Cornworthy (early fifteenth century) and Whalley (lobby of inner gatehouse, 1480)] are memorable for having tunnel vaults panelled with transverse and longitudinal ribs.

Groin vaulting may have been commonly employed in the early medieval period, but is now practically non-existent in gate-halls, with one possible instance at Cartmel, and this as late as the fourteenth century, the date usually attributed to the main fabric of the gatehouse.

Many gate-halls were vaulted in a ribbed quadripartite pattern, a popular style which lasted for most of the medieval period. Early specimens had either no ridge ribs [e.g. Peterborough main (twelfth century)] or added transverse ridge-ribs [e.g. Bristol Abbey Gatehouse (*c*.1165), Kirkstall (twelfth and thirteenth centuries)], the latter feature clearly revealing the internal bay divisions. Later ones [e.g. Burnham Norton (early fourteenth century), Oxford St Bernard's (mid-fifteenth century), Morwell (sixteenth century)], have longitudinal ridge ribs added.

Most of the later gate-halls with vaulting have tierceron or lierne vaults. Fourteenth-century tierceron vaults still exist at Beaulieu (inner gatehouse), Bridlington and Butley, fifteenth-century instances at Canterbury Christ Church (Prior Selling's Porch), Durham, Montacute, Norwich (Bishop's Gateway), and one sixteenth-century example at Clerkenwell. These gate-halls are one, sometimes two bayed, with star-shaped rib patterns. The lierne vault was designed slightly later than the tierceron vault and so the instances found at Norwich (St Ethelbert's Gate, *c.*1328) and Worcester (lobby of Edgar Tower, early fourteenth century) are remarkably early. Other instances are found at Canterbury Christ Church (Christ Church Gate, 1507–17), Colchester (fifteenth century), Ely (Palace gatehouse, late fifteenth century), Gloucester (inner gatehouse, fifteenth century), Kingswood (lobby, late fourteenth century), St Albans (Great Gateway, 1360+) and St Osyth (Great Gatehouse, *c.*1475). With most of these vaults, the lierne ribs form an octagon around which the tiercerons form a star shape. Unusually, at Gloucester, the lierne ribs of the inner gatehouse form a square, and at Kingswood a complex and probably unique pattern.

Though designed and introduced after the lierne vault, the fan vault figures only in two portals, these being the porch-towers of Cerne (*c.*1500) and Forde (1528).

One or two other types of vaulting survive as single instances. At Tewkesbury there is some rare sexpartite vaulting, constructed in the fifteenth century but using a design common two centuries earlier. The five bays of Thornton, which are placed with four in front of the cross-wall and one behind, have double quadripartite vaulting otherwise described as lattice-ribbed (Clapham, 1951, p. 9).

Internal wall decoration of gate-halls

Quite a number of gate-halls, especially if capacious or were part of gatehouses of important monasteries, had their side walls embellished. A common device was to cover the walls with blind or blank arcading, a popular form of wall adornment in every century between the Norman Conquest and the Dissolution. It is, moreover, possible to identify gate-halls from all periods with such features.

A few ruined gatehouses, such as the late twelfth-century Great Gate of York St Mary's or the Priory Gate (*c.*1160) of

Hexham, still display early examples of such arcading. In the gate-halls of at least nine complete gatehouses, the arcading survives in virtually unspoilt condition. Possibly the oldest arcading (*c*.1139/43) exists at Evesham in the North Gate where on each side three semicircular arches rest on thin triple shafts. Other Norman arcading is found at Bristol (Abbey Gatehouse) and Peterborough (main gatehouse) where both sets of work date from the second half of the twelfth century. The arcading at Bristol (Photograph 21) comprises interlaced arches with small capitals and cones and plain shafts, redolent of the wall ornamentation in the chapter-house there. In the Peterborough gate-hall, on each side there are three semicircular blind arches plus one higher arch to accommodate a doorway.

Thirteenth-century arcading is represented by the Abbot's Gatehouse at Peterborough. Probably erected in the second part of the century, the blind arcading consists of slender arches with Y-tracery, thought to be similar to that displayed on the west wall of the conventual (now cathedral) church. From the first nine years of the fourteenth century comes the Fyndon Gate of Canterbury St Augustine's. It possesses wall arcading with tiny, open-bottomed trefoils on the caps (Newman, 1969, p. 227).

Slightly later came the Great Gate (1327–46) of Bury St Edmunds. Both the outer and inner sections of its gate-hall possess what is probably better described as wall panelling rather than arcading, wall panelling that is displayed as flowing (even flamboyant) tracery. The lobby also has its walls embellished with coats of arms of donors and benefactors.

The most recent surviving gatehouse to have been given wall arcading is that at Durham, built *c*.1500. Its gate-hall has arcading which is plain compared with the earlier examples just described. This decoration consists of repeated triples of pointed and recessed arches along its two sides.

These types of arcading and panelling were designed specifically as ornamental work for the walls, but some gate-halls have walls that were given a different type of surface decoration. This was in the form of shafting, which was intended primarily to underpin the springing of roof-vaulting. This is seen in the gate-halls of several gatehouses where the shafting, sometimes elaborately carved, rises from the floor to a point varying between six and ten feet up the wall where it gives way to the springing of the gate-hall vault. Such long shafts in effect divide the wall-space into panels. Examples of such treatment within gate-halls may be seen at Gloucester St Mary's Gate (thirteenth century), Kirkham (late thirteenth century), Battle (1338), St Andrews Pends (late fourteenth century), Canterbury Christ Church (Prior Selling's Porch, 1472–94) and Morwell (sixteenth century).

Notwithstanding the examples mentioned in the previous paragraph, it was probably more usual for internal shafting to rise not from the floor, but from six or eight feet up the wall for two or three feet before giving way to the vault-springing. Instances include the fourteenth-century outer gatehouses of Maxstoke and Whalley, where the vaulting ribs of the gate-hall spring from points halfway up the side-walls thereby minimising the wall-panelling effect.

Seating
Stone benches attached to interiors of walls in conventual churches and chapter-houses were quite common. Gatehouses were also fitted with benches, though with what frequency is not known. A few gate-halls as at Arbroath, Battle and Furness (cemetery gatehouse), still possess stone seating placed there for the convenience of visitors awaiting admittance. Sometimes the benches were placed in arched recesses along the side(s) of the gate-hall, as at Cleeve (inner gatehouse).

Doors
Not surprisingly, few of the original timber doors of gate-halls are in existence, though frequently their iron hinge-crooks are still in place (e.g. Bermondsey). Thornton has a pair of badly decayed doors attached to its cross-wall. There are timber gates of the fifteenth/sixteenth century at Leez (outer) with refined trefoil-headed panels believed to have been moved from the inner gatehouse of the same priory. Other complete doors which are substantially original exist at Norwich (Bishop's Gate) (Pevsner, 1962, p. 230) and Whalley (inner) (Ashmore, 1981, p. 14).

UPPER STOREYS

Typically the storey immediately above the gate-hall consisted of a single chamber which had a variety of uses. Sometimes it served as a chapel, as at Barking (dedicated to the Holy Rood), Durham (dedicated to St Helen) or at the outer gatehouse of Whalley (dedication unknown). The inner gatehouse at Beaulieu even had two chapels placed side by side in this position. At Bury St Edmunds the front upper chamber of the Great Gate was a guardroom from which the portcullis could be raised or lowered. Thornton exhibits a similar arrangement in the great chamber in the second storey over the gate-hall, and this kind of use seems common enough in gatehouses that had a marked defensive role, such as Ewenny or Tynemouth.

The greater portion of the presently undivided middle-floor apartment at Thornton almost certainly served as the great hall or courtroom, the abbot occupying the whole of the gatehouse, and it is equally likely that the extant upper chamber at Montacute, equipped with two oriels, was occupied by the prior. There are several instances where the chamber was almost certainly used as a prison or courtroom as at Bridlington, Ely Porta Gate and St Albans (Great Gateway). Two portals are used for ringing as they were before the Dissolution: one is the St James' Tower at Bury St Edmunds and the other is the bell tower at Evesham.

Sometimes the needs of pilgrims or visitors were catered for over the gate-hall, as at Blanchland where the room may have been the hospitium, at Minster-in-Sheppey where the room may have been a dormitory (and the room above it a lodging for the nunnery priests), and at Worksop where the room served as a guests' chamber. Upstairs accommodation may also have been provided for corrodians, as possibly at Monk Bretton. Given all these different uses, we are probably on firmer ground in noting that the accommodation over the gate-hall was probably used most frequently as a lodging (rather than an office which would have been downstairs) for the gatekeeper or porter (e.g. Walsingham).

Descriptions of the accommodation of two gatehouses
Of the lesser monastic houses, the accommodation of the

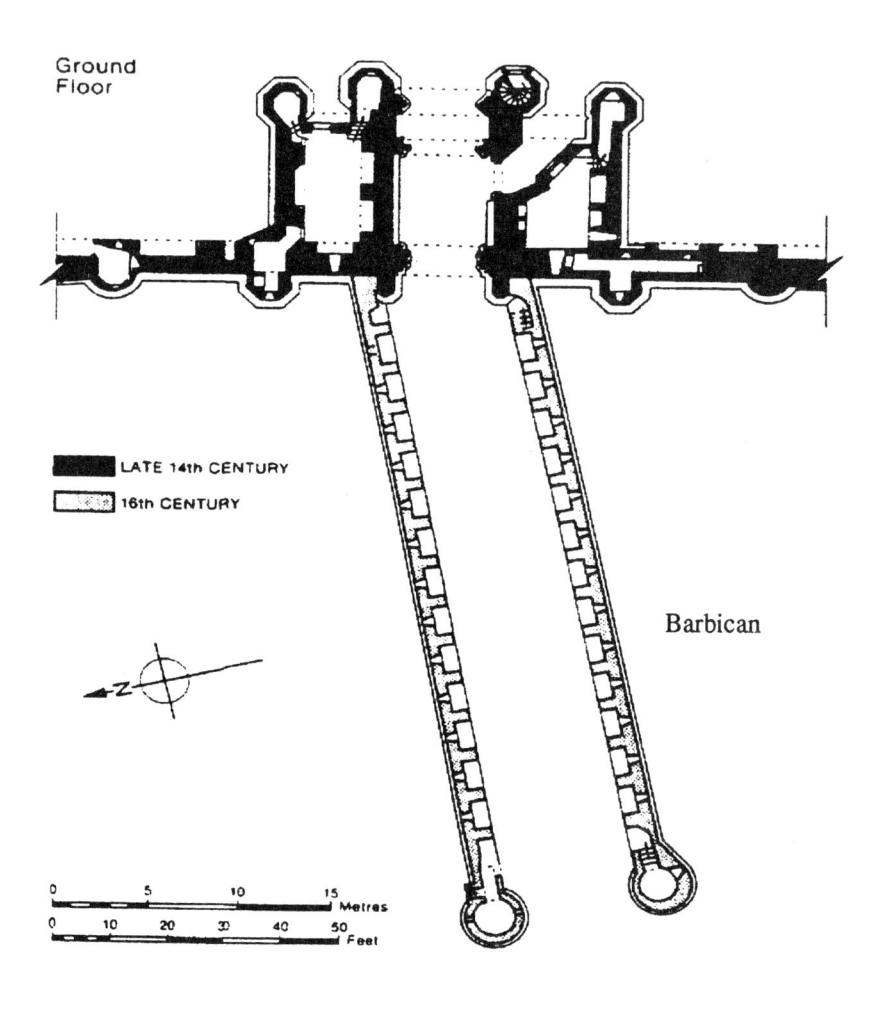

Figure 22 Thornton Abbey: Storey Plans

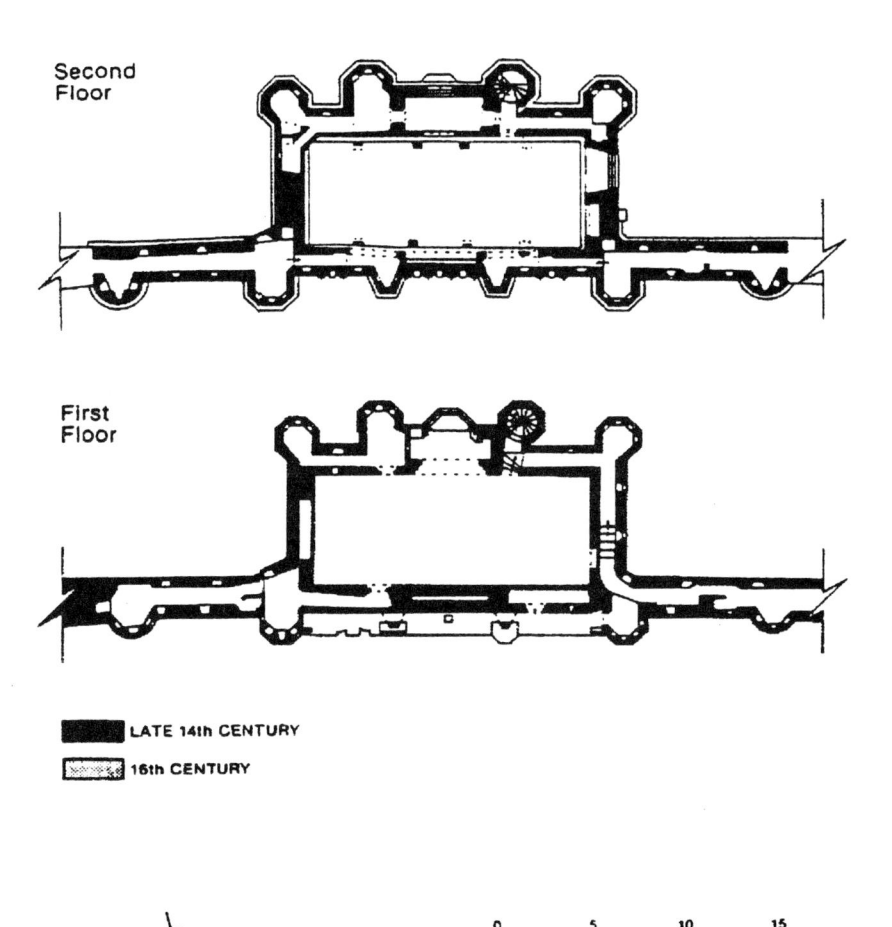

[From Clapham, A. & Baillie Reynolds, P.K. (1989) " Thornton abbey ", pp. 16, 18.]

gatehouse of **Wetheral** (Photograph 22) is perhaps typical. There are three storeys at this gatehouse which is substantially complete probably due to the fact that it was used as a vicarage for some time after the Dissolution. Other than that the floor between the first and second storeys has perished, the main building survives intact. To the right of the gate-hall is a chamber which may well have served as the porter's office. On the outside of the side walls of the gatehouse are inverted 'Vs' which signify attached ancillary buildings or ranges now gone, the purposes of which are unknown. A spiral staircase attached to the building at its north-east corner leads to the two upper storeys which provide the same accommodation as each other. Thus on each floor was a large chamber fitted with a fireplace and having a small privy leading off. The fireplace of the lower chamber still exists, but that of the upper room appears to have been blocked. The front wall of the gatehouse has been made to project forward a few feet, almost like an oriel, with slit windows at the sides giving the occupant of the upper chambers views along the road outside the gatehouse. The ample nature of this accommodation on two upper floors suggests that the gatehouse may have provided a lodging for the prior rather than the porter.

The great gatehouse at **Thornton**, reputedly the abbot's residence (or administrative headquarters) consists of three storeys (Figure 22). On the ground floor there are two large vaulted chambers on either side of the gate-hall. That to the right was clearly the porter's office, but the use of the other chamber is uncertain. The upper storeys are accessible via a spiral stairway in one of the rear turrets which is entered through an external doorway behind the gatehouse. The middle storey is mainly taken up by a large apartment which has a wide fireplace at its left-hand end. This apartment was probably originally divided by a partition into a smaller antechamber at the right-hand end near the stairs, and a larger hall at the other end in which was the fireplace. To the rear of the hall is a small chapel entered through a wide, four-centred archway which probably used to be filled by an open screen. The chapel is illuminated by a canted oriel, below which is a sill displaying signs of having served as an altar. On either side are a piscina and aumbry. The top storey also now contains a large apartment which was originally divided by partitions into possibly three chambers. To the front of this apartment are three archways, from the middle of which descended the gatehouse portcullis. All three storeys have an elaborate pattern of wall passages or galleries leading to small rooms sometimes fitted with fireplaces and privies.

UNDERCROFTS

That monastic gatehouses, like other buildings standing on an abbey or priory precinct, should have possessed undercrofts may be regarded as unexceptional, but in practice such accommodation is rarely encountered. What may be a unique instance survives below the Steeple Gate at Ely. Probably dating from the fourteenth century, the undercroft consists of three bays, two under the gate-hall and one to the right of it below the other accommodation. The ribbed stone vaulting, which is infilled with red brick, springs from piers lacking capitals. The undercroft's original use is unknown.

6

SURVIVORS AND ADAPTATIONS

Portals vary considerably in the structural treatment they have received since they were first built, especially after the Dissolution. Accordingly we may recognise them as belonging to several distinct groups.

The complete and unaltered group
These are portals which are more or less in the condition they were in when originally built (or rebuilt) before the Dissolution, and which normally continue to serve as entrances (though not, of course, to monasteries except in one or two modern cases, such as Aylesford and Malling). The medieval fabric of a portal may include the work of more than one century or building campaign. Since the Dissolution a portal belonging to this group may have lost small items such as a minor roof, a lean-to building or even a floor. Any portal which was restored in the nineteenth or twentieth century broadly in keeping with its medieval design is also included in this group.

The complete and rebuilt/remodelled group
Some portals were rebuilt as passageways or entrances to buildings with, broadly speaking, changed uses after the Dissolution (e.g. the Abbey Gateway leading to Chester cathedral, formerly abbey), or to buildings erected on sites of former monasteries (e.g. the outer gatehouse of London Charterhouse). Though the reconstruction of these portals may only match the original design approximately, the later work is normally characterised by a post-Dissolution architectural style involving in most cases the rebuilding of the upper storey (or storeys).

The adapted group
These are former portals, structurally altered or enlarged after the Dissolution to serve entirely different non-conventual uses. In the majority of cases, adaptation involved conversion to a domestic house, the alteration perhaps consisting of little more than blocking the main archways of a gate-hall (e.g. Montacute). In others whole new additions, such as the provision of a new wing (e.g. Beaulieu inner gatehouse), were made to the original building. In a few cases as we shall see, some strange and non-domestic adaptations occurred

The partially dismantled group
There is a fine distinction between partially dismantled portals on the one hand and ruined and fragmentary portals on the other. The former include all those buildings whose ruinous condition appears to have been the result of deliberate demolition rather than weathering or vandalism. For instance, the upper storey (or storeys) may have been pulled down, leaving the ground floor intact for use, say as a barn or cow-shed (e.g. Cornworthy). In another instance, the single archway of a gatehouse may have been retained to highlight the entrance to a property (e.g. Lanercost). In a third, the part-demolished portal may have been kept as a landscape feature (e.g. Bayham), while in a fourth, partial removal of the fabric may have been achieved in order to make room for road-widening (e.g. Neath).

The ruined group
These are portals which were permitted or encouraged to deteriorate after the Dissolution through neglect, the effects of weather, stealing of materials, and so on. In the case of some portals, ruination did not occur until quite recently (e.g. the beginning of the nineteenth century). The group includes a number of portals that have retained a considerable portion of their fabric. At one extreme a portal may have lost little more than its roof (e.g. Thetford); at the other, not much more may have survived than, say, a recognisable ground plan and low-standing walls (e.g. Furness inner).

The fragmentary group
Included in this group are portals identified by a small

feature such as the jamb (or jambs) of an archway (e.g. Bradsole south-east), or a length of recognisable walling which may enroach on the boundaries of another, later building (e.g. Culross). In all these cases, destruction has proceeded further compared with portals identified as belonging to the previous group. Such a fragment may equally be the product of demolition, neglect, weathering, theft of materials, and so on.

Altogether in England, Wales and Scotland there are 230 portals which, varying in condition from being complete to being fragmentary, may be allotted to the six groups:

complete and unaltered	105
complete and rebuilt/remodelled	18
adapted	35
partially dismantled	35
ruined	22
fragmentary	15

Although the first group is numerically by far the largest, this must be matched against another, more compelling one, namely that of 1000 or so monastic houses that existed in England, Wales and Scotland in medieval times, the vast majority of their portals have disappeared without trace.

If now we allocate all the existing portals to the century from which their earliest surviving and identifiable fabric dates, we find that the middle and later medieval periods are numerically better represented than the earlier ones:

Twelfth century (to 1200)	22 portals
Thirteenth century (1201–1300)	25 portals
Fourteenth century (1301–1400)	71 portals
Fifteenth century (1401–1500)	76 portals
Sixteenth century (1501–1600)	17 portals

This distribution is not surprising, as many early portals must have been completely destroyed to make way for newer and more ornate ones built nearer in time to the Dissolution. Moreover the smaller total figure of 211 is explained by not being able to date 19 existing portals with accuracy.

We now turn to review the surviving portals in terms of their general structural condition and the styles of medieval architecture that they exhibit.

TWELFTH CENTURY AND EARLIER

It is not known whether Anglo-Saxon abbeys possessed portals, that is, formal entrances to their monasteries. If as possibly they did, they were probably constructed in the form of simple gateways in a wall, earthen bank or hedge. The Normans did rather better than this, probably modelling their earliest monastic portals on the entrance to a castle, the design being in the form of a gateway in a high wall sometimes flanked by towers, with a drawbridge over a steep ditch. There is a tantalising suggestion of such an arrangement at Battle, where there are remnants of late eleventh-century Norman towers at each end of the existing gatehouse range built in the fourteenth century, with vestiges of a stone pathway inside the porter's ground-floor apartment immediately to the right of the present gate-hall. It is likely, however, that most of the gateways constructed in this early period were soon replaced by gatehouses. Thus the earliest surviving monastic portals with substantial Norman work date from the twelfth century. All of them are gatehouses, and they range in height from one to four storeys.

Most of them, like Battle, were refaced or remodelled in the later medieval or post-Dissolution centuries. Probably the earliest surviving complete gatehouse with the original (i.e. unaltered) Norman architecture is the four-storeyed St James' Tower at Bury St Edmunds which was built in the period 1120–48. Another outstanding instance, though somewhat remodelled in the fifteenth century, is the North Gate (c.1153+) at Canterbury Christ Church. The single-storeyed gatehouse of c.1180 at Cirencester, though not quite as ancient as these two, is also largely unaltered.

All the other surviving Norman gatehouses exhibit subsequent alterations of considerable magnitude. Slightly earlier than the Canterbury gatehouse is the Evesham North Gate (c.1139-43) (Photograph 23) which, though retaining its original stone Norman lower storey, now has a late medieval half-timbered upper storey with an attic. The Abbey Gatehouse at Bristol, with Norman work dating from c.1165, is undoubtedly one of the most elegant and attractive gatehouses in England. This is because it was completely remodelled c.1500 when it was provided with elaborate façades to the front and rear. The abbot's gatehouse also at Bristol is similar in having a Norman lower storey constructed about the same time, but an upper storey replaced probably after the Dissolution.

Several others may also be attributed to the Norman period. They include, among others, the main gatehouse at Peterborough and the Town Gate at Tavistock. The first of these though endowed with a substantial Norman core, was remodelled 1302–07 when it was provided with a façade and front super-arch, behind which was kept the original Norman arch. The Tavistock gatehouse survives in its entirety, admittedly with little of its original Norman architecture now visible, having received considerable attention especially in the fifteenth century and again in the nineteenth, when it was finally restored.

One adapted Norman gatehouse of twelfth-century and then thirteenth-century date is sited at Kirkstall. Converted into a house after the Dissolution, its original identity is verified externally by the survival of the now-blocked outer arches of its gate-hall. Another is the twelfth-century Pentise Gate at Canterbury Christ Church which was reconstructed (c.1400) as part of a new guest-house, now the Archdeacon's House.

Twelfth-century gateways are uncommon. The unadorned Lindores gateway probably dates from the late twelfth/early thirteenth century, soon after the abbey was founded in 1191. The earlier Norman gateway ornamented with zig-zag mouldings and relocated to the entrance to the Kent Memorial Garden of Canterbury Cathedral (see Newman, 1969, p. 217), is also one of the few surviving portals of that century.

In addition, several dilapidated Norman gatehouses exist in fairly recognisable condition. They include the Priory Gate at Hexham (c.1160) where the upper storey was removed in 1818, the late twelfth-century gatehouse at Guisborough, of which three arches remain, and the great gatehouse at York St Mary's of the twelfth century, also with its upper storey missing. Part of the great gatehouse survives at Byland, where most of the cross-wall and some of the south wall of the building still stands. Of Buckfast's twelfth-century North Gate, the lower portion of the left-hand side of its gate-hall and its rear archway survive.

Of fragmentary gatehouses, that at Rievaulx is probably the only extant example of the century. Sited in a lane near the parish church, it displays a few courses of stone along one side of the lane including the respond of one of the cross-wall arches.

THE THIRTEENTH CENTURY

This century is represented by several portals displaying easily recognisable Early English work, but considered as a whole, the surviving fabric is hardly more extensive than the Norman work of the previous century. It is, moreover, likely that many portals constructed in the thirteenth century, as in the previous century, were rebuilt in the fourteenth, fifteenth or sixteenth century, the older work having been eliminated or covered up.

Complete gatehouses in the Early English architectural style which have escaped subsequent restoration or reconstruction are limited to two or three only. The chief survivor is the Abbot's Gatehouse at Peterborough, which dates from the later part of the century. One of the larger gatehouses, it is outstanding in its use of external and its internal shafting, and statuary, all of which survive unspoilt. One other gatehouse virtually unaltered is the small outer one at Beaulieu, apart from one or two later lancet windows. St Mary's Gate at Gloucester also belongs to this group of unaltered portals, its membership of the group marred by missing shafts on its façades and the loss of carving detail through erosion.

Thirteenth-century gatehouses which have been subsequently reconstructed or restored are slightly more numerous. They include the severe-looking gatehouse of Minster-in-Sheppey which, while retaining older work in its rear turret, was largely rebuilt in the fifteenth century. At Ewenny the south gatehouse, the main section of which is complete, was largely reconstructed in the fifteenth century. The Reading gatehouse was heavily restored in the nineteenth century. Its present appearance suggests that much of its original thirteenth-century external detail was not replaced by the Victorians, and its authenticity as a thirteenth-century building is therefore questionable.

One thirteenth-century gatehouse which was the subject of conversion after the Dissolution, is that at Llanthony. Converted into a barn or cattle-byre, it had its outer archways blocked, but is still reasonably intact.

Several thirteenth-century gatehouses have been part-dismantled. They include Fountains (early thirteenth century), Kirkham (late thirteenth century), Lanercost, Lewes, Neath, Repton (late thirteenth century) and Roche (late thirteenth/ early fourteenth century). Fountains and Roche were probably taken down to improve the view of the abbey buildings from the west side. Kirkham lost most of its rear façade but not its superb front façade, while Lanercost had the whole of its front façade and gate-hall removed. The Neath gatehouse has had one side of its building dismantled to permit road-widening. At Repton the gatehouse was demolished except for its front archway, which now provides the main entrance to the school. In the nineteenth century the fabric at Lewes, which until then had survived more or less intact, was mischievously altered, part of it (the pedestrians' archway?) being re-positioned.

One gateway (*c*.1300) survives, and this is at Furness. Partly reconstructed after the Dissolution on the site of the outer portal of the abbey, next to the *capella-ante-portas*, it comprises a wall with a pedestrians' smaller archway and vehicular larger archway.

Of ruined thirteenth-century portals, several good specimens exist. Otherwise roofless but standing to its full height, the inner gatehouse at Cleeve, which was considerably reconstructed in the later medieval period, and the unreconstructed one at at Easby (*c*.1300) are probably the most impressive. Another high-standing ruin is the north gatehouse at Ewenny, like its southern partner also designed for defensive purposes. Arbroath gatehouse which dates from *c*.1300, was considerably remodelled *c*.1500. The gate-hall section of this building though now roofless, also displays much of its original fabric.

One gatehouse fragment of this century is at Furness. The inner (great) gatehouse is remarkable for displaying in a few courses of well-tooled stone the whole plan of the gate-hall and right-hand wing.

THE FOURTEENTH CENTURY

There are many more portals dating from this century and the next than from the two previous centuries. Taking this century first, a number of fine gatehouses have survived which are materially the same as when first constructed. Their external appearance varies from the austere to the highly ornamented, and in size from the small if not insignificant to the monumental. Pride of place goes to the Thornton gatehouse which was erected soon after 1382. The building, which stands to its full height of three storeys, is a magnificent structure with octagonal towers, a fine array of canopied niches (some of which are occupied by their original statues) and the remnant of a later barbican.

Three other complete gatehouses compare with Thornton in size if not magnificence. The Great Gate at Bury St Edmunds (1327–46) displays to its front a great ogeed arch equipped with portcullis and a series of long niches in which once stood statues. The St Albans Great Gateway, which was constructed somewhat later (1360+), is generally a more serviceable-looking building and lacks any decorative work on its front and rear exteriors. Later still is the Porta Gate at Ely (1396–97) which compares more with the St Albans than the Bury gatehouse in respect of an absence of decoration (except for a few now-empty niches).

Medium-sized complete fourteenth-century gatehouses include Bridlington Bayle Gate, Canterbury St Augustine's Fyndon Gate, Malling, Norwich St Ethelbert's Gate, Pentney and Worksop. The Bridlington gatehouse of 1388 is somewhat unusual in that its lower two-thirds are constructed of stone and the upper one-third of brick. This three-storeyed building is devoid of ornamentation except for the arms of the priory, which are displayed on its front façade. Of the two gatehouses of St Augustine's Abbey at Canterbury which have survived, the Fyndon Gate dates from the period 1300–09. It is an elegant building of two storeys with octagonal turrets at the front and smaller square ones at the back. It was severely damaged in the Second World War, but has now been carefully restored.

One of four complete portals still marking the precinct limits at Norwich, the St Ethelbert's Gate of $c.$1328 displays a surfeit of flushwork in the form of large circles and gabled niches. Of the late fourteenth (or even early fifteenth) century, the gatehouse at Pentney stands in a remote rural corner of Norfolk. Though its interior vaulting has gone, this gatehouse is more or less complete with wings on either side. Its appearance includes turrets and embattled parapets. Otherwise plain, it is more suggestive of the entrance to a military rather than a religious establishment.

The Worksop gatehouse was built in the early years of the fourteenth century, and then had a special porch with curvilinear tracery added later in the same century. The porch serves as an entrance to a delightful little chapel. Above its main entrance the gatehouse possesses a fine six-light window. Malling's gatehouse also has a chapel, but this one is attached to the rear of the building. The chapel's flowing tracery and the detail of the archways suggest later dates (say, mid fourteenth and fifteenth century) for the construction of this gatehouse.

Other and mostly smaller complete portals of the fourteenth century vary significantly from each other in their design. The group includes two friary gatehouses, the first at Burnham Norton and the second at Stamford Greyfriars. The Burnham Norton building, which is two-storeyed, stands immediately to the west of what is probably part of the conventual church. Dating from the beginning of the century, it displays an early example of flushwork. The gatehouse at Stamford was constructed slightly later, say mid-fourteenth century. Also possessing two storeys, it has a niched and pinnacled front on which have been placed several blank coats of arms.

Alnwick has a gatehouse (Photograph 24) which was constructed about the same time as the Stamford one, in the middle of the century. It is an imposing affair with four large towers projecting at the corners. The front is decorated with statue niches and coats of arms. The small priory at Bromfield and the somewhat more important abbey at Polesworth are today each represented by a gatehouse constructed of stone below, but which is half-timbered in its upper storey. Both buildings are otherwise plain in appearance. The gatehouse at Cartmel which, incidentally, is sited at a distance from the conventual church beyond the river, is also a plain structure. It has a high archway and two windows with ogeed lights. At Dover is a two-storeyed gatehouse with overhanging roof-eaves. Probably erected in the first half of the fourteenth century, the building is devoid of external decoration. Another small gatehouse is at Stoneleigh and was probably erected towards the middle of the century. This portal is attached to a hospitium, also of fourteenth-century date. The Sacrist's Gate at Ely (1325–26) is another edifice flanked on one side by a coeval building, the latter being the sacristy. The main decorative feature of its front façade is a stepped parapet.

Two gatehouses, at Dunfermline and Torre, share an important characteristic. Unusually, each is attached to the south-west corner of the cloister buildings. The three-storeyed Dunfermline gatehouse or Pends, which faces north-west, fills an irregularly shaped space between the refectory, kitchens and guesthouse (later royal apartments); in consequence, it has an awkward shape. The refectory is reported as having been drastically repaired in 1329 (Gifford, (1988) p. 183), and it is therefore likely that The Pends was erected about this time. The Mohun (inner) Gatehouse at Torre, which dates from *c.*1320 when it was probably rebuilt, is also three storeys high. Like the Dunfermline portal, it is plain in appearance though it does possess battlements. It is regularly shaped and faces west.

A rare example of a complete yet unrestored gateway of the period is the late fourteenth-century gateway of the Whitefriars at King's Lynn. One-storeyed, it possesses one noteworthy ornamental feature, a set of three empty niches above the entrance arch.

This brings us to reconstructions, that is portals partly rebuilt after the fourteenth century, the rebuilding usually involving the replacement of the upper fabric. Instances include two that were reconstructed long after the Dissolution: the main gatehouse at Chester, where the upper storey was partly rebuilt in the early nineteenth century, and Walsingham where the Knight's Gate, a postern, was largely refashioned in the middle of the same century.

Six gatehouses were adapted as private houses. This was normally done by walling off the gate-hall at each end and constructing additional accommodation. Instances displaying such alterations include two that are now stately homes: these are the inner gatehouse (mid-fourteenth century) at Beaulieu, now known as Palace House, and the gatehouse (early fourteenth century) at Bolton now called Bolton Abbey. Three more with equally visible alterations are located at Butley (1320–25), Canterbury St Augustine's (Cemetery Gate, *c.*1390) and Maxstoke (inner, fourteenth century). The great gatehouse at Evesham (*c.*1316/1332) qualifies as the sixth member of this domestic group but, unlike the other four, its monastic fabric is concealed within post-Dissolution work, and all that is externally visible is the tell-tale curve of a section of the great archway at the rear of the building.

Several unusual adaptations also derive from fourteenth-century portals. These include the alteration of Beauvale's gatehouse into part of a farm building. At Tavistock the fifteenth-century west tower of the parish church may have been erected over the cemetery gatehouse, evidence for which is supplied by blocked north and south fourteenth-century archways at the base of the tower. The most bizarre post-Dissolution use of a gatehouse was to convert one at St Benet of Holme into a windmill in the eighteenth century.

Partly dismantled portals of the period may be seen at Bayham, Gloucester, Kenilworth, St Osyth, Waltham and West Acre. At the first of these, bits and pieces of fabric have been subtracted and added to make a now-ruined eighteenth-century Gothick summerhouse. Road-widening accounts for the demolition of much of King Edward's Gate at Gloucester, where a turret and part of another attached to a house are all that remain of the gatehouse to the south of the abbey (now cathedral) church. At Kenilworth the upper storey (or storeys) has been removed; at St Osyth a semicircular archway, believed by some to be the original main portal, stands together with a wall forming the front elevation of an otherwise demolished building near and at right-angles to the main gatehouse. The Waltham watergate appears to have lost what may have been flanking towers and possibly an upper storey, while at West Acre, though the front façade is complete to its full height, much of the rear portion of the gatehouse has been destroyed and removed.

There are several ruined portals dating from this century. Belonging to the group are Dunwich, Furness (cemetery and west), Maxstoke (outer), Monk Bretton, St Andrews (Pends) Thetford, Tynemouth and Whalley (outer). Of these, Maxstoke, Monk Bretton, St Andrews, Thetford, Tynemouth and Whalley are virtually complete, except for their missing roofs and apart from Maxstoke, any vaulting they may have had. Because of the noble simplicity of its design, the Thetford gatehouse may be regarded as the finest of the group, with St Andrews and Whalley coming close behind. The Thetford building is constructed almost as a square and is three storeys high. The rear elevation but not the front, is bounded by two octagonal turrets and the whole of the exterior is faced with knapped flint and stone dressings. At St Andrews the gatehouse now shares with that at Whalley the indignity of being part of a public highway. Both gatehouses are long, two-storeyed buildings with the Whalley building dating from the first half of the fourteenth century (*vide* its flowing window tracery), and the St Andrews gatehouse dating from the end of the century. Whereas serviceability rather than appearance seems to have been uppermost in the mind of the designer at Whalley, great pains were taken at St Andrews to match the architectural detail of The Pends with that of the west front of the cathedral-church.

Of the other three roofless gatehouses, Tynemouth is in a different category from the remaining two at Maxstoke and Monk Bretton. The Tynemouth gatehouse served as a dual-purpose portal for the castle which surrounded and protected the Augustinian priory placed within its walls. It is therefore a castle gatehouse with a typically harsh (that is to say, plain and dark) appearance with the substantial remnants of barbicans to its front and rear. The Maxstoke gatehouse has a high gable roof into which reaches a tall two-light window at the front flanked by two empty niches. The two-storeyed gatehouse at Monk Bretton which, apart from its roof, has lost its flooring and some of its walling, is almost devoid of decorative features and thus unremarkable to look at. Less substantial as ruins are the cemetery and west gatehouses at Furness, both little more than roofless and archless gate-halls. At Dunwich there is a gateway with a vehicular and a pedestrians' entrance, the latter decorated with some flushwork characteristic of East Anglia.

Fourteenth-century fragments exists at Abbotsbury where the jamb of an archway represents the outer portal, and Evesham where some rough masonry may be all that survives of the Barton Gate.

THE FIFTEENTH CENTURY

Pride of place must be awarded to the Great Gatehouse of St Osyth Abbey as a complete and unaltered portal of this century. It is a large and magnificent building dating from *c.*1475 and has a façade covered with flushwork simulating blind arcading. Few of the other gatehouses of the period approach that of St Osyth in size, though some do in terms of gracefulness. One contender is the St John's gatehouse at Colchester and another, Montacute. The former, a well-proportioned structure probably erected in the first rather than the second half of the century, displays elaborately decorated niches and octagonal turrets but has a minimum of flushwork. The Montacute gatehouse is notable for the quality of its oriels, friezes and embattled parapets.

Other complete and unaltered portals of the period, nearly all two storeys high, are quite numerous and we shall restrict our description to mentioning only some of them, starting with those of the cathedral-priories and Gloucester. The one surviving gatehouse (*c.*1500) at Durham is typical of the basic box-like form. It is of two storeys and the ornamentation on its front is applied sparingly, with two niches, one on either side of the large three-light window; its rear façade, however, displays no niches. Unlike the Durham gatehouse, the Bishop's Gate (*c.*1436) at Norwich has a central niche with flanking lancet-style windows at the front and a single three-light window at the rear. Gloucester's Inner Gate is a gatehouse with a lierne vault but nothing by way of external ornament. The Prior's Gate at Rochester is equally plain, with only a nineteenth-century replacement window to illuminate its inner face.

Four fifteenth-century gatehouses of the great abbeys next draw our attention: those of Abingdon, Barking, Glastonbury and Walsingham. The late fifteenth-century Abbey Gate at Abingdon is a two-storeyed gatehouse which stands between the church of St Nicholas and the former Hospital of St John the Baptist. As modest in appearance as the gatehouses of some cathedral-priories, it possesses on its front a single niche, on either side of which is a two-light window. The great abbey at Barking, otherwise destroyed, has left a gatehouse known as the Curfew or Fire Bell Gate ($c.$1460), a portal which, though unaltered, now serves as the lich-gate of the parish church. Probably a medieval cemetery gate (cp. Evesham or Tavistock), it is a building of tower-like appearance with embattled parapet. Over its front archway is a single niche, above which is a three-light window to illuminate the upper chamber. At Glastonbury the great gatehouse (late fifteenth/ early sixteenth century) has a gate-hall which is closely enveloped by the roof, the upper storey of the building being restricted to the domestic accommodation placed to the hall's left. The front façade is therefore restricted in area, and completely lacking in external decoration over the gate-hall. The gatehouse of $c.$1440 at Walsingham, though hemmed in on either side by other buildings, is fairly typical of fifteenth-century two-storeyed portals, with two niches (possibly three) at the front and none at the rear.

A number of other well-preserved examples of portals of the period may be identified, notably at Blanchland, Hyde, Michelham, Wetheral and Whalley. Taking them in alphabetical order, the Blanchland gatehouse ($c.$1500) has the plainest appearance of the group. Two storeys high, it is devoid of ornamentation except for an embattled roof parapet. Hyde possesses a one-storeyed gatehouse which is somewhat like the Glastonbury building, in that the porter's lodge is to the side. Michelham's gatehouse is a square and solid structure of three storeys. Apart from having four two-light windows and an embattled roof parapet, its front façade is lacking in decorative features. Of red sandstone and constructed in three storeys, the embattled gatehouse of Wetheral priory is a building of considerable quality and less plain. The Whalley inner gatehouse, which dates from 1480, is smaller than its fourteenth-century outer counterpart. At the front it has a single archway over which is an empty niche with a coat of arms on each side.

There are a few complete gateways which may be attributed to the fifteenth century. Among others, they include gateways at Brecon and Canterbury Christ Church (Mint Yard Gate) which have vehicular and pedestrians' archways, the Little Abbey Gateway at Chester, an archway in the extensive precinct wall at Coventry Charterhouse, and the now-blocked Austinfriars' entrance at King's Lynn. The gateway at Pluscarden which has a small prison cell attached to it, also may date from this century.

Several gatehouses of the period come within the category of complete but rebuilt/remodelled, all having reconstructed upper storeys. The list includes Gloucester (St Michael's Gate), London Charterhouse (outer), Norwich (Pull's Ferry), Rochester (Cemetery and Sextry Gates) and Worcester (watergate).

At King's Lynn Priory is a gatehouse which is unusual in that it forms part of the south or refectory range of the cloister. It is two-storeyed with a single carriageway which separates stone arches at the front and back, and it is devoid of ornamentation. Though the gate-hall is still used for communication between the front and rear of the range, the whole building at the sides and over the gate-hall has been divided into a number of self-contained cottages.

There are a few fifteenth-century gatehouses that have been adapted as mansions or houses. Probably the least altered of these is Montacute which apart from having its great archways partly blocked and fitted with smaller doors, is little different than in monastic times. In a somewhat similar state of adaptation is the inner gatehouse at Abbotsbury where the front vehicular archway has been blocked and fitted with windows. Cerne's conversion is less obvious but a section of the great archway provides evidence as to its former identity as a gatehouse (cp. the great gatehouse at Evesham). At Canonsleigh is a little-known gatehouse of generous proportions, also converted with minor alterations into a private house.

An intriguing example of adaptation is provided at Sudbury where there is a ground-floor front façade comprising timbered vehicular and pedestrians' entrances. Whether behind and above these features any more of a gatehouse survives is an open question. We are on more certain ground at Ely where Bishop Alcock (1486–1501) constructed a palace for himself just to the west of the south-west tower of the cathedral. The red brick east tower of this palace is a gatehouse (Photograph 25) which retains at ground-floor level a room with lierne vault, still recognisable as the gate-hall. Dunkeswell's gatehouse teeters between ruination and adaptation. The greater part of it became ruined, and the right-hand side became part of a cottage (cp. Culross). Pevsner (1958, p. 206) reports that the gatehouse at Hinton is now inextricably part of the dwelling house.

One or two portals have been adapted for non-domestic purposes. The later fifteenth-century Letheringham gatehouse (Photograph 26) has one of its two main archways totally blocked, the building now serving as a stable. Bruton supplies an example of a large gateway blocked off to complete the precinct-wall now fronting a house near the parish church. Pittenweem's gatehouse, though possessing an unaltered front except for a parapet, has lost its rear section including the archway and gate-hall, and has been converted into a church hall.

What partially dismantled fifteenth-century portals can be identified? Binham Jail Gate which stands some distance to the west of the abbey church, was probably retained after the Dissolution as a lich-gate to mark the main approach to this church. It has lost most of its upper work, but enough survives of the fabric of the ground floor to indicate that there were separate vehicular and pedestrians' entrances at the front. Similarly, Broomholm's gatehouse with a rear main arch in position has a contrived look suggesting that it was deliberately kept as an entrance to the long driveway leading to a farmhouse. The gatehouse of Cornworthy, with much of its upper storey and all of its ground storey, stands in a field where it has been used as a barn for many years. One of the strangest demolition jobs was undertaken at Ramsey where half the great gatehouse of $c.1500$ was transported to Hinchinbrooke House and re-erected. The relocated parts include the front façade, vehicular and pedestrians' archways and gate-hall. The portion retained at Ramsey, which is by no means insignificant, consists of a highly ornamented wing which stood on the left-hand side of the relocated part. Among partially dismantled portals is the watergate at York St Mary's. This vestige, which is adjacent to the abbey guesthouse, retains vehicular and pedestrians' archways and a small two-light upper window all in its rear wall, suggesting that the portal was a gatehouse rather than a gateway.

Several gatehouses exist in a ruined form. Of these, Castle Acre's stands almost to the maximum height of its upper storey in the main range. Its front still exhibits a wealth of decorative features, which include brick facings to doorways and windows, and shields in sunk panels. The other gatehouses are all severely ruined. The Dryburgh gatehouse retains its rear archway and wall at the end of the gate-hall, but much of the remainder of the building has disappeared. This brings us to the last of ruined gatehouses of the period, namely at Dunstable where remnants exist of the ground floor of the building (*c.*1450) including its front two archways.

THE SIXTEENTH CENTURY

As the period of construction in the century lasted only 40 years in England and Wales – and not much longer in Scotland – not many portals were built or reconstructed then. It is possible to identify seven complete portals that are datable to between 1501 and 1539. Taking them in approximate order of erection, the gateway (*c.*1503) known as the Postern Gate at York St Mary's has two entrances, one for vehicles (a segmental arch) and a smaller one for pedestrians (a shouldered arch). At the side is a tower which may have been the porter's lodging. Built about the same time as the postern at York, St John's Gate at Clerkenwell (1504) was considerably restored in the nineteenth century. This brings us to Christ Church Gate (1507–17) at Canterbury Christ Church, probably the finest of sixteenth-century gatehouses and one which befits the chief approach to the cathedral. A much smaller portal but quite as richly decorated as Christ Church Gate is the Prior's Gateway at Peterborough which dates from 1510. The last gatehouse marked with a date to be built before the Dissolution in England is that at Carlisle (1527), a plain building clearly built with defence in mind. The majestic porch-tower built by Abbot Chard at Forde a year later and the great bell tower of Evesham built 1529–39 supply the last two members of this group.

Besides these, there are two other dated portals which survive in a severely adapted form. The first is a large gatehouse (1502) at the entrance to the outer court of Holyrood Abbey and Palace, erected by James IV of Scotland. Most of it was subsequently destroyed, but one wall was incorporated into an adjacent building. The other is the porch of the Bishop's Lodging hall (1527) of St Osyth, of which the fascia survives.

Five other portals of the period deserve mention, all of them more difficult to date within the century than those already described. Two of these are the complete and unaltered gatehouses at Leez. Both are constructed of brick, the outer gatehouse comprising two storeys and the inner, three. In Scotland is the three-storeyed gatehouse of formidable appearance at Crossraguel constructed 'to give a show of strength in the time of the last abbots' (New, 1988, p. 90). At Usk is the small gatehouse which possesses plain semicircular arches at either end of the gate-hall and small square-headed windows in the upper storey. The fifth is the partially dismantled gatehouse at Coverham which may date from the early part of the century.

Of the gatehouses mentioned above, those at Carlisle, Coverham and Usk have semicircular arches, indicative perhaps of the impending classical revival in architecture.

GEOGRAPHICAL DISTRIBUTION

Almost all the surviving monastic portals whether complete or in varying stages of demolition or ruination, are found in England. Of 230 identifiable instances, only 17 are found in Scotland and 10 in Wales. The 203 English portals are scattered throughout the country with five counties possessing double figures: Devon 14, Gloucestershire 11, Kent 26, Norfolk 19 and Yorkshire 18. The remaining English counties each have between one and nine portals, except for five counties (Buckinghamshire, Cornwall, Rutland, Staffordshire and Westmorland) which have now lost any monastic portals they may have had.

The full distribution is as follows:

Bedfordshire	1	Leicestershire	1
Berkshire	2	Lincolnshire	3
Buckinghamshire	0	Middlesex	3
Cambridgeshire	4	Norfolk	19
Cheshire	4	Northamptonshire	5
Cornwall	0	Northumberland	7
Cumberland	4	Nottinghamshire	2
Derbyshire	2	Oxfordshire	2
Devon	14	Rutland	0
Dorset	7	Shropshire	2
Durham	1	Somerset	8
Essex	8	Staffordshire	0
Gloucestershire	11	Suffolk	8
Hampshire	4	Surrey	2
Herefordshire	2	Sussex	6
Hertfordshire	2	Warwickshire	7
Huntingdonshire	1	Wiltshire	3
Kent	26	Worcestershire	7
Lancashire	7	Yorkshire	18

It is not possible to assess whether there is any significance in this distribution, except to note that several of the stone-bearing counties (Devon, Gloucestershire, Kent, Norfolk, Yorkshire) seem to have retained more of their portals than any of the others.

INVENTORY

The Portals Classified in Groups

THE COMPLETE AND UNALTERED GROUP

Abbotsbury Benedictine abbey
gateway
A fifteenth-century plain gateway standing on its own which may have been repositioned after the Dissolution. Its stone archway is segmental and chamfered.

Abingdon Benedictine abbey
gatehouse: Abbey Gate
The two-storeyed building which dates from the late fifteenth century, is sandwiched between the church of St Nicholas and the Hospital (i.e. hospitium) of St John the Baptist. At the front of the gatehouse there are three arches, of which the right-hand one was inserted in the nineteenth century when the building was restored. There is one niche in the front façade placed over the middle archway and said to contain an original figure of St Mary the Virgin. The rear façade is similar to the other, but without a niche. Internally the gate-hall possesses a quadripartite vault of three cross-bays, that is, which run across the gatehouse rather than along it.

Alnwick Premonstratensian abbey
gatehouse
Apart from a small conduit house, this two-storeyed building is all that survives of the abbey. Dating from the middle of the fourteenth century, it presents a military appearance,

equipped as it is with an array of corner turrets, battlements and machicolations. The front and rear arches leading into the gate-hall are segmental, while the gate-hall itself has an unribbed stone vault also segmental in cross-section. There is a small single-storeyed range now roofless attached to the right-hand side of the main building, the purpose of which is uncertain.

Aylesford Carmelite friary
outer gatehouse
Dating in all likelihood from the latter part of the fifteenth century, this substantial but plain-looking gatehouse is of two storeys. It was restored in 1590 (according to a date over a door in the gate-hall). The windows at the front and rear are square-headed and mullioned, and these were probably inserted as replacements for earlier ones at this later time. The gate-hall is entered at the front through a labelled four-centred arch and is exited through an unlabelled arch at the rear. The ceiling of the hall is plastered between crossbeams.

Barking Benedictine abbey (nuns)
gatehouse: Curfew Gatehouse or Tower, Fire Bell Gate
A minor gatehouse and the only surviving one of the great abbey, this stone portal is of *c.*1460 date and may have originally served as a cemetery gate. Today it is used as as the lich-gate of the parish church. Wingless, it is of two storeys with a single turret staircase at its rear. In the upper room is a worn twelfth-century stone rood, once the object of pilgrimage. The gate-hall has a cross-beamed ceiling and a four-centred arch at each end.

Battle Benedictine abbey
great gatehouse
This exceptionally fine three-storeyed building is one of the great surviving gatehouses of England. It is a wide structure which includes a range on each side of the square gate-hall. To the right the range includes the porter's lodge, with twelfth-century work in its outer walls. The left-hand range, which is now roofless, was probably the almonry. In 1338 or soon afterwards the gatehouse and the two ranges were

largely rebuilt, the present building largely the outcome of this work. Both the front and rear façades, which are alike, are richly ornamented chiefly with bands of panelling that encompass the turrets as well as the walls over the arches leading into the gate-hall. The latter is rib vaulted in two bays, each bay of vaulting being subdivided to accommodate the vehicular and pedestrians' separate passageways.

Battle Benedictine abbey
gateway: postern opposite parish church
A small doorway in the precinct wall having a two-centred arch. Dating from the late thirteenth/early fourteenth century, it has continuous mouldings of a double flat chamfer separated by a quirk.

Battle Benedictine abbey
gateway: postern to left of gatehouse
Details similar to those of the above gateway.

Beaulieu Cistercian abbey
outer gatehouse
The little two-storeyed gatehouse which is lacking in external decoration, dates from the late thirteenth century and must have been used since the Dissolution as a lodge for the gate-keeper of Palace House. The portal possesses a lean-to on each side, and these may well have been built or enlarged after the medieval period to increase the gatekeeper's accommodation. Over the small gate-hall is a chamber with lancet windows.

Blanchland Premonstratensian abbey
gatehouse
Typically of medieval buildings in border lands (Northumberland in this case), this gatehouse was constructed for defence and thus has no ornamentation except for an embattled parapet. Made of stone in two storeys, the gatehouse (*c.*1500) has a wing on the right-hand side which may have provided guests' accommodation. The building has square-headed windows to the front and rear, and the arches leading into the gate-hall have semicircular heads. The gate-hall has a tunnel vault with no ribs.

Brecon Benedictine priory
gateway
The fifteenth-century gateway led into the outer court of the priory. It is of the double type, having a small pedestrians' entrance with a two-centred pointed arch, and a large vehicular entrance with a segmental top. Over the latter are two empty, rectangular-shaped niches and above these an embattled parapet.

Bridlington Augustinian priory
gatehouse: Bayle Gate
Constructed in 1388, this wide gatehouse consisting of gatehall and two wings, is constructed of stone below and brick above, probably indicative of large-scale repairs carried out at a later date. The building is lacking in external decoration except for the arms of the priory prominently displayed over the vehicular arch at the front. The central section of the portal comprises two storeys, the gate-hall having a tierceron vault in the shape of a star. Above is a large chamber that was used, probably from before the Dissolution, as a courtroom. The right wing was the porter's lodge, and the left wing the 'Kydcott' or prison.

Bristol Augustinian abbey
main gatehouse: Abbey Gatehouse (now cathedral)
First dating from *c*.1165, the stately gatehouse still displays work of this period in the gate-hall and semicircular arches leading to it. The pedestrians' passageway is completely separated from the gate-hall by a longitudinal septum. The vehicular passageway consists of two bays with a twelfth century ribbed vault and some fine blind intersecting arches along the walls. About 1500 this Norman portal was restored and a new and bigger gatehouse built around it. The ornate work of the upper two storeys and the tower block adjoining it to the rear on the left-hand side belong to this later date.

Bromfield Benedictine priory
gatehouse
A small double-winged building built probably in the fourteenth century. Its ground-floor storey is made of stone and

its upper storey is half-timbered. The central gate-hall has a plastered ceiling and is entered via single two-centred archways, one at the front and the other at the rear.

Buckfast   Cistercian abbey
porch-tower: Abbot's Tower
The four-storeyed building is sited towards the southern end of the modern west range. Apart from a small undercroft, it is the only remaining portion of the claustral buildings to have survived the Dissolution. Dating from the fourteenth century, it possesses several two-light windows, but is lacking in external ornamentation.

Burnham Norton   Carmelite friary
gatehouse
This is one of the very few friary gatehouses that is complete. Built early in the fourteenth century, its only missing feature is the tracery in the big three-light window above the front archway. The two-storeyed building is faced with knapped flint and has jambs, etc., of tooled stone. The gatehouse is ornamented with flushwork panelling, an early instance of this type of decoration in East Anglia. The gate-hall is vaulted in stone with ribs and wall-shafts.

Bury St Edmunds   Benedictine abbey
main gatehouse: Great Gate
Except for the vaulting inside the gate-hall and two small turrets, the gatehouse is complete and provides one of the best surviving examples of this type of fourteenth century work. It was built in two campaigns, the first taking place somewhere between 1327 and 1346 and the second lasting from 1353 to *c.*1384. It is a handsome structure, well ornamented with niches, panelling, shafting, and so on, in the Decorated style, but not extravagently so. The narrow lobby of the gate-hall is entered through the single front archway which unusually retains its portcullis. In turn, this lobby leads into a wide gate-passage. Both sections of the gate-hall have side walls into which blind arches have been inserted. The accommodation over the gate-hall was occupied by guards (not porters) who were in charge of the gatehouse, men who could raise or lower the portcullis.

Bury St Edmunds   Benedictine abbey
gatehouse: St James' Tower or Gate
This great gatehouse of four storeys is one of the earliest to survive virtually unspoilt and unchanged. It was built during the period which lasted from 1120 to 1148. Besides giving access to the abbey church, it also served as the belfry of the neighbouring church of St James, a service it continues to fulfil on behalf of the present cathedral. The great Norman tower is characterised by having its faces taken up with a series of semicircular arches and pilasters, and in possessing an ornate high arch at each end of the gate-hall.

Caldey   Tironensian priory
gatehouse
Possibly on account of its small size, the priory never had a normal layout of buildings round the cloister. Thus the two-storeyed portal, and so-called gatehouse, was placed at the south end of the west range where it abutted the church. Possibly dating from the thirteenth century, the gatehouse which formed a major component of the range, gave direct access to the cloister and had a guest room over the gate-hall.

Canterbury Christ Church   Benedictine cathedral-priory
main gatehouse: Christ Church Gate
This is a splendid building which provides a fine approach to the cathedral church. The gatehouse probably replaced the North Gate as the chief portal of the cathedral-priory. It was constructed between 1507 and 1517, and may not have been finally completed before 1521. Its importance architecturally is that the Renaissance influenced aspects of its design. The building consists of three storeys and possesses a wealth of ornamentation on its front façade, but much less on its rear. Its gate-hall has a large lierne vault in the form of a star.

Canterbury Christ Church   Benedictine cathedral-priory
gatehouse: Forrens Gate
Constructed in the fifteenth century, the gatehouse has a front portion which appears to have been added to or extended from the front of the existing earlier range (i.e. bakehouse/brewhouse/granary). The gate-hall is long, has plain internal walls of knapped flint and a beamed and

plastered ceiling. To its front Forrens Gate presents a neat, two-storeyed appearance with an embattled parapet.

Canterbury Christ Church   Benedictine cathedral-priory
gateway: cemetery gate, entrance to Kent War Memorial Garden
The gabled twelfth-century semicircular archway with zig-zag moulding on one side and a spiral moulding on the other now stands east of the cathedral Corona where it provides a fitting entrance to the Kent War Memorial Garden. In the early nineteenth century it was taken from its position south-east of the south-east transept where it had stood between the monks' cemetery and the lay cemetery, and moved to its present location.

Canterbury Christ Church   Benedictine cathedral-priory
gateway: Mint Yard Gate
This portal appears to have served as an outer gateway leading to North Gate and thence to the outer or Green Court. The existing gateway which dates from the fifteenth century, is double with a larger vehicular arch (four-centred) and a smaller pedestrians' arch which is two-centred. The structure consists of knapped flint interspersed with larger pieces of tooled stone. Above the arches is a tiled capping.

Canterbury Christ Church   Benedictine cathedral-priory
gatehouse: North, Court or Latter Gate
First built *c.*1153 or later, the present building exhibits strong Norman work in its ground floor, notably the single large arches at the front and rear, the decorative blind arcading on the front façade, and the large arched recesses at the sides of the gate-hall. However, the gatehouse was extensively restored in the fifteenth century, when a two-arched wall was inserted across the gate-hall immediately behind the front archway and a single one was inserted at the opposite end. At the same time the upper storey was renewed. The gate-hall has a plastered barrel vault which could equally be a product of the earlier or later work.

Canterbury Christ Church   Benedictine cathedral-priory
porch-tower: Prior Selling's Porch
Facing the Green Court, the porch-tower of Prior Selling

was built some time between 1472 and 1494. It is a two-storeyed building of knapped flint with stone facings, and was the entrance to the prior's lodgings. Internally, its gate-hall of two bays possesses a handsome tierceron double-star vault which springs from shafts ascending from the floor.

Canterbury St Augustine's　　　　　　Benedictine abbey
main gatehouse: Fyndon or Great Gate
An outstanding example of a complete fourteenth-century gatehouse. Its construction was effected in the period which lasted from 1300 to 1309. It was damaged during the Second World War and was restored from 1942 onwards. Flanked by two octagonal turrets at the front, its outward façade presents an upper storey elaborately ornamented with niches and windows, all of which have been given small but steep gables. Below, the gate-hall is entered through a segmental archway which has been placed under a dominant super-arch. The rear façade is much plainer than the front and has a modest two-centred archway. The gate-hall has plain blind arches along its side walls and a ribbed quadripartite vault.

Canterbury St Augustine's　　　　　　Benedictine abbey
gateway
This fifteenth-century portal is a four-centred tall gateway that stands next to Fyndon Gate and at right angles to it. It is made of brick and is inserted into a flint-knapped section of the abbey's precinct wall. The gateway is surmounted with a label and has a tiled wall-top.

Carlisle　　　　　　Augustinian cathedral-priory
gatehouse
An unadorned building typical of gatehouses to be found in border areas. This two-storeyed stone gatehouse may be accurately dated, as the year of its construction is given in an inscription on the rear arch, 1527. The gate-hall, which has a barrel vault devoid of ribs, is entered at each end via semi-circular archways which possess continuous mouldings of the chamfered kind. The small windows are square-headed with cuspless round-arched lights.

Cartmel Augustinian priory
gatehouse
Built *c*.1330, the small gatehouse of two storeys is hemmed in by neighbouring buildings, one of which to the right has enroached upon its front façade, while to the rear both sides of the archway are also partially hidden behind other buildings. The portal lacks decorative features except for a moulded stone surround that originally housed a statue or coat of arms. Constructed of stone, the façades have both been rendered giving a generally dismal appearance to the building, a look compounded by the grey slate roof. Internally, the gate-hall exhibits traces of having once been partly ribbed, but the vault, which is plastered, appears to be groined.

Castle Acre Cluniac priory
porch-tower: Prior's House Porch
Of an attractive domestic appearance, the porch was constructed in the early years of the sixteenth century. It stands in front of a much earlier porch placed halfway along the west range, this earlier porch forming the main entrance in the twelfth century. Though portions of the prior's house have been destroyed, the outer porch is complete, standing two storeys tall with a high timbered gable. The lower walls are faced externally with knapped flint, and a large section between the ground-floor and first-floor levels is covered with chequered flushwork. The porch is entered from the front through a wide four-centred arch, above which is a label with blank shields in the spandrels.

Cerne Benedictine abbey
porch-tower: Abbot's Hall Porch
The abbot's hall which probably occupied the west range has completely disappeared, but its porch (*c*.1500) which faces west, probably gave access to it from the west side. The porch-tower stands three storeys high and has a handsome oriel at the front that rises through the middle and top storeys. The porch-hall has a fine fan vault. A spiral stairway leads to the abbot's chamber on the first floor. Evidence provided by the fabric at the rear of the porch indicates that it was formerly joined to another building.

Chester   Benedictine abbey
gateway: Kaleyards Gate   (now cathedral)
A small gateway with a square head. The gateway tunnels under the lower part of the city wall which at this point probably did dual service as the abbey's precinct wall. The portal provided access to the garden immediately beyond the wall where the monks grew vegetables.

Chester   Benedictine abbey
gateway: Little Abbey Gateway   (now cathedral)
A much-weathered portal consisting of a fifteenth-century segmental arch, to the left-hand side of which is a short piece of precinct walling.

Cirencester   Augustinian abbey
gatehouse: Saxon Arch, Spital Gate
Essentially a one-storeyed building with accommodation of sorts placed in the roof. The gatehouse which dates from *c*.1180, is therefore Norman not Anglo-Saxon. Of stone construction it possesses a large vehicular and a small pedestrians' archway at the front, and a large common archway at the rear. There is no external ornamentation, and the interior of the gate-hall has a plastered ceiling.

Clerkenwell   Knights Hospitallers' priory
gatehouse: St John's Gate
Judging from early pictures, the building which dates from 1504, had become quite rundown by the beginning of the nineteenth century, during which century it was restored to its pristine condition. Consisting of two storeys, the gatehouse presents a clean appearance to its front, which has a middle (gate-hall) section which separates a tower-wing on either side. The large chamber over the gate-hall is used as the council chamber of the reconstituted Order of St John in England. The gate-hall has a tierceron vault in the form of a four-pointed star.

Colchester St John's   Benedictine abbey
gatehouse
This is a superb piece of architecture constructed in the East Anglian style with plenty of flushwork panelling. Built in the

fifteenth century and restored in the nineteenth, the gatehouse competes for acclaim with its neighbour down the road, St Osyth. Two-storeyed, it displays pinnacled turrets at its four corners, and niches and two windows to the front and one window to the rear. The common gate-hall is entered from the front through two arches of dissimilar size, the larger or vehicular one being four-centred and the smaller or pedestrians' two-centred. At the rear is a single four-centred arch. The vault of the gate-hall is a particularly fine example of the lierne type, having ribs added to form a cross superimposed on a star. To the left of the gate-hall section is a roofless porter's lodge with walls standing two storeys high.

Coventry Whitefriars   Carmelite friary
outer gatehouse
Though the small building has been given modern windows, the front and rear walls which consist of ashlar (part crumbling and part renewed), are largely original. The vehicular arches and two of four (*sic*) pedestrians' arches are four-centred and suggest a fifteenth-century date for the gatehouse. The side walls of the gate-hall are made of stone which has been faced on the right side with brick and on the left with half-timbering and nogging. The ceiling consists of cross-beams with a plastered infill. The gatehouse with its two small lateral wings is divided into two cottages, one of which is now used as a museum.

Crossraguel   Cluniac abbey
gatehouse
It stands to the south-west of the conventual church and gives access to the outermost or south court. Built in the sixteenth century, the gatehouse was raised to three storeys to give a show of strength in the time of the last abbots (New, 1988, p. 90). With circular turret and corbelled-out parapet (the uppermost part of which is missing) and no external decoration, it strongly resembles a castle. Its small gate-hall, which is segmentally vaulted in stone, is entered via a semicircular headed archway at either end. To the right of the gate-hall is a slender room that was used by the porter. The accommodation of the middle and top

storeys is identical, consisting of a large square chamber equipped with window seats front and back, fireplace, cupboard and privy.

Dover   Augustinian priory
gatehouse
This portal dates from the fourteenth century and was restored late in the nineteenth. It now forms part of Dover College and is currently used as a library. The building, which is constructed of knapped flint, is two-storeyed and is winged on each side. The gate-hall also has walls of knapped flint, its ceiling consisting of timber boarding.

Dunfermline   Benedictine abbey
gatehouse: The Pends
This building is placed in an unusual position at the west end of the refectory range. It is sandwiched between the refectory to one side and the kitchen and guest wing/palace to the other, forming a kind of bridge between the two groups of buildings. Dating from the second half of the fourteenth century, it is a gaunt-looking portal from both front and rear, having no external decoration. It consists of three storeys with stone-vaulted ceilings at each level. Because of the juxtaposition of neighbouring buildings, the ground plan of the gate-hall is irregular, as is its ribbed vaulting. A line of corbel-stones at the top of the rear of the gatehouse indicates the probable position of a missing parapet.

Dunster   Benedictine priory
gateway: near Prior's House
The portal stands approximately 100 yards north-west of the conventual (now parish) church. It possesses a segmental head and coped parapet above. There is insufficient detail to put a date on the gateway. The head, however, may have been reconstructed after the Dissolution.

Dunster   Benedictine priory
gateway: next to monastic barn
A plain arch, approximately 150 yards due north of the east end of the church. Its details are similar to those of the above gateway.

Durham   Benedictine cathedral-priory
gatehouse
Giving access to the College or green of the cathedral from North Bailey, the stone gatehouse of *c*.1500 is a building of modest proportions and appearance that was quite extensively restored in the nineteenth century. The portal has a three-light window at the upper storey level both at the front and the rear. However, niches on either side of the front window are absent at the rear. The porter's lodging forms a wing on the right-hand side, behind which is a turret staircase providing access to the upper storey. The gate-hall has a wide two-centred archway at each end, and is divided by a cross-wall halfway along. Its vaulting on either side of the cross-wall consists of a tierceron-ribbed star, and it has plain blind arches inserted into its side walls.

Ely   Benedictine cathedral-priory
gatehouse: Porta or Walpole's Gate, South Gatehouse
One of the surviving great gatehouses of the medieval monastic era, the portal was built in 1396–97. A wide building, it consists of three storeys and has turrets at the four corners. Its only external decoration consists of four widely spaced empty niches on the front façade (and none on the rear), an indication that the main gatehouse of the cathedral-priory was sited elsewhere. The square-shaped gate-hall now lacks its vaulting, though the shafting and springing in the corners of the hall are still evident.

Ely   Benedictine cathedral-priory
gatehouse: Sacrist's or Sextry Gate
Built between 1325 and 1326, the stone gatehouse is sandwiched between the sacristry to the left and another range, the Old Choir House (almonry?), to the right. With its stepped parapet and high blind arcading, the front façade presents quite an impressive appearance. Internally, there is a barrel-ribbed vault over the gate-hall.

Ely   Benedictine cathedral-priory
gatehouse: Steeple Gate
Possessing a crypt which dates from the fourteenth century

(or possibly earlier) under the gate-hall, this is one of the most interesting surviving gatehouses in the country. Above ground the building, which dates from *c.*1500, is half-timbered, a feature more evident at the rear than the front. The upper storey of the gate-hall is supported at both ends on carved beams, of which the front one displays the arms of the cathedral-priory.

Evesham   Benedictine abbey
gatehouse: North, Norman or Cemetery Gate,
Abbot Reginald's Gateway
Built by Abbot Reginald (or Reynold) Foliot between *c.*1139 and 1143, the gatehouse leads from the market square into the north section of the abbey precinct. It is two storeys high, the lower being constructed in stone and dating from the above-mentioned period. Although only the jambs of the archways at the ends of the gate-hall have survived, the Norman arcading along the sides of the hall remain in position. Overhead, the ceiling of the hall consists of plasterwork and cross-beams. Though the upper storey may have originally been made of stone, a half-timbered storey with an attic was constructed in the fifteenth century, and with the Norman lower storey this has survived to the present day.

Evesham   Benedictine abbey
gatehouse or gate-tower: cemetery gate,
Abbot Lichfield's Bell Tower, New Tower
The tower was constructed as a dual-purpose portal and bell tower and was sited between the town cemetery to the west and the monks' cemetery to the east. Conjecturally, like the cemetery gate at Furness, it may have enabled townspeople to visit the monks' graves. Constructed in the period between 1529 and 1539, it represents the last flowering in English monasteries of the late Perpendicular or Tudor style. The detached building consists of three stages with the front and rear façades of identical appearance. We must assume that the west side of the tower on which is placed the clock face, is the front of the building. The one-bay gate-hall displays springers in its corners for vaulting which appears never to have been installed.

Ewenny Benedictine priory
south gatehouse
As befitted a fortified priory, the two-storeyed gatehouse displays to its exterior an embattled parapet, loop-holes, small windows but no ornamentation. It consists of a main section with gate-hall flanked to the right by a wing which served as a porter's lodge (the roof and intermediate floor of which have gone). The wing which displays one or two lancets and trefoiled-headed single-light windows, is probably of thirteenth-century origin, but the gate-hall and chamber overhead belongs to the fifteenth century and must have been rebuilt at this time. The gate-hall interior has an unribbed barrel vault which is pierced by murder-holes.

Exeter St Nicholas Benedictine priory
porch-tower
Constructed of three storeys, the late fifteenth- or early sixteenth-century tower, which was equipped with a staircase, was undoubtedly built to give better access to the upper floor of the west range where there was accommodation for the prior and his guests. Given the erection of towers as porches in the same position at other monasteries (e.g. at Forde described below), there is a likelihood that this tower was intended to be used (or for a short time actually was used) as a porch affording external access from the west. Evidence for this is provided by the high and wide relieving arch which may be seen in the west wall of the tower from outside above the modern three-light window (itself a replacement for an earlier window). The size of the relieving arch appears to be more suited to the support of an entrance-arch than a window.

Forde Cistercian abbey
porch-tower: Abbot Chard's Tower
One of the last monastic buildings to be constructed in England before the Dissolution, the tower (Photograph 27) was finished in 1528, the date coupled with Abbot Chard's name in a Latin inscription given at the top. The stately three-storeyed building is sited on the west side of the west range where it leads directly into the great hall (also

Chard's work). The tower with its superb oriel which rises from the middle to the top storey, is one of the jewels of surviving monastic architecture anywhere in the country. It is entered at ground-floor level from the south side through a basket arch into a lobby with a sumptuous fan vault, beyond which is a labelled and four-centred inner doorway.

Forde   Cistercian abbey
west gatehouse
A small fifteenth-century gatehouse of two storeys, it stands on the west side of the abbot's lodging to which it is joined. Its other side was attached to a barn now removed, indicated by a roofline on the wall of the gatehouse. Its probable use, indicated by a hatch in the side wall of the gate-hall, was to regulate the movements of guests on their way to Abbot Chard's Tower. The gate-hall itself has a four-centred archway at each end and a beamed ceiling.

Glastonbury   Benedictine abbey
gatehouse
One of the few instances of a one-storeyed gatehouse, though the substantial domestic accommodation to the left of the gate-hall looks altogether too grand for a porter. This accommodation, which carries an impressive array of transomed windows, is two-storeyed. Constructed of stone in the late fifteenth or early sixteenth century, the gatehouse has a modern pantile roof. The gate-hall is completely divided by a longitudinal wall, the main hall for vehicles being boarded overhead, not vaulted. However, the pedestrians' passageway has a ribbed quadripartite vault.

Gloucester   Benedictine abbey
gatehouse: Inner Gate   (now cathedral)
A small fifteenth-century gatehouse that led from the outer court to the abbot's quarters and great court. Of two storeys it lacks external ornamentation, its front and rear façades being partly plastered and partly stone, but its gate-hall has a rather attractive lierne vault of an unusual square pattern, with fleurons at the rib intersections. Its arches at either end of the hall are badly worn and need renewing.

Gloucester Benedictine abbey
outer gatehouse: St Mary's or Great Gate (now cathedral)
Before King Edward's Gate became the chief gatehouse of the abbey, St Mary's Gate probably fulfilled this role. Mainly constructed in the thirteenth century, the two-storeyed portal displays much of the work of this century, especially on the front and rear façades and in the gate-hall. Thus, the capitals of the shafting all have stiff-leaf foliage. However, a number of the shafts are missing, a feature which gives the building a run-down look. The gate-hall interior is amply provided with wall-shafting which rises six feet from the floor to a point where capitals give rise to the springing of a ribbed vault. Behind the wall-shafting are semicircular blind arches which, with the chevron-mouldings of some of the ribs suggest that this part of the gatehouse may be even older than the thirteenth century. Contiguous with the gatehouse on the right-hand side is a sixteenth-century half-timbered house which may have been, or have replaced, the almoner's lodging.

Hulne Carmelite friary
main gatehouse
The two-storeyed fifteenth-century portal which forms part of the precinct wall includes a porter's lodge on its right-hand side. It has a narrow gate-hall, at the ends of which are semicircular archways. The gate-hall has rough barrel vaulting which is devoid of ribs. On the right, behind the precinct wall, a flight of steps leads to the upper storey which appears to be incomplete.

Hyde Benedictine abbey
gatehouse
Another instance of a one-storeyed gatehouse. The fifteenth-century main section of the building has vehicular archways to the front and rear which are four-centred. To their left are two pedestrians' archways, the front one blocked, and to the left again is a small range, also one-storeyed, which was probably the porter's lodging.

King's Lynn Whitefriars Carmelite friary
gateway
A small portal which dates from the late fourteenth century.

Constructed of brick with stone facings, it is about six feet deep from front to back and has a design approaching that of a gatehouse. The front of the building has three empty niches set at the 'upper-storey' level, the middle one higher than the flanking ones. Below the middle niche is a four-centred front archway which leads into a small 'gate-hall' having a depth from front to back of perhaps five feet. At the rear of this is another archway with an obtuse and plain head.

Leez   Augustinian priory
inner gatehouse
This stately building now stands on its own, low remnants of neighbouring brick ranges showing that this was not always so. The gatehouse dates from the sixteenth century. The complete absence of religious symbols or motifs suggests that the gatehouse could have been erected immediately after the Dissolution by the new owner of the priory, Lord Rich. However, the timber gates (removed from the inner to outer gatehouse), which have trefoil-headed panels, are certainly monastic. Constructed of brick with stone facings (arches, windows, etc.), the gatehouse is three storeys high and possesses four corner turrets, the brickwork being panelled and displaying diaper-work. The superb four-centred front archway which has the Tudor rose and fleur-de-lis in its spandrels, leads into a plain gate-hall with a timbered ceiling and this hall is exited via another four-centred archway to the rear.

Leez   Augustinian priory
outer gatehouse
A more modest building of the sixteenth century than its inner partner, this portal of two storeys now forms part of an outer range which today serves as the core of the privately owned mansion. Its brick construction and general external appearance are similar to that of the inner gatehouse, the chief difference being that its top, including the turrets, is embattled. Like the inner gatehouse, the gate-hall which is plain, has a four-centred archway at each end.

Leigh (Buckfast)   Cistercian abbey
gatehouse
Leigh, near Churchstow, was a grange of Buckfast Abbey,

and it includes a remarkable set of complete medieval buildings, including a small fifteenth-century gatehouse. Built of stone, it is two-storeyed with two gables at right angles to its front/rear axis. The building is continuous, left and right, with a short precinct wall. The two-centred front archway leads into a small gate-hall having a beamed ceiling, while to the rear is a semicircular archway. The chamber overhead has a fireplace.

Lindores Tironensian abbey
gateway
The abbey, according to Gifford (1988, p. 331), was enclosed by an outer wall with a round-arched hoodmoulded south-west gateway. The latter, indeed, survives up to the level of a ragged parapet which is immediately over the big archway. New (1985, p. 203), however, describes this archway as being part of a former gatehouse. Careful examination of the portal, which may be dated as late twelfth/early thirteenth century, reveals it to be a double gateway with its pedestrians' pointed archway now blocked. There is no visible evidence to support that it was the front wall of a gatehouse, and excavation would be needed to prove the point one way or the other.

London Charterhouse Carthusian priory
inner gateway
A four-centred tall archway which is constructed of brick and has a tiled top. It dates from the early sixteenth century.

Malling Benedictine abbey (nuns)
gatehouse
A small chapel projects to the rear from the left wing of the gatehouse. This chapel displays mid-fourteenth-century work (e.g. a window with Kentish tracery). However most of the gatehouse which also has a wing to the right of the gate-hall section, dates from the fifteenth century when it must have been largely rebuilt. The front is made of stone, but the upper storey at the rear is jettied, half-timbered and plastered. The front of the gatehouse is characterised by three chimneys, which give it a domestic look. The wall also carries shields emblazoning symbols of the Passion, placed

over large and small archways leading to the interior. The gate-hall has partly timbered walls as well as a beamed and plastered ceiling.

Malvern Benedictine priory
gatehouse: Abbey Gateway
Though heavily restored in 1891, the stone gatehouse (or Abbey Gateway as it misnamed) retains a substantial amount of its original structure which dates from the fifteenth century as early pictures (by Buck, 1731) show. It is a wide building with wings on either side of the gate-hall section. It consists of two storeys which are reflected in the two dazzling arrays of panelling which ornament the front from side to side. The upper-storey array is broken by an attractive oriel which is placed immediately over the central archway; the lower-storey array is broken by this archway which is four-centred with quatrefoils in its spandrels. The rear of the building is much more pedestrian in character, having a series of square-topped windows at the side of and above the four-centred archway. The gate-hall has a timbered partition which served as a cross-wall, and overhead, a ceiling composed of cross-beams and boarding. The gatehouse is presently used as a museum.

Michelham Augustinian priory
gatehouse: watergate, Gateway Tower
Standing immediately before a bridge over a moat where in medieval times there was a drawbridge, the gatehouse dates from $c.1395$. It consists of three storeys, its walls made of chalk and flint faced with Eastbourne greensand. It has narrow wings on either side of the gate-hall section that were offices of the porter. Though it possesses a staircase-turret at the rear, the building is devoid of buttresses and has a tower-like profile. Ornamentation is limited to battlements and two string-courses. The upper storeys are each occupied by a great room lit by (mostly) two-light windows at the front and sides. The front archway, which is segmental, is recessed. No doubt this was to accommodate the drawbridge when raised. The gate-hall, which has a similar archway at its rear, lacks vaulting.

Minster-in-Sheppey　　　　　　Augustinian priory (nuns)
gatehouse
A small piece of work involving the rear turret (right-hand side) and displaying lancets dates from the thirteenth century. Otherwise the fabric of the stone gatehouse was erected in the fifteenth century, when substantial reconstruction took place. The building has a gate-hall to the left and a porter's office to the right, and overhead there are two more storeys. Though the top is embattled, there is no external ornamentation except for some string-courses. The rear appears to retain more of its original work than the front, where modern windows have been inserted. The gate-hall, which has a boarded ceiling, is entered via two arches (large and small) at the front and one at the rear. The gatehouse is currently used as a local history museum.

Morwell (Tavistock)　　　　　　Benedictine grange
gate-tower
Reminiscent of the Town Gate at Tavistock on which it may have been modelled, the sixteenth-century portal leads into a quadrangle on the four sides of which stand the grange buildings, including a barn. The gate-tower, of two storeys only, has a front façade given additional height by twin flanking turrets and middle gable. The labelled basket arch at ground-floor level leads into a two-bay gate-hall which has a ribbed quadripartite vault. A winding stairway gives access to the upper chamber, which is equipped with a fireplace and privy, and which displays evidence (blocked doorways) of having formerly communicated with the standing ranges on either side of the gate-tower. Though gabled, the rear façade lacks turrets and is plain in comparison with the front.

Norwich　　　　　　Benedictine cathedral-priory
gatehouse: Bishop's Gate or Bishop Alnwick's Gateway
This building, built *c.*1436, is flanked to the left by the former fifteenth-century granary and to the right by a former prison, now the gatehouse cottage. The gatehouse is less adventurous in its design and ornamentation than the Erpingham and St Ethelbert's gatehouses. Of two storeys, its decoration on the front façade is restricted to an embattled

parapet, and a central niche between two small windows. At ground-storey level are a large and small archway, both two-centred, and over these but under the niche a panelled frieze. The square gate-hall has a tierceron star vault and a single two-centred archway at the rear. The rear façade is plain, having two flanking turrets and a small central two-light window.

Norwich Benedictine cathedral-priory
gatehouse: Erpingham Gate
One of the most exciting fifteenth-century portals, the gatehouse provides the chief mode of access to the west end of the cathedral-church. With its tall archway which rises two-thirds of the total height of the gatehouse, from the front it appears to be of one storey only. From the rear, however, it is clear that there is an upper storey entered from a range on the left-hand side of the gate. The front arch is flanked by polygonal buttresses, and both arch and buttresses are highly decorated with heraldry and sculpture. Over the archway the gable, which is faced with knapped flint, has a niche. The rear archway, however, is plain and plastered. The gate-hall has a plastered barrel ceiling.

Norwich Benedictine cathedral-priory
gatehouse: St Ethelbert's or Great Gate
Though heavily restored in the nineteenth century, St Ethelbert's Gate is believed substantially to represent the building erected *c.*1328. It consists of two storeys, though this is more obvious from the rear where there is one large three-light window with reticulated tracery at the upper-storey level with dummy windows in flushwork left and right. The front façade is ornate, with geometrical shapes of flushwork at the top, a series of canopied niches and friezes of chequerwork and quatrefoils in the middle, and carved figures and more niches on either side of the archway. The gate-hall is vaulted in two bays, each with lierne ribs forming an octagon inside a star, an early example of this type of vault.

Osney Augustinian abbey
gateway
Standing next to a fifteenth-century medieval building which

may have been a mill is a segmental gateway with a straight parapet. This portal, which is of similar date to that of the mill, is near the river and may have been a watergate.

Oxford St Bernard's   Cistercian college
gate-tower   (now St John's college)
The front of Front Quad stands on St Giles, and the mid-fifteenth-century gate-tower (Photograph 28) is placed between two two-storeyed ranges. The gate-tower is three storeys high with an embattled parapet. The front of the ground storey has a wide, four-centred archway that occupies the whole of the tower's frontage. At first-floor level there is a canted oriel with canopied niches left and right containing an ecclesiastical and academic figure respectively. The centre of the façade of the top storey has another canopied niche containing an original statue of St Bernard flanked by two more windows. The gate-hall has a two-bay ribbed quadripartite vault, while to the rear is another four-centred archway leading into the quadrangle.

Peterborough   Benedictine abbey
gatehouse: Abbot's Gatehouse   (now cathedral)
Possibly the finest surviving thirteenth-century gatehouse. Constructed during the second half of the century, it overshadows the main gatehouse in size and in its refined but not excessive use of decorative features. The latter include multi-ordered arches, niched figures, shafting and string-courses externally, and quadripartite rib vaulting and wall-shafting inside the gate-hall. The cobblestoned floor of the gate-hall is probably original.

Peterborough   Benedictine abbey
gateway: cemetery gate   (now cathedral)
A small embattled portal of the fourteenth or fifteenth century that stands next to the Prior's Gate. Leading to the north side of the cathedral church, it probably served as a cemetery gate. Its arch, which is chamfered, has a segmental head.

Peterborough   Benedictine abbey
main or outer gatehouse   (now cathedral)
This two-storeyed building was evidently first erected in the

twelfth century and later reconstructed without total demolition in 1302–07. The earlier work consists of the gate-hall, notably its ribbed quadripartite vault and interior wall arcading, as well as the two great single semicircular arches at each end. In the early fourteenth century a new and pointed arch was erected over the front arch, and the upper storey rebuilt.

Peterborough   Benedictine abbey
gateway: Prior's Gateway   (now cathedral)
A single-storeyed construction dating from 1510, it possesses a wall-walk overhead which is fronted by ornamented battlements. The gateway is of the double type with high vehicular arch to the left and low pedestrians' arch to the right. The gateway as a whole is characterised by its rich ornamentation.

Pluscarden   Benedictine cell
north gateway
Though starting life as a Valliscaulian priory, the house became a dependency of Dunfermline abbey in 1454. The fifteenth-century gateway, which forms part of one of the most extensive sections of surviving precinct wall in Scotland, has an attached small chamber thought by some to have been used as a prison cell (see New, 1985, p. 244). Examination of the masonry of the gateway does not establish conclusively whether or not it was part of a gatehouse.

Polesworth   Benedictine abbey (nuns)
gatehouse
This is one the few gatehouses to display half-timbered work, this being in the upper storey with brick infilling. The lower storey, however, is made of stone. A long range of stone, possibly the almonry, projects to the right of the gate-hall section, while to the left is a wing, the porter's accommodation. Most of the above fabric dates from the fourteenth century, but it is possible that the gate-hall stone section, which lacks architectural detail, may be earlier. The pedestrians' and vehicular passageways are quite separate. The ceiling of the vehicular passageway (gate-hall proper) is composed of asbestos sheeting(!), a measure of the need to restore this portal.

Quenington Knights Hospitallers' commandery
gatehouse: Knights' Gate
The building is one of only two surviving gatehouses belonging to the Knights Hospitallers, the other being at Clerkenwell in London. The small two-storeyed gatehouse dates from the early fifteenth century. Its front façade has a niche which contains the figure of a knight. The gate-hall possesses two arches at the front, one large and three-centred and the other small and two-centred. At its rear, there is not an arch but a square-shaped opening with a timber lintel. A door on the right-hand side of the gate-hall leads into a two-storeyed range that may have provided the porter with accommodation. On the left-hand side of the gate-hall is a one-storeyed range that may have been stables.

Reading Benedictine abbey
inner gatehouse: Abbey or Inner Gate
A gatehouse rather spoilt when restored in the nineteenth century by Sir George Gilbert Scott, it now lacks replacements of some of its missing earlier decorative features such as parapet, niches, and so on. The building consists mostly of ashlar below and knapped flint above. The core dates from the thirteenth century, the gatehouse's style of windowing pointing to this period. The rear façade is similar in appearance to the front façade in having a 'hard' look and in lacking ornamental detail. The gate-hall is divided by a cross-wall with a single archway. The porch has a stone barrel vault, while the gate-passage behind the cross-wall has a timber-boarded ceiling.

Rochester Benedictine cathedral-priory
gatehouse: Prior's Gate
An unexceptional two-storeyed building dating from the fifteenth century, it is almost totally devoid of external ornamentation. It possesses a small single-light window at the front and a slightly larger two-light window at the rear. Even its parapets are plain. The gate-hall is square, with a ribbed quadripartite vault.

Saighton (Chester) Benedictine grange
porch-tower
All that is left of the medieval grange at Saighton near

Chester is this embattled porch-tower which now stands in front of a Victorian mansion (currently used as a school) to which it is joined. The porch-tower, which was built by Abbot Ripley c.1490, is made of red sandstone and consists of three storeys. The porch-hall, which has a timbered ceiling, is entered through a single pointed archway. The most attractive feature of the building is the oriel which is placed at first-floor level on the left-hand side of the entrance where it faces left.

St Albans Benedictine abbey
main gatehouse: Great Gateway (now cathedral)
A very substantial building (1360+) of knapped flint with stone facings, it was used as a gaol after the Dissolution and is now part of school premises. The building is double-winged and there are turrets to the rear on either side of the central archway. The gatehouse consists of three storeys, and both at the front and rear there are a number of two- and one-light windows all under square heads. External ornamentation is restricted to embattled parapets at the front and back. The gatehouse has a large (vehicular) and small (pedestrians') archway at the front and a single archway at the rear. The chief feature of the gate-hall is its fine lierne vault in the form of an octagon inside a four-pointed star.

St Andrews Augustinian cathedral-priory
gateway: Cemetery Gate
A single round-arched gateway which could date from the late twelfth/early thirteenth century. Located immediately to the north-east of the cathedral-church, it afforded access to the cemetery area to the east of the great church. As this area had probably been the churchyard of a parish church, the gateway was almost certainly provided so that lay people could visit the graves of relatives subsequently located within the precincts of the cathedral-priory. The gateway was probably restored in the sixteenth century at the same time as the precinct wall to which it was joined.

St Andrews Augustinian cathedral-priory
gateway: Sea Yett or Mill Port
This is a portal with a semicircular arched opening flanked

by loopholes. Over the archway is a coat of arms and immediately above this an empty niche. The parapet of the gateway appears to be incomplete. The portal, like the precinct wall to which it is joined, was probably constructed in the fourteenth century and restored in the sixteenth.

St Osyth Augustinian abbey
gatehouse: Great Gatehouse
One of the finest half-dozen monastic gatehouses in the country, this splendid building dates from *c*.1475. It is of considerable size, having a wing on each side of the central gate-hall section and beyond these wings, further ranges. The gatehouse is three-storeyed with two broad octagonal turrets to the front and four small square turrets to the rear, its front and rear façades being covered with a glorious array of flushwork panelling which extends downwards from the embattled parapets to the ground. The two-centred central archway is flanked, unusually, by two small archways for pedestrians, while to complete the decorative ensemble three prominent niches are placed over these three arches. The spandrels of the large archway have carvings of a dragon in one and St George or St Michael in the other. At the rear of the building, which is generally plainer than the front, is a single archway, also two-centred, with quatrefoils in the spandrels. The gate-hall, which is square with no wall panelling, has a vault divided into two bays with a complex lierne pattern of octagon and star in each.

Stamford Greyfriars Franciscan friary
gatehouse
Standing on the site of a modern hospital, the gatehouse is all that survives of the friary and is one of the very few gatehouses of the mendicant orders to have outlasted the Dissolution. Built in the middle of the fourteenth century, the two-storeyed stone building is in remarkably good condition. Considering that the gatehouse is small, it is well decorated on its front face, with square buttresses, pinnacles, empty niches and blank shields. The rear façade is also decorated but less so. The front archway leads into a small gate-hall which has a ribbed barrel vault with curved ashlar between the ribs.

Stoneleigh Cistercian abbey
gatehouse
The fourteenth-century stone gatehouse, which consists of a gate-hall section and a large range to its left, is in complete condition. The building consists of two storeys with a deep gabled roof. There is little by way of external ornamentation front or back, but the twin-light windows have flowing tracery. The gate-hall possesses no vault, being timber-floored above. The long range at the side was the hospitium, part of which also belongs to the fourteenth century and part to the Elizabethan portion of the sixteenth century when it was remodelled.

Tavistock Benedictine abbey
main gatehouse: Town, Court or Higher Abbey Gate
The gatehouse was originally built in the twelfth century, this period represented by the core of the building. It was then reconstructed in the fifteenth, when it was given new external archways and windows. Finally, it was severely restored in the nineteenth century before being converted to use as a public library. The building, devoid of medieval ornamentation, now consists of two storeys, its pinnacles and battlements apparently having been replaced in the nineteenth-century restoration. The gate-hall is divided by a twelfth-century cross-wall with two arches, the front half having a plastered barrel vault and the rear half a beamed and boarded ceiling.

Tewkesbury Benedictine abbey
gatehouse: Abbot's Gatehouse
The two-storeyed embattled gatehouse was built in the fifteenth or sixteenth century and restored in 1849 by J. Medland. The front archway, which takes up most of the ground-storey, though pointed is almost semicircular. Above is an empty niche with two two-light windows left and right. A charming touch is provided by gargoyles below the parapet which are not bizarre, as they usually are, but in the form of angels. Apart from lacking a niche, the rear façade is similar to that at the front. The gate-hall is divided by a cross-wall with two arches, placed one-third of the distance from the front archway. Its stone vaulting is unusual in that the bays are placed across the hall rather than along it, with three

bays in front of the cross-wall and two behind it. The vaulting, which is ribbed, is basically sexpartite.

Thornton   Augustinian abbey
gatehouse
Probably the largest and most elaborately designed gatehouse of all, it was in all likelihood occupied by the abbot either as his lodging or as his administrative quarters It is a building which owes its survival to having been used as housing after the Dissolution. Dating from 1382, the main gate-hall section and two wings flanking it are complete. However, the high walls beyond the wings appear to be incomplete or unfinished. Moreover, the barbican, which is composed of two parallel walls in front of the main archway, and which was built later than the gatehouse (sixteenth century), is partly ruined. The gatehouse itself is made mostly of brick but much stone is also used, not all of it for facings. The building consists of three storeys and has several turrets both at the front and back. Though equipped with military features such as loopholes, barbican and portcullis, it is doubtful whether these were intended for anything more than show. The upper part of the front of the gatehouse is ornamented with a battery of canopied niches, several of which still retain their original statues. The rear of the building has more of a domestic appearance, a fine oriel being the focal point at the level of the middle stage. The gate-hall has a cross-wall with a single arch through which horses and vehicles passed, but immediately in front of the cross-wall is a passageway for pedestrians leading off the gate-hall to the right. This took them past the porter's office which was situated on this side of the gate-hall. The ribbed vault of the gate-hall is unusual, consisting of four bays in front and one bay behind the cross-wall, the whole being divided by a transverse rib into eight and two units respectively. On the first floor is a large apartment, measuring 48ft × 20ft, in which is a wide fireplace. On the second floor there is another large room from which was operated the gatehouse portcullis.

Tisbury (Shaftesbury)   Benedictine grange (nuns)
inner gatehouse
Place Farm (Pevsner and Cherry, 1975, p. 523) is the re-

markable survival of a grange of the nunnery of Shaftesbury, with farmhouse, barn and outbuildings dating from the fourteenth and fifteenth centuries. The small, two-storeyed gatehouse which leads to the house from the outer court is a product of the fifteenth century. It has a narrow gate-hall with a plastered ceiling, and its front and rear façades are plain except that each possesses a two-light window. An external stairway leads to the upper chamber.

Tisbury (Shaftesbury)   Benedictine grange (nuns)
outer gatehouse
This building is as large as the gatehouse of many of the smaller abbeys and priories. It gives access to the outer court from the public highway. Its front façade, which is characterised by possessing five tall and prominent buttresses, has a large vehicular archway and a smaller pedestrians' archway. These lead into a gate-hall divided into two almost equal parts by a longitudinal wall in which is an arch. The ceiling of both parts is beamed and boarded. The rear façade displays two archways at ground level which are almost equal in size (cp. Canonsleigh). External ornamentation is absent, both front and rear façades exhibiting two two-light windows in the upper storey. An external stairway leads to the upper chamber.

Torre   Premonstratensian abbey
porch-tower: Abbot's Tower
The tower stands halfway along the west range to which it is joined at its rear. Erected during the fifteenth century, it is a much plainer looking porch-tower than others of the same date and type. It consists of four storeys, is embattled at the top and has a rendered exterior. The first floor and second floor have labelled, square-topped windows facing the front, while at the third-floor level above these windows is a clock face. The main doorway at ground level is insignificant (compared with that, say, at Forde).

Torre   Premonstratensian abbey
inner gatehouse: Mohun Gate or Gatehouse
Named after the family who were lords of the manor locally and whose arms appear on corbels in the gate-hall, the stone

gatehouse dates from *c*.1320 when it probably replaced an earlier one. It is sited in an unusual but not unique location, namely at the south-west angle of the claustral ranges. There is one main storey over the gate-hall, while to the right is a wing providing the porter's suite which rises through three storeys from the ground floor. The front façade, including two flanking octagonal turrets, lacks decoration except for an embattled parapet. The gate-hall is entered by a large and small arch from the front, and is divided by a longitudinal wall (in which there are two arches) into a broad and high section for vehicular traffic and a small one for pedestrians. The whole gate-hall has a ribbed quadripartite vault of two bays divided by the longitudinal wall into four vault units, two large and two small. The rear façade, which also has two archways, is flanked by one octagonal turret only, this to the right.

Usk   Benedictine priory (nuns)
gatehouse
This building of simple appearance consists of two main storeys plus an attic. Its plain semicircular archways at the front and rear probably date from the sixteenth century when the Romanesque architectural style was enjoying a revival. It has square-headed windows with lights devoid of cusps in their heads. The building lacks decoration of any kind.

Walsingham   Augustinian priory
main gatehouse
Located in the main street, the gatehouse of *c*.1440 is placed tightly between two ranges, of which judging from its rear windows the left-hand one is medieval and may have been the hospitium or almonry. The portal stands two storeys high, but has lost its parapet. The upper storey, housing a room used by the porter, is equipped with squints which enabled him to see along the street in either direction. The front façade has a wide, four-centred archway, while overhead, ornamentation consists of two niches placed either side of a modern window above which is a quatrefoil filled with a carving of the porter's head. The rear façade has a larger window than that at the front. Inside the gate-hall, the vaulting which has gone has been replaced by blocks of concrete.

Wetheral Benedictine priory
gatehouse
This fine, unspoilt gatehouse probably owes its survival to having been used as a vicarage after the Dissolution. Built of stone in the fifteenth century, it stands three storeys high, and has a wing on the right-hand side probably used as the porter's office downstairs, and a turret with staircase to the left rear. Roof-lines indicate the locations of two other buildings attached to the gatehouse. Ornamentation at the front and rear is restricted to battlements and string-courses. The gate-hall has a tunnel vault which is entered via a single archway at the front and by another at the rear. Though not obvious when viewed from the front, the wall over the archway with its windows at first- and second-storey levels projects forwards, making an oriel of sorts. Slit-windows placed in the wall at the ends of the oriel enabled observation to be made of visitors approaching the gatehouse.

Whalley Cistercian abbey
inner gatehouse: North-east Gateway
Two-storeyed and constructed of stone, the gatehouse (1480) gave access to the great court of the abbey. It is modestly ornamented with an embattled parapet and a niche flanked by coats of arms over the front archway. The rear façade lacks the niche and coats of arms, but is embattled. The gate-hall is entered via a large archway at the front, and is exited through another, equally large one at the rear. The hall is divided into two equal sections by a double-arched cross-wall, the front section having a tunnel vault and the rear a timbered ceiling. The heavily studded doors in the cross-wall are probably original (fifteenth century). A small range to the left was the porter's lodging.

Wigmore Augustinian abbey
inner gatehouse
The abbot's lodging which forms the core of the post-Dissolution house, stands to the west of the site of the south (refectory) range of the abbey. In turn, the fourteenth-century inner gatehouse (Photograph 29) winged on either side, is placed to the west of the abbot's lodging with which it is contiguous. The lower section of the gatehouse is made

of stone and the picturesque upper portion, which overhangs the lower part at the front, is half-timbered. The gate-hall has a beamed and boarded ceiling, above which is not an upper storey as such, but an attic taking up the space of the roof.

Winchester Benedictine cathedral-priory
gateway: Prior's or St Swithun's Gate
Constructed in the fifteenth century, the portal has a wide, four-centred stone archway above which is a tablet dated 1968 displaying the arms of Elizabeth II. The gateway, which is single-storeyed, has solid flanking walls, an embattled parapet and a lean-to roof behind this parapet. The gateway surround is faced with knapped flint and squared-off pieces of stone. The timber gates may be original.

Worcester Benedictine cathedral-priory
main gatehouse: Edgar Tower or Great Gate
Over-restored in the nineteenth century (for instance in the renewal of niches and the provision of statues), the large, two-storeyed and double-winged gatehouse substantially dates from the early fourteenth century. The front and rear faces are flanked by octagonal turrets which are embattled. Both faces are largely occupied by windows and ornate, statue-filled niches, the front face more so than the rear. The gate-hall is entered and departed from via large, single archways. Its interior is equally divided by a two-arched cross-wall into a lobby and gate-passage. Both areas are vaulted, but whereas the lobby has a lierne vault, the gate-passage has a ribbed quadripartite vault.

Worksop Augustinian priory
gatehouse
This impressively large gatehouse dates from the early part of the fourteenth century, and was substantially restored in the nineteenth. Its front is asymmetrical owing to the porch of a ground-floor chapel. This porch is placed immediately to the right of the gate-hall archway and to the anterior of the chapel, the latter occupying the front ground portion of the right-hand wing of the gatehouse. Apart from the porch, which possesses a large, three-light window with reticulated

tracery, a pierced gable-parapet and four niches, the front façade of the two-storeyed gatehouse is not excessively ornamented, its main decorative features being a large six-light window flanked and topped by statue-filled niches. The rear façade is plainer and partly taken up by an external stairway to the upper floor. The gate-hall, which is entered via a large archway at each end, is divided by a cross-wall with a large and small archway and has a beamed and plastered ceiling. The gatehouse is currently used as an arts centre.

York St Mary's Benedictine abbey
gateway: postern or Postern Gate
Built in 1503 in honour of Princess Margaret, daughter of Henry VII, who was the guest of the abbot for two days on her journey to Scotland as the bride of James IV of Scotland, the gateway has two arches, the large vehicular arch being segmental and the small pedestrians' arch shouldered. The gateway is single-storeyed, with a low, embattled parapet overhead. To the right of the gateway and contiguous with it is a two-storeyed porter's lodge.

THE COMPLETE AND REBUILT/REMODELLED GROUP

Aylesford Carmelite friary
gatehouse: watergate
Leading from the River Medway during earlier centuries, the watergate provided an important means of entry to the friary. It forms one end of a long range, of which the Pilgrims' Hall occupies the opposite end. Apart from later windows, the ground floor of the gatehouse area probably dates from the fifteenth century or even earlier, but the upper storey in particular was reconstructed by John Sedley *c.*1590. His work included the insertion of new windows at ground- and first-floor levels, and dormers in the roof.

Bristol Augustinian abbey
gatehouse: abbot's gatehouse (now cathedral)
The lower storey of this building was erected *c.*1165. It possesses a Norman arch at each end of a rectangular-

shaped gate-hall leading from the exterior to a little cloister. The upper storey consists of post-Dissolution work (possibly of seventeenth-century date) which in turn has been restored more recently.

Buckfast Cistercian abbey
south gatehouse: South Gate
This portal was almost entirely rebuilt in the twentieth century when what was left of the original gatehouse, probably the side-walls of the gate-hall, was incorporated into the new structure.

Canterbury Christ Church Benedictine cathedral-priory
gatehouse: Larder Gate
This portal was virtually demolished in the Second World War and had to be almost completely rebuilt. Now called the Larder Gate Memorial Building, the modern range is faced with knapped flints. It maintains its continuity with the past by retaining its original front arch which gave access to the gate-hall. Of fifteenth-century date, the arch of stone is four-centred.

Canterbury Christ Church Benedictine cathedral-priory
gatehouse: Pentise Gate
Located immediately to the west of the Archdeacon's House of which it now forms part, the gatehouse consists of three storeys. The ground floor, originally of two bays, was built in the twelfth century and still displays plain semicircular vaulting arches in the gate-hall (now of three bays). The upper storeys, which incorporate rooms called Heaven and Paradise, were reconstructed by Prior Chillenden *c.*1400 when he built the Archdeacon's House as additional guest lodgings. These storeys which are half-timbered, were further altered after the Dissolution when, for example, new windows were inserted.

Carmarthen Augustinian priory
gatehouse
The original structure now forms part of a row of terraced houses which at the time of writing has recently been modernised. The whole set of buildings is rendered with plaster and it is thus impossible to distinguish old work from

new. The gate-hall, which is complete, permits pedestrians and wheeled traffic to pass from one side of the houses to the other. It possesses a doorless single archway at the front and another at the rear.

Chester Benedictine abbey
main gatehouse: Abbey Gateway (now cathedral)
Constructed of dark red sandstone, the fourteenth-century lower storey of the gatehouse (Photograph 30) presents two archways to the front and one to the rear. Part of the upper storey, especially at the front which is a lighter coloured sandstone than below, was rebuilt probably towards the beginning of the nineteenth century. The vaulting of the gate-hall is plain, consisting of three ribbed quadripartite bays.

Furness Cistercian abbey
outer gateway
As with some other Cistercian abbeys, the outer portal of *c*.1300 was probably always a gateway rather than a gatehouse. Of the double type (i.e. with pedestrians' and vehicular arches), it stands close to the west end of the *capella-ante-portas* to which its masonry is joined, its other side being connected to a short length of precinct wall. Although it is quite possible that some of the gateway fabric may have been reassembled or strengthened in the interests of conservation, its general appearance would suggest that what is seen now may not be very different from what it looked like in medieval times.

Gloucester Benedictine abbey
gatehouse: St Michael's or Cemetery Gate (now cathedral)
The front portion of the fifteenth-century lower storey of this gatehouse is constructed of stone. It possesses a wide, four-centred archway which is flanked by two empty niches. The upper storey, which is constructed of brick, is post-Dissolution in date.

Hulne Carmelite friary
south-west gateway
Probably a postern, the small, two-centred gateway has three lancet windows overhead retained in a common blank arch.

Corbel-stones to the rear suggest that the gateway originally possessed a lean-to roof.

King's Lynn Augustinian priory
gatehouse
This portal forms part of the south or refectory range of the priory. The surviving portion of the gatehouse consists of a fifteenth-century gate-hall with a four-centred arch at each end. The left side of the gate-hall is half-timbered and it has a beamed ceiling. The range was converted after the Dissolution into a row of cottages, one of which includes the upper storey of the gatehouse.

London Charterhouse Carthusian priory
outer gatehouse
Of the medieval gatehouse only the lower storey, mainly built of stone survives, this of fifteenth-century date. To the front it displays vehicular and pedestrians' archways both four-centred, the pedestrians' archway being constructed in brick somewhat later than the vehicular. Overhead are two storeys of brick, with sash windows. These were erected in 1716 and, judging from old pictures, replaced a half-timbered earlier superstructure. It now serves as accommodation for the Master of Charterhouse.

Norwich Benedictine cathedral-priory
gatehouse: watergate, Pull's Ferry
John Pull was a nineteenth-century ferryman-cum-innkeeper and for some unknown reason the watergate (Photograph 31) was named after him. Built in the fifteenth century, it was sited to guard the River Wensum approach to the cathedral-priory. The ferryman's house above the lower storey was constructed soon after the Dissolution. The building was restored and re-roofed in 1949. Of special interest are the completely divided gate-hall (for pedestrians and vehicles) and the turret on the right of the building which may be older than the main structure.

Rochester Benedictine cathedral-priory
gatehouse: Cemetery, College or Chertsey's Gate
The lower storey is faced with bands of knapped flint

alternating with ashlar. Possessing four-centred main arches to front and rear, it dates from the fifteenth century. The upper storey, including an attic in the roof gable is timber-clad with sash windows. This upper storey was either totally rebuilt or extensively remodelled after the Dissolution.

Rochester Benedictine cathedral-priory
gatehouse: Sextry or Deanery Gate
The ground floor of this gatehouse has walls made of mixed tooled stone and flint. Its two archways, though four-centred, are almost semicircular. It could date from the fourteenth or fifteenth century. The upper storey, which has clearly been rebuilt or remodelled since the Dissolution, has plastered walls and sash windows, and there is an attractive tiled roof.

St Albans Benedictine abbey
gatehouse: Waxhouse Gate (now cathedral)
This provided the north entrance to the abbey precinct from the town. Pevsner and Cherry (1977, p. 321) report that of this portal, the springers of pointed arches are visible beneath the eighteenth-century archway.

Walsingham Augustinian priory
gateway: Knight's Gate
A fourteenth-century postern, heavily restored in the nineteenth century when the embattled parapet was probably added. Set in the original precinct wall of the priory, it consists of a small doorway with a pointed arch.

Worcester Benedictine cathedral-priory
gatehouse: watergate, Ferry Gate
Located close to a wharf at the side of the River Severn, the fifteenth-century lower storey of the watergate is constructed of stone in two bays. At the front are portcullis grooves. The upper storey, which has brick walls and modern windows, is post-Dissolution in date. It is now part of a private house.

THE ADAPTED GROUP

Abbotsbury Benedictine abbey
inner gatehouse
Originally standing two storeys high, the fifteenth-century gatehouse is now a private house with additional accommodation placed in the attic. Viewed from the road, its vehicular arch is seen to have been filled with stone and fitted with post-Dissolution windows, but the gatehouse retains some of its medieval two-light windows. Inside is a large and unaltered pointed archway of coeval date, which formerly led from the gate-hall to the exterior.

Aylesford Carmelite friary
inner gatehouse
Judging from the shape of the two large archways which may be seen on either side of a late sixteenth-century range (now used as a reception office), the inner gatehouse was constructed in the fifteenth century and probably originally was an adjunct of the west range of the friary. The arches, which are four-centred, are now each filled with a small doorway and flanking post-Dissolution windows.

Beaulieu Cistercian abbey
inner gatehouse
The large fourteenth-century building now forms the core of a mansion, Palace House, constructed by Sir Arthur Blomfield in 1872. The front elevation displays the chief archway, blocked and given a modern window, together with original buttressing, central niche (filled with a modern statue of the Mother and Child) and a pair of two-light windows. There is some doubt as to whether the vaulting of the gate-hall is all original work or was altered by Blomfield. The upper storey still displays evidence (e.g. piscinas) that, unusually for a gatehouse, it had two chapels.

Beauvale Carthusian priory
gatehouse
This building has been considerably altered and is now a granary. Its fourteenth- or fifteenth-century origin is recognisable with some difficulty internally and probably not at all

externally. The two great arches of the gate-hall have been blocked, but their jambs, visible from inside, survive at the front and rear, the arches themselves having been cut off at their springing. Some of the fascia walls of the gatehouse also survive up to the level of the top of the ground-floor storey.

Bermondsey   Cluniac abbey
east gatehouse
On the south side of Grange Walk is the south or left-hand wall of a gate-hall. Though rendered and forming the front of a post-Dissolution house, it displays some large iron hinge-crooks from which one of the monastic gates was hung.

Bolton   Augustinian priory
gatehouse
Like the inner gatehouse at Beaulieu, this gatehouse, which dates from the early fourteenth century, also forms the core of a post-medieval mansion. The latter was altered and almost certainly enlarged in 1806 to a design of Joseph Michael Gandy and, judging from its general appearance, again later in the nineteenth century. A large archway may be seen at the front, blocked by a wide chimney-breast. At the rear a small medieval doorway is inserted into the archway on that side. Internally, the cross-wall and vaulting have been retained.

Bruton   Augustinian abbey
gateway
A blocked four-centred gateway of the fifteenth century, constructed as part of the high precinct wall of the abbey in a street called The Plox.

Butley   Augustinian priory
gatehouse
One of the most elaborately decorated gatehouses to survive in the country, it was built 1320–25 and exemplifies the Decorated style of architecture in all its luxuriance. Though adapted as a house, the gatehouse has front and rear façades which retain all their ornamental features such as

coats of arms, flushwork, niches, buttresses and window tracery. Viewed from the front, apart from the blocked main archway, there is little to indicate a significant departure from the former use of this large and imposing winged gatehouse.

Calder Cistercian abbey
gatehouse
Though the rear archway of this fourteenth-century gatehouse is open, the front archway has been blocked and a small doorway inserted in it, and the intermediate floor between the lower and upper storeys has been removed. These appear to have been the only alterations made when the portal was converted to a barn after the Dissolution. Externally, the gabled and roofed building appears never to have been decorated except minimally. The cobbled floor, which extends along the roadway beyond the front of the gatehouse, may well be original.

Canonsleigh Augustinian abbey (canonesses)
gatehouse
The massive, two-storeyed, fifteenth-century gatehouse is substantially complete and is sited in Canonsleigh Barton farmyard. After the Dissolution the high vehicular archway and low pedestrians' archway in the front wall were blocked off, the resultant confined space in the gate-hall being used for storage purposes. At the time of writing the gatehouse is being carefully restored for private occupation. What makes the ground-floor of the building unusual is that, viewed from the rear, the gate-hall is seen to have been divided by a continuous longitudinal wall into two equally sized sections, the rear arches both segmental of the same size. Why this was done is not known. The vehicular section of the gate-hall also possesses a cross-wall placed one-third of the distance from the front of the gatehouse. Inserted into this cross-wall is a high, four-centred arch which is ornamented on its front with a series of well-carved fleurons. The large chamber occupying the whole of the first-floor possesses the usual privy and fireplace. The façades of the gatehouse lack ornamentation apart from an empty niche placed between two two-light windows at the front.

Canterbury Christ Church   Benedictine cathedral-priory
gateway: in The Borough
A late fourteenth-century two-centred archway composed of brick which is now blocked. Bordering The Borough, a section of the precinct wall of the cathedral priory is constructed of knapped flint interlarded with pieces of stone, and the archway was inserted in it. Overhead are two sets of brick trefoils separated by what may have been a niche, now filled in.

Canterbury St Augustine's   Benedictine abbey
gatehouse: Cemetery Gate
From the front the gatehouse (*c*.1390) appears to be unaltered, except for its blocked main archway. Though not as elaborate as its neighbour the Fyndon Gate nearby, its façade survives displaying its original appearance, but inspected from the rear the building which now serves as a hall of residence for students, has been considerably altered and added to. Internally, the gate-hall, now being used as a study-bedroom, has either lost its vaulting or has had the vaulting masked by a flat ceiling inserted below it in recent times.

Cerne   Benedictine abbey
main gatehouse
A large house built in the eighteenth century round the gatehouse hides nearly all of the medieval fabric which belongs to the fifteenth century. However, part of the springing of the outer great arch is visible from the front of the house, thus providing evidence for the origin of the present building.

Dale   Premonstratensian abbey
gatehouse
One hundred yards or more west of the site of the conventual church and on the opposite side of the road behind the Methodist church is a building believed to consist of a remnant of the abbey gatehouse. The latter was converted after the Dissolution into a prison which in turn now appears to be in use as a garden store. It is not possible to date the medieval portion of the building as architectural detail is lacking. Today its lower part is composed of large

tooled pieces of stone, and there are portions of buttressing at the corners. The upper part is brick and there is a tiled roof. There are no external signs of gate-hall archways, and the building seems too small to have been the main section of a gatehouse.

Dunkeswell   Cistercian abbey
gatehouse
The fifteenth-century building is mostly ruined, with the front archway broken at the springing of the arch. On the left-hand side of the gate-hall is a high-standing ruined wing which may have been the porter's accommodation or almonry. The right side of the gatehouse has been converted into a thatched cottage.

Ely   Benedictine cathedral-priory
gatehouse: Palace gatehouse
A four-storeyed building which stands in an awkward location immediately west of the cathedral-church. A casual glance to the front does not reveal the portal's origin, but a closer look shows where brickwork and a square-headed window was used to seal off the front archway. Internally, the gate-hall still possesses its rear four-centred archway and a rich lierne vault. The gatehouse was built by Bishop Alcock (1486–1501), and used to be connected to the west porch or galilee of the cathedral-church by a gallery, now removed. The building today forms part of a Sue Ryder Home.

Evesham   Benedictine abbey
main gatehouse: Great Gatehouse
A large house of *c*.1711 was built over and round the great gatehouse of the abbey. This earlier building which was constructed between *c*.1316 and 1332, is almost completely hidden within the fabric of the house. However, when viewed from the yard behind the house, part of the rear main arch, now blocked, is visible together with a smaller unblocked arch which may originally have been the pedestrians' rear doorway.

Hinton Charterhouse   Carthusian priory
gatehouse
Pevsner (1958, p. 206) mentions a gatehouse which 'is now

inextricably part of the dwelling house. It seems to have been built in the fifteenth century'.

Holyrood   Augustinian abbey
gatehouse
This was built by James IV of Scotland in 1502 to the design of the master mason Walter Merlioun. Most of it was subsequently pulled down and the remainder, the walling of the right-hand wing, was incorporated into another building which stands at the edge of the forecourt of the abbey and palace. The right side wall of the gate-hall displays vestiges of the vaulting within the gatehouse and the position of a cross-wall.

Jervaulx   Cistercian abbey
gatehouse
To the south-west of the abbey precinct is a large private nineteenth-century house in which is entangled medieval work, especially towards its west end. Though there is no external indication of a gate-hall or its archways, this medieval work is believed to be the remnant of the inner gatehouse. A broken arch of a ground-floor doorway possesses a water-leaf capital, suggesting that some of the work may date as early as the late twelfth century.

King's Lynn Austinfriars   Augustinian friary
gateway
All that survives of the friary is a complete fifteenth-century elliptical arch surmounted by a low parapet and with short lengths of precinct wall on either side. The arch is made of brick with the usual stone facings, and is blocked. The gateway probably continued to be used for a time after the Dissolution and was subsequently walled off.

Kirklees   Cistercian priory (nuns)
gatehouse
Mentioned by Midmer (1979, p. 184), part of a gatehouse exists incorporated in farm buildings. He suggests that it owes its survival to having been part of a house which was built on the site of the priory. Pevsner (1959, p. 291) states that the gatehouse which is largely post-Reformation,

consists of fabric some of which is timber-framed and some stone. Apparently there is no sign of archways or gate-hall.

Kirkstall   Cistercian abbey
inner gatehouse
Forming a substantial part of a post-Dissolution house constructed in the nineteenth century (now the abbey museum), the gatehouse is easily recognisable for what it was before adaptation. Dating from the twelfth century (mainly) and thirteenth centuries, the portal retains its two chief arches as well as its internal cross-wall and rib-vaulted gate-hall. These outer arches are semicircular, but are now blocked. The cross-wall has two archways, the bigger semi-circular and the smaller pointed.

Lacock   Augustinian abbey (canonesses)
gatehouse or gateway
There is some mystery concerning the whereabouts of a gatehouse at Lacock. Pevsner (1975, p. 288) refers to a main gatehouse of stone in the outer courtyard with half-timbered dormers and a half-timbered clock-turret. The building at the north-west corner of the courtyard next to the brewery, which seems to meet this description, was erected by Sir William Sharington in the period 1540–53. There is, however, a blocked archway containing a two-light modern window at the north end of the west range beyond the medieval kitchen. Of fifteenth-century date this arch, which is four-centred, led from the west through the north-extended west range towards the courtyard. It may have been the outer arch of a gate-hall (cp. Aylesford friary inner gatehouse).

Leicester St Mary's   Augustinian abbey
inner gatehouse
After the Dissolution the gatehouse became either the entrance to or part of Cavendish House, a post-Dissolution mansion built nearby. This house was later plundered and burned by Royalist troops in the Parliamentary Wars, the gatehouse not escaping the destruction. The surviving section of the gatehouse is a high-standing wall connected to the ruins of the house.

Letheringham Augustinian priory
gatehouse
Constructed of brick in the closing years of the fifteenth century, this small gatehouse now in use as a stable is virtually complete. It is roofed but has lost its intermediate floor. The rear archway has been totally blocked, while the front has had a small doorway inserted for the animals to use.

Llanthony Augustinian priory
gatehouse
The building is now in use as a barn. Its great arch at the front has been filled with stone and the rear section made longer after the Dissolution. The floor between the lower and upper storeys has been removed, as has the cross-wall. Though these alterations seem quite extensive, in actual fact the building, which dates from the thirteenth century, is easily recognisable as a gatehouse. On the left-hand side are the remains of a lean-to building, probably the porter's lodging.

Maxstoke Augustinian priory
inner gatehouse: Inner or Middle Gatehouse
Probably of similar date (fourteenth century) to the outer gatehouse, this portal extending as a wing to the left-hand side served as the prior's lodging until the Dissolution, after which it became an Elizabethan private dwelling-house. The main arches of the gatehouse which are visible from the exterior are now blocked, the gate-hall being converted into the dining hall of the house.

Montacute Cluniac priory
gatehouse
This great fifteenth-century gatehouse, possessing a long wing to the left and a short wing to the right of the high gate-hall, is almost complete, even to the extent of displaying all the original ornamental detail of its front and rear façades. The two main arches are blocked, not with stone but with timber screens. The gate-hall, which retains its tierceron vault in two bays, is now used as a reception room of the house into which the gatehouse has been converted.

Pittenweem　　　　　　　　　　　　Augustinian priory
east gatehouse
This fifteenth-century building still exists in somewhat mutilated form and is forbidding in appearance, with a small round-headed entry and an upper floor with heavy machicolation (New, 1985, p. 239–240). The rear of the gatehouse, which has lost its archway, appears to have been completely rebuilt with a lean-to roof. It is now used as accommodation for a nearby church.

St Benet of Holme　　　　　　　　Benedictine abbey
gatehouse
Roofless and with walls standing mostly to the height of the main arches, the gatehouse dates from the early fourteenth century. At the rear may be seen the high, two-centred archway. The front archway, however, is concealed within an eighteenth-century brick windmill erected partly outside and partly inside the area of the gate-hall. A fragment of the stone vaulting of the gate-hall is also hidden within the windmill.

St Osyth　　　　　　　　　　　　Augustinian abbey
porch: Bishop's Lodging hall porch
The so-called Bishop's Lodging in reality was the abbot's lodging built by Abbot Vyntner in 1527. The lower part of its front façade survives from this time and is so dated. The fine oriel at first-floor level was reconstructed when the building behind the late medieval ground-floor façade was rebuilt in 1865. The central vehicular archway and flanking pedestrians' doorways probably led into a large porch below the abbot's hall before this latest rebuilding.

Sudbury　　　　　　　　　　　　Dominican friary
gatehouse: Priory Gate
Two fifteenth- or sixteenth-century arches abutting Friars Street stand side by side. They form part of the lower front wall of a half-timbered house which overhangs them. The vehicular archway, which possesses some attractively carved spandrels, is now blocked and contains a modern window. The present house has probably developed from the friars' gatehouse of which the front façade may be all that survives of the original late medieval building.

Tavistock Benedictine abbey
gatehouse: cemetery gate
The west tower of the parish church was constructed in the fifteenth century over what seems to have been an early fourteenth-century gatehouse which probably afforded entry to the lay cemetery. The gatehouse possessed large, pointed openings to the north and south, each decorated with shafted rib arches. These openings, now blocked, have been incorporated into the fifteenth-century structure of the tower.

Wenlock Cluniac priory
gatehouse
Some distance to the west of the conventual church is 'a square featureless tower, connected probably with the outer courtyard of the priory' (Pevsner, 1958, p. 211). Though its lack of detail makes it undatable, its position suggests that it may have been part (e.g. the right-hand wing) of a gatehouse of the priory.

THE PARTIALLY DISMANTLED GROUP

Bayham Premonstratensian abbey
gatehouse: Kentish Gate
Probably the lesser of two gatehouses (the other has completely vanished), this small two-storeyed building was partly dismantled and then 'reconstructed' in the eighteenth century when it was converted into a summerhouse. Since then it has deteriorated and is more of a ruin than a summerhouse. At the present time little more of the original early fourteenth-century portal survives other than the gabled front façade which has lost the tracery from its large two-light window.

Binham Benedictine priory
gatehouse: Jail Gate
Considerable remnants of this fifteenth-century portal survive up to the level of the top of the ground-floor storey, although all the chief archways are broken. The gatehouse's survival since the Dissolution may be because, sited directly

to the west of the church, it served for some of the intervening period as a lich-gate. On the left side of the rear arch is a squint which is in line with the middle of the great west door of the church.

Broomholm (Bacton) Cluniac priory
gatehouse
A four-centred arch at the rear of this fifteenth-century gatehouse was retained to mark the entrance to the farmhouse which occupies the priory precinct. The upper storey was demolished leaving the side walls and broken arches at the middle and front of the gate-hall.

Buckfast Cistercian abbey
north gatehouse: North Gate
This twelfth-century building has been partly dismantled, leaving intact the rear semicircular archway and the left-hand wall to the level of the top of the ground-floor storey. Traces of masonry on the inner side of this wall show that the gatehouse interior consisted of perhaps two bays of groin vaulting divided by a cross-wall.

Byland Cistercian abbey
inner gatehouse
The surviving parts of this late twelfth-century gatehouse are the cross-wall (except for most of the pedestrians' arch) and the right-hand wall of the gate-hall, the remainder having perished. The doorway leading to the porter's office, though blocked, is located in this side wall. Why the gatehouse still straddles a public highway rather than having been totally cleared away is not known.

Cornworthy Augustinian priory (canonesses)
gatehouse
The early fifteenth-century building is complete except for its roof and several courses of stone in the walls of the upper storey which are missing. The building, especially its lower storey, was probably retained after the Dissolution for use as a barn or cow-byre. The gate-hall is divided both by a cross-wall and, for the whole of its length, by a solid longitudinal wall, all four sections retaining all their vaulting. The

vehicular sections possess ribbed and panelled barrel vaulting, an unusual design for the period.

Coventry Charterhouse Carthusian priory
gateway
This small, fifteenth-century portal (Photograph 32), probably a postern, is located in a long run of near-perfect precinct wall. Though the wall continues over the gateway uninterruptedly, nearly all the moulded stone which formed the jambs and head of the arch has been removed, leaving a mutilated opening.

Coverham Premonstratensian abbey
gatehouse
The building which probably dates from the early sixteenth century, has suffered much since the Dissolution and is now reduced to its ground-floor storey. The small, two-bay gate-hall has lost its front arch except for the responds but not its semicircular rear arch. Though the hall's vaulting has gone, there are springers on either side, as well as the respond of an archway of a cross-wall. To the left and right of the gate-hall are wings now in use as stables which still possess tunnel vaults.

Dunstable Augustinian priory
gatehouse
Built *c.*1450, the gatehouse has largely been demolished and all that survives today is the front wall and its two four-centred archways. This façade, which rises to a level just above the vehicular archway, was probably retained as an entrance to a mansion.

Fountains Cistercian abbey
inner gatehouse
This building has been largely destroyed, probably like that at Roche, to open up the view of the ruins of the abbey from the west. Standing one storey high, the whole of the left wall of the gate-hall survives, together with a smaller section of the right wall. More walling, probably belonging to the porter's lodging, survives beyond the left-hand side of the gate-hall. The gatehouse dates from the early thirteenth century.

Gloucester Benedictine abbey
gatehouse: King Edward's Gate (now cathedral)
The building dates from the fourteenth century and may have been erected and named to mark the inhumation of Edward II in the abbey church. Most of the gatehouse has been pulled down, probably to permit the widening of the main roadway leading to what is now the cathedral church. The surviving portion consists of work located on the left-hand side of the gate-hall: a left-rear turret and some walling decorated with blind panelling.

Gloucester Lanthony Augustinian priory
gatehouse
At the entrance to the site of the priory stands part of the front wall of the late fourteenth-century gatehouse. Still embattled and buttressed to upper-storey level, it is the portion of the building that displays the pedestrians' archway and the springing of one side of the vehicular archway. Above the pedestrians' archway appear coats of arms, including those of the Bohuns, founders and patrons of the priory.

Guisborough Augustinian priory
gatehouse
The front bay of this late twelfth-century gatehouse stands to the height of the ground-floor storey, its great semicircular archway still in position. At the rear of this bay is a complete cross-wall with its two semicircular arches. Behind the cross-wall the gatehouse has been pulled down.

Hexham Augustinian priory
gatehouse: Priory Gate, St Wilfrid's Gateway
This building was constructed *c.*1160. It now rises to the height of the ground-floor storey with two complete semi-circular arches at the ends of a three-bay layout. The upper storey was taken down in 1818.

Kenilworth Augustinian abbey
gatehouse
Dating from the fourteenth century, the gatehouse was dismantled down to the upper limit of the ground-floor

storey. Thus the vaulted and arched gate-hall is undamaged, as is the porter's accommodation which is situated on the right-hand side of the building. However, there seems to have been another wing or extension on the left side of the gate-hall which was demolished. It is not certain what use was made of the building after its partial demolition.

Kingswood *gatehouse* Cistercian abbey

Only the front bay of this gatehouse from ground-level to the tip of the roof gable survives, everything behind the cross-wall to the rear having been demolished. The surviving portion is now sealed off by means of the cross-wall and a modern wall erected over this cross-wall. The building dates from the late fourteenth century, the period illustrated for instance by the complex lierne vault over the front bay. It was refurbished if not rebuilt in the sixteenth century when some of the ornamental features of the front façade (e.g. the big central window) were inserted. Parts of the ranges to the left and right of the main section of the gatehouse survive too, these also dating from the sixteenth century.

Kirkham *gatehouse* Augustinian priory

The well-ornamented front façade of this gatehouse survives almost in its entirety, a joy to behold. The remainder of the late thirteenth-century gatehouse, however, was largely demolished, leaving little more than the left-hand wall of the gate-hall and sections of walling of the porter's lodging (on the righthand side of the building). A range to the left of the gate-hall, possibly the almonry, has also largely disappeared. Almost certainly the gatehouse offers a rare post-Dissolution instance of the preservation of part of a building because of its beauty.

Lanercost *gatehouse* Augustinian priory

This gatehouse was demolished except for the thirteenth-century rear main arch which was used to mark the main entrance to the priory church, vicarage and post-Dissolution mansion occupying part of the site of the claustral buildings.

Langley   Premonstratensian abbey
inner gatehouse
Both New (1985, p. 232) and Pevsner (1962, p. 242) confirm the existence of a fourteenth-century gatehouse at the site of this abbey. The front wall still exists, with modern brickwork used to block off the main archway. The remainder of the gatehouse appears to have been pulled down and replaced by a modern building.

Lewes   Cluniac priory
gatehouse: Great Gate
What is left of the thirteenth-century portal stands immediately to the east of Southover Parish Church. It survived as a fairly complete gatehouse until the nineteenth century when it was largely demolished, some of the fabric including a small archway being repositioned on site. The remains standing to lower-storey height consist of a section of walling which displays the responds of two major arches.

Mount Grace   Carthusian priory
gatehouse
Built in the fifteenth century, the two-bay gatehouse is sandwiched between two guest-houses of which one was integrated into a post-Dissolution house and the other allowed to become ruinous. The upper storey of the gatehouse has been removed, leaving the lower storey intact with front and rear archways, and an arched cross-wall midway between these two arches.

Neath   Cistercian abbey
gatehouse
One side only survives of this gatehouse, owing to road widening which necessitated the removal of at least two-thirds of the original building. The gate-hall has gone, leaving a long rectangular area, possibly the porter's accommodation, bounded by walls of ground-storey height which are pierced by several arches. The remnant dates possibly from the thirteenth century.

Ramsey   Benedictine abbey
gatehouse
One of the most fascinating instances of the conversion of a

monastic gatehouse from its former use. Dating from *c*.1500 and judging from its size and decoration, the portal was almost certainly the abbey's great or main gatehouse. At the Dissolution, the lower part of the front façade, including the vehicular and pedestrians' archways, were taken down and removed some half a dozen miles to Hinchingbrooke. Here the masonry was reassembled and made into a gatehouse for the seventeenth-century mansion. At Ramsey the partially demolished medieval gatehouse, shorn of its gate-hall and consisting chiefly of its left-hand wing, became a lodge for the post-Dissolution mansion constructed over the abbey site.

Repton   Augustinian priory
gatehouse
This is another example of a gatehouse that has been totally demolished except for one of its main arches, which continues to serve as the entrance to the public school. The front façade of the portal, dating from the closing years of the thirteenth century, has been stripped down to the ground-floor storey, leaving little more than a buttressed wall which contains the single great archway.

Roche   Cistercian abbey
gatehouse
Dating from the late thirteenth or early fourteenth century, the portal has been partly demolished leaving its ground-floor storey largely intact (though the area occupied by the porter's lodge on the left-hand side has been razed to the ground). This partial demolition was probably done in the eighteenth century so as not to impede the view of the abbey ruins from the west. Access to the upper storey, which may have been a chapel for lay people, was provided by a spiral stairway still largely intact, leading from the gate-hall.

Rochester   Benedictine cathedral-priory
porch-tower
Attached to the west claustral range on the latter's west side, the porch tower retains work of the fourteenth and fifteenth centuries. It has a façade which appears to have been preserved after the Dissolution as a gateway to the open area of the cloister. Though not now used as an

entrance, the façade's archway is crowned with a modern parapet. Behind the façade, the side and rear walls and vaulting of the porch-hall have been partly demolished (or permitted to deteriorate).

St Andrews Augustinian cathedral-priory
gatehouse: Teinds Yett or Tithe Gate
The front façade of this fourteenth-century building stands to the upper part of its second storey. It displays two archways, each two-centred, the larger for vehicular traffic and the smaller for pedestrians (Butler and Given-Wilson, 1979, p. 336). However, the rear sections of the gatehouse appear largely to have been pulled down. The upper storey with small windows was probably the porter's quarters (New, 1988, p. 268). As its name implies, it served the monastic barn which stood to its rear. The façade was obviously retained after the Dissolution as walling for the property that lay behind it.

St Osyth Augustinian abbey
gateway or gatehouse
This fourteenth-century portal stands on the left-hand side of the main gatehouse and is at right angles to it. It forms part of the windowed east wall of a range now demolished. The gateway, which is quite high, has an arch that is almost round. It has been suggested that it provided the chief entrance to the monastery before the main gatehouse was erected a century later.

Tavistock Benedictine abbey
west gatehouse: Betsy Grimbal's Tower
This fifteenth-century gatehouse which was the abbot's lodging, includes a substantial wing to its left and is joined to a long length of precinct wall to the right. It is largely complete though some of the upper storey, especially over the gate-hall has been demolished. Its chief feature, as seen from the front, is the pair of bold flanking towers standing on either side of the main four-centred archway. The latter leads into an unribbed barrel-vaulted gate-hall, on the further side of which is a four-centred rear arch, now blocked.

Tintern   Cistercian abbey
gateway: watergate
A fourteenth-century two-centred arch placed in an incomplete high-standing piece of walling. The cobbled slipway, which originally led to the edge of the River Wye but which is now separated from it by a modern embankment, also survives.

Tynemouth   Benedictine priory
military gatehouse
The roofless building dates from the late fourteenth century. Until 1783 it kept its medieval appearance, but in that year considerable alterations and additions were made to the fabric by the War Office. However, in recent years these additions have been removed, leaving the shell of the building as it used to be. Including the wings on either side of the gate-hall, the building stands to its full height of three storeys though the battlements have been removed. The gate-hall, which retains its barrel vault, is protected by outer and inner barbicans. The gatehouse is said to have been copied from that at Alnwick castle.

Waltham   Augustinian abbey
gateway or gatehouse: watergate
The portal was constructed on the bank of a small river and is approached by means of a bridge over the river. Both portal and bridge date from *c.*1370. In the medieval period the portal was flanked by two turrets or watch-towers, of which part of the right-hand one survives. It is quite possible that originally the portal was in the form of a gatehouse, but in its present condition its fabric amounts to little more than a double gateway with a tiled parapet overhead.

West Acre   Augustinian priory
gatehouse
The front bay of this fourteenth-century gatehouse is complete, together with its quadripartite vaulting. The bay together with its façade stands to roof level, although any parapet that there may have been has gone. The fabric behind this bay has also largely disappeared, while to the right of the gate-hall there are traces of a demolished wing or

range. The gatehouse now serves as an entrance to a mansion occupying the site of the priory.

Wigmore Augustinian abbey
outer gatehouse
Two fourteenth-century buildings are located at a distance north-west of the inner gatehouse where they border the public highway. The modern entrance to the farm and abbey site passes between these two buildings. New (1985, p. 451) suggests that these buildings may have been a long range broken through to form lodges after the Dissolution. An alternative explanation might be that the buildings which display no evidence at all of having been the wings or ranges of a gatehouse, are undoubtedly located where one would expect an outer portal to have been. It is thus possible that a gateway originally placed between these buildings may have been pulled down after the Dissolution to make way for highly loaded wagons entering or leaving the farmyard.

York St Mary's Benedictine abbey
gatehouse: watergate
All that survives of this late fifteenth-century building is its rear wall, which continues to stand two storeys high, adjacent to the guest-house. It displays a pedestrians' four-centred small archway and a vehicular four-centred large archway, both complete. The exterior of the wall is made of stone and the interior of brick. There is no sign of vaulting.

THE RUINED GROUP

Arbroath Tironensian abbey
main gatehouse: Abbey Pends
Standing to the west of the conventual church, the middle section of the gatehouse of *c.*1300 is largely intact, though its roof and gate-hall vaulting has gone. It consists of two storeys and is gabled at its front and rear. The four-bay gate-hall was originally divided equally by a cross-wall. The gatehouse possesses a long range on each side. One of these, between the middle section of the gatehouse and the conventual church, is a roofed and complete range of two storeys

(also *c*.1300), thought to have been a guest-house. The other range, which is on the opposite (right-hand) side of the middle section, is of the same date and is now gone except for its front wall. This second range which housed the Regality Court, terminates at its outer end in a complete four-storeyed tower, the Regality Tower.

Boxley Cistercian abbey
gatehouse
Standing mostly to lower-storey height, the two stone side walls of the gatehouse (fourteenth or fifteenth century) mark the entrance to a private house. Though the front arch has disappeared, the rear is represented by its two brick responds. The left of these is more or less complete.

Bury St Edmunds Benedictine abbey
gateway: postern
A small mutilated fifteenth-century archway leading through the precinct wall on the south east-side of the abbey.

Castle Acre Cluniac priory
main gatehouse
Dating from the late fifteenth or early sixteenth century, the two-storeyed gatehouse stands almost to the height of the eaves. The windows at both levels are square-headed, a factor which supports a later rather than an earlier date of construction. The portal is built of knapped flint and has brick facings to the windows, doors, and so on. Any vaulting that there may have been has disappeared. Over the pedestrians' archway at the front are the arms of the priory.

Cleeve Cistercian abbey
inner gatehouse
The two-storeyed stone building has a complex history of building and reconstruction. Originally dating from the thirteenth century, it was altered in the fourteenth, and then reconstructed quite extensively in the fifteenth, for instance in the replacement of windows. The main section of the building stands up to and includes its gabled roof, and is fairly complete. However, the porter's lodge to the right and the almonry to the left have largely vanished. The gate-hall,

which has lost its vaulting, is notable for the thirteenth-century wide recesses placed along its sides.

Dryburgh   Premonstratensian abbey
gatehouse
This is a small, late fifteenth-century building which is located immediately to the south of the claustral buildings beyond an old watercourse. The front wall and archway are destroyed, the rear wall and segmental archway surviving unscathed. The gatehouse used to be joined to the refectory range by a roofed passage supported on a bridge over the watercourse, but the passage and bridge have disappeared.

Dunwich   Franciscan friary
gateway
This is a double gateway, that is it possesses a pedestrians' archway (smaller) to the left and a vehicular archway (larger) to the right. The two are separated by a run of walling of about 15 feet. The gateway dates from the late fourteenth or early fifteenth century. Both archways which are four-centred, are complete, but some of the high walling over them has disappeared.

Easby   Premonstratensian abbey
gatehouse
This building (*c*.1300) may well have been the main if not the only gatehouse of the abbey. Except for its missing gabled roof, it is complete even to the extent of retaining window tracery. As was frequently the case with early gatehouses, it is characterised by its length and comprised three bays marked internally by quadripartite vaulting and externally by pilasters.

Ewenny   Benedictine priory
north gatehouse
The chief section of this thirteenth-century stone gatehouse is roofless and has lost its parapet, but otherwise is reasonably intact. It is attached to the curtain wall of the fortified priory on either side. As befits such a gatehouse, externally it lacks ornamentation, while in the barrel-vaulted gate-hall are portcullis grooves and murder holes.

Furness   Cistercian abbey
gatehouse: cemetery gate
This portal is located at the entrance to the monks' cemetery on the north-east side of the conventual church. Dating from the early years of the fourteenth century, it retains a fairly complete ground-floor storey. Its upper storey, however, has disappeared. Along each side of the gate-hall are stone benches.

Furness   Cistercian abbey
west gatehouse
Its overall dimensions confirm that it was a subsidiary not a main portal. The ruin now consists of two high walls with windows at the upper-storey level. The walls stand on either side of a metalled road which runs through the roofless gate-hall.

Inchcolm   Augustinian abbey
gatehouse
The fifteenth-century gatehouse is combined with the dorter where it forms a bridge to the reredorter/infirmary (New, 1988, p. 165).

Leiston   Premonstratensian abbey
porch-tower
Dating from the late fifteenth century, the porch-tower leads into the west range. Constructed of brick, half of the porch has vanished, but the remainder, which consists mainly of a flanking turret, still stands quite high.

Lindisfarne   Benedictine priory
inner gatehouse or porch-tower
The building, which is severely ruined, stands to a maximum height of perhaps not more than several feet. Built in the thirteenth century, it is located at the south-west corner of the refectory range and connects with a cross-passage leading to the cloister . It was fortified in the fourteenth century by the addition of a barbican which leads from the outer court.

Maxstoke   Augustinian priory
outer gatehouse
Another roofless gatehouse which stands to its maximum

height. Constructed in the fourteenth century, the building retains a high wing to its right and unusually still has the precinct wall connected to it on either side. Externally, it displays niches and traceried windows, while internally the gate-hall retains its quadripartite vaulting and double-arched cross-wall. There was some talk of reroofing this gatehouse, but to date this has not been done.

Monk Bretton　　　　　　　　　　　　Benedictine priory
gatehouse
Nearly all of this gatehouse survives to roof height, although some of its internal walling has been lost. Though the lower courses of an earlier gatehouse (identified by smaller pieces of stone) remain, the major existing fabric of this complex building belongs to the early fifteenth century. The gate-hall is flanked on either side by roofless winged accommodation, part of which (on the right-hand side) served as the almonry. The building does not appear to have had internal stone vaulting.

Neath　　　　　　　　　　　　　　　Cistercian abbey
porch-tower
Ascribed to the fourteenth century, this gabled and two-storeyed porch-tower is joined to the mid-point of the west side of the west range. It is complete except for its missing roof and one or two pieces of upper masonry. The porch-hall which leads at its rear into a vaulted slype, retains a ribbed quadripartite vault. Some of the stone benches along its wall interiors also survive, as do fragments of blind arcading over these benches.

Pentney　　　　　　　　　　　　　Augustinian priory
gatehouse
Constructed either towards the end of the fourteenth or the beginning of the fifteenth century, this ambitiously designed gatehouse is not all it seems to be when viewed from the front. From this aspect it appears to be complete with octagonal towers and wings flanking the single carriageway and with an embattled parapet running from wing to wing. However, behind the façade all the vaulting has gone and some of the walling has collapsed. The building requires urgent repair if it is to be saved.

St Andrews Augustinian cathedral-priory
gatehouse: The Pends
This roofless shell, through which now runs a busy road, has lost most of its upper storey(s) and its gate-hall vaulting. The building is known to date from the second half of the fourteenth century. Its front façade though incomplete, still displays a series of seven trefoiled arches similar to those of the west front of the cathedral church, from which they were undoubtedly copied. The trefoils are not ogeed, and point to an old-fashioned style of design employed at this time at St Andrews. The gate-hall consists of four bays with a cross-wall between the first and second bays.

Thetford Cluniac priory
gatehouse
A three-storeyed fourteenth-century building which stands to its full height except for its parapets. It is almost square in ground plan, and is buttressed at the front and turretted at the rear. Internally it lacks its floors. Though not possessing the usual decorative features such as niches and the like, its exterior is enhanced by its knapped flint walls, stone dressings and label-headed windows.

Whalley Cistercian abbey
outer gatehouse: North-west Gateway
This early fourteenth-century roofless building stands to the height of its eaves. It is characterised by its overall length and division into eight internal bays. External ornamentation is largely absent, although several of its upper-storey windows retain their flowing tracery. Traces of a piscina and aumbry in the upper room indicate its former use as a chapel, possibly for guests.

York St Mary's Benedictine abbey
main gatehouse: Marygate, Great Gate
This late twelfth-century building became a courthouse after the Dissolution and survived intact until the last steward of the court died in 1722. After this it gradually lapsed into disrepair and, finally, ruination. The core of the gatehouse comprises its ground-floor storey now devoid of vaulting, but with the main front arch still standing. On the west side

of the gate-hall is a complete fifteenth-century three-storeyed range used for housing important guests.

THE FRAGMENTARY GROUP

Abbotsbury   Benedictine abbey
outer gatehouse
All that is now visible are the responds of an archway and some walling, probably fourteenth century.

Bradsole   Premonstratensian abbey
north gatehouse
Two pieces of undatable high walling stand at right angles to one another. One wall may be part of the almonry.

Bradsole   Premonstratensian abbey
south-east gatehouse
This remnant consists of a narrow but tall piece of stone masonry. At a height of perhaps ten feet a short length of brickwork springs from this masonry, the commencement of which was probably a main arch. The brickwork indicates a possible date of the fourteenth or fifteenth century.

Chertsey   Benedictine abbey
gatehouse
A blocked archway in a piece of walling at the north-west corner of the precinct, opposite a medieval barn on the other side of a lane, is probably the right-hand wall of the gate-hall of one of the abbey's lesser gatehouses.

Cleeve   Cistercian abbey
outer gateway or gatehouse: watergate
A two-arched stone bridge across a small river stands immediately before the site of this gateway or gatehouse which, because of its position, may be described as a watergate. It is identified by one of the moulded responds of a main arch.

Coupar Angus   Cistercian abbey
gatehouse
Though only a fragment of this building survives, much may

be deduced as to what it originally looked like. The fragment comprises the lower right-hand portion of the front wall of the gatehouse. The masonry is pierced to a depth of perhaps three yards to the rear by a barrel-vaulted passageway. Immediately to the right of the semicircular arch of this passageway is a very large diagonal buttress. The scale of the buttress and arch suggests that the passageway was the pedestrians' entrance and that next to it, on the left-hand side, was the vehicular archway now vanished, separated from it by a longitudinal wall The date of construction of the arch and passageway could be late twelfth/early thirteenth century, and that of the buttress, fourteenth century.

Culross   Cistercian abbey
gatehouse
Remnants of the gatehouse are attached to Chapel Barn Lodge at the entrance to Abbey House, the west gable reported as being original (New, 1988, p. 98).

Dunfermline   Benedictine abbey
gatehouse: Abbey Lower Gate or Netheryet
One of three outer gates to the precinct, this fragment is all that is visible of a gatehouse. It consists of the left respond and springing of an arch, say ten feet from the ground. The mouldings, for example a recessed concave, suggest a fourteenth-century date of construction.

Evesham   Benedictine abbey
gatehouse or gateway: Barton Gate
Rough masonry protruding from the west wall of the almonry is possibly the left-hand side of the portal. Built between 1316 and 1336 by Abbot Cherington, it had a battlemented tower which served as the monks' pigeon house (Cox, 1980, p. 4).

Furness   Cistercian abbey
inner or main gatehouse
A metalled road now runs through the site of the gate-hall, the building itself represented by several courses of well-preserved stone. These give a good indication of the ground plan of the gatehouse which apparently had a substantial

wing to the right of the gate-hall section. Mouldings suggest the thirteenth century for the date of the building.

Langdon   Premonstratensian abbey
gatehouse
Traces of a gatehouse exist beside the approach lane to the abbey site (reported by New, 1985, p. 231).

Peterborough   Benedictine abbey
south east gatehouse   (now cathedral)
Part of a gatehouse survives to the south-east of the conventual church. This consists of the lower portion of the right-hand wall of the portal's gate-hall, now retained as part of a precinct wall. Visible are one of the responds of a cross-wall arch and one vaulting-shaft.

Rievaulx   Cistercian abbey
inner gatehouse
Slight remnants of the building stand on either side of a lane near the parish church (formerly the *capella-ante-portas*). The remains consist of a few courses of ashlar and the respond of a cross-wall arch. Nearby in a garden is a twelfth-century semicircular arch that may have been reset.

Stamford Whitefriars   Carmelite friary
gateway
The responds of a wide gateway on St Leonard's Lane stand to an approximate height of ten feet between lengths of precinct wall. Judged by its width and position, this gateway was probably the chief entrance to the friary.

Sweetheart   Cistercian abbey
gatehouse
According to New (1988, p. 292), part of a gatehouse pier is visible on the west side of the abbey precinct.

APPENDIX 1

Monastic Houses Mentioned in the Text

Abbey Dore Abbey,
   Herefordshire (Cistercian)
Abbotsbury Abbey, Dorset (Benedictine)
Abingdon Abbey, Berkshire (Benedictine)
Alnwick Abbey, Northumberland (Premonstratensian)
Arbroath Abbey, Angus (Tironensian)
Aylesford Friary, Kent (Carmelite)
Bardney Abbey, Lincolnshire (Benedictine)
Barking Abbey, Essex (Benedictine nuns)
Battle Abbey, Sussex (Benedictine)
Bayham Abbey, Sussex (Premonstratensian)
Beaulieu Abbey, Hampshire (Cistercian)
Beauvale Priory, Nottinghamshire (Carthusian)
Bermondsey Abbey, Surrey (Cluniac)
Binham Priory, Norfolk (Benedictine)
Blanchland Abbey,
   Northumberland (Premonstratensian)
Bolton Priory, Yorkshire (Augustinian)
Bordesley Abbey, Worcestershire (Cistercian)
Bourne Abbey, Lincolnshire (Augustinian)
Boxley Abbey, Kent (Cistercian)
Bradsole Abbey, Kent (Premonstratensian)
Brecon Priory, Breconshire (Benedictine)
Breedon-on-the-Hill Priory,
   Leicestershire (Augustinian)
Bridlington Priory, Yorkshire (Augustinian)
Bristol Abbey, Gloucestershire (Augustinian)
Bromfield Priory, Shropshire (Benedictine)
Broomholm Priory, Norfolk (Cluniac)

Bruton Abbey, Somerset	(Augustinian)
Buckfast Abbey, Devonshire	(Cistercian)
Burnham Norton Friary, Norfolk	(Carmelite)
Burton Abbey, Staffordshire	(Benedictine)
Bury St Edmunds Abbey, Suffolk	(Benedictine)
Butley Priory, Suffolk	(Augustinian)
Byland Abbey, Yorkshire	(Cistercian)
Calder Abbey, Cumberland	(Cistercian)
Caldey Priory, Pembrokeshire	(Tironensian)
Canonsleigh Abbey, Devon	(Augustinian canonesses)
Canterbury Cathedral-Priory, Kent	(Benedictine)
Canterbury St Augustine's Abbey	(Benedictine)
Carlisle Cathedral-Priory, Cumberland	(Augustinian)
Cartmel Priory, Lancashire	(Augustinian)
Castle Acre Priory, Norfolk	(Cluniac)
Cerne Abbey, Dorset	(Benedictine)
Chertsey Abbey, Surrey	(Benedictine)
Chester Abbey, Cheshire	(Benedictine)
Christchurch Priory, Hampshire	(Augustinian)
Cirencester Abbey, Gloucestershire	(Augustinian)
Cleeve Abbey, Somerset	(Cistercian)
Clerkenwell Priory, Middlesex	(Knights Hospitallers)
Colchester St Botolph's Priory, Essex	(Augustinian)
Colchester St John's Abbey, Essex	(Benedictine)
Cook Hill Priory, Worcestershire	(Cistercian nuns)
Cornworthy Priory, Devon	(Augustinian canonesses)
Coventry Cathedral-Priory, Warwickshire	(Benedictine)
Coventry Charterhouse Priory, Warwickshire	(Carthusian)
Coventry Friary, Warwickshire	(Carmelite)
Coverham Abbey, Yorkshire	(Premonstratensian)
Crossraguel Abbey, Ayrshire	(Cluniac)
Croxden Abbey, Staffordshire	(Cistercian)
Culross Abbey, Fifeshire	(Cistercian)
Dale Abbey, Derbyshire	(Premonstratensian)
Dorchester Abbey, Oxfordshire	(Augustinian)

Dover Priory, Kent	(Augustinian)
Dryburgh Abbey, Berwickshire	(Premonstratensian)
Dunfermline Abbey, Fifeshire	(Benedictine)
Dunkeswell Abbey, Devon	(Cistercian)
Dunstable Priory, Bedfordshire	(Augustinian)
Dunster Priory, Somerset	(Benedictine)
Dunwich Friary, Suffolk	(Franciscan)
Durham Cathedral-Priory, Co. Durham	(Benedictine)
Easby Abbey, Yorkshire	(Premonstratensian)
Edington Priory, Wiltshire	(Bonhommes)
Ely Cathedral-Priory, Cambridgeshire	(Benedictine)
Evesham Abbey, Worcestershire	(Benedictine)
Ewenny Priory, Glamorganshire	(Benedictine)
Exeter Polsloe Priory, Devonshire	(Benedictine nuns)
Exeter St Nicholas Priory, Devonshire	(Benedictine)
Forde Abbey, Dorset	(Cistercian)
Fountains Abbey, Yorkshire	(Cistercian)
Furness Abbey, Lancashire	(Cistercian)
Glastonbury Abbey, Somerset	(Benedictine)
Gloucester Abbey, Gloucestershire	(Benedictine)
Gloucester Lanthony Priory, Gloucestershire	(Augustinian)
Guisborough Priory, Yorkshire	(Augustinian)
Hexham Priory, Northumberland	(Augustinian)
Heynings Priory, Lincolnshire	(Cistercian nuns)
Hinton Charterhouse Priory, Somerset	(Carthusian)
Holmcultram Abbey, Cumberland	(Cistercian)
Holyrood Abbey, Midlothian	(Augustinian)
Hulne Friary, Northumberland	(Whitefriars)
Hyde Abbey, Hampshire	(Benedictine)
Inchcolm Abbey, Fifeshire	(Augustinian)
Inchmahome Priory, Perthshire	(Augustinian)
Iona Abbey, Argyllshire	(Benedictine)
Jervaulx Abbey, Yorkshire	(Cistercian)
Kenilworth Abbey, Warwickshire	(Augustinian)
King's Lynn Friary, Norfolk	(Austinfriars)

King's Lynn Friary, Norfolk	(Whitefriars)
King's Lynn Priory, Norfolk	(Benedictine)
Kingswood Abbey, Gloucestershire	(Cistercian)
Kirkham Priory, Yorkshire	(Augustinian)
Kirklees Priory, Yorkshire	(Cistercian nuns)
Kirkstall Abbey, Yorkshire	(Cistercian)
Kirkstead Abbey, Lincolnshire	(Cistercian)
Lacock Abbey, Wiltshire	(Augustinian canonesses)
Lanercost Priory, Cumberland	(Augustinian)
Langdon Abbey, Kent	(Premonstratensian)
Langley Abbey, Norfolk	(Premonstratensian)
Leez Priory, Essex	(Augustinian)
Leicester St Mary's Abbey, Leicestershire	(Augustinian)
Leiston Abbey, Suffolk	(Premonstratensian)
Lenton Priory, Nottinghamshire	(Cluniac)
Letheringham Priory, Suffolk	(Augustinian)
Lewes Priory, Sussex	(Cluniac)
Lindisfarne Priory, Northumberland	(Benedictine)
Lindores Abbey, Fifeshire	(Tironensian)
Llanlugan Priory, Montgomeryshire	(Cistercian nuns)
Llanthony Priory, Monmouthshire	(Augustinian)
London Charterhouse Priory, Middlesex	(Carthusian)
Malling Abbey, Kent	(Benedictine nuns)
Malvern Priory, Worcestershire	(Benedictine)
Margam Abbey, Glamorganshire	(Cistercian)
Maxstoke Priory, Warwickshire	(Augustinian)
Merevale Abbey, Warwickshire	(Cistercian)
Michelham Priory, Sussex	(Augustinian)
Minster-in-Sheppey Priory, Kent	(Augustinian canonesses)
Monk Bretton Priory, Yorkshire	(Benedictine)
Montacute Priory, Somerset	(Cluniac)
Mount Grace Priory, Yorkshire	(Carthusian)
Neath Abbey, Glamorganshire	(Cistercian)
Norton Abbey, Cheshire	(Augustinian)

Norwich Cathedral-Priory, Norfolk	(Benedictine)
Nun Monkton Priory, Yorkshire	(Benedictine nuns)
Osney Abbey, Oxfordshire	(Augustinian)
Oundle, ancient house, Northamptonshire	(Benedictine?)
Oxford St Bernard's College, Oxfordshire	(Cistercian)
Penmon Priory, Anglesey	(Augustinian)
Pentney Priory, Norfolk	(Augustinian)
Peterborough Abbey, Northamptonshire	(Benedictine)
Pittenweem Priory, Fifeshire	(Augustinian)
Pluscarden Cell, Morayshire	(Benedictine)
Polesworth Abbey, Warwickshire	(Benedictine nuns)
Portchester Priory, Hampshire	(Augustinian)
Quenington Commandery, Gloucestershire	(Knights Hospitallers)
Ramsey Abbey, Huntingdonshire	(Benedictine)
Reading Abbey, Berkshire	(Benedictine)
Repton Priory, Derbyshire	(Augustinian)
Rievaulx Abbey, Yorkshire	(Cistercian)
Roche Abbey, Yorkshire	(Cistercian)
Rochester Cathedral-Priory, Kent	(Benedictine)
St Albans Abbey, Hertfordshire	(Benedictine)
St Andrews Cathedral-Priory, Fifeshire	(Augustinian)
St Benet of Holme Abbey, Norfolk	(Benedictine)
St Germans Priory, Cornwall	(Augustinian)
St Osyth Abbey, Essex	(Augustinian)
Shaftesbury Abbey, Dorset	(Benedictine nuns)
Shap Abbey, Westmorland	(Premonstratensian)
Sherborne Abbey, Dorset	(Benedictine)
Shrewsbury Abbey, Shropshire	(Benedictine)
Smithfield St Bartholomew's Priory, Middlesex	(Augustinian)
Stamford Friary, Lincolnshire	(Greyfriars)
Stamford Friary, Lincolnshire	(Whitefriars)
Stoneleigh Abbey, Warwickshire	(Cistercian)
Sudbury Friary, Suffolk	(Dominican)

Sweetheart Abbey, Dumfriesshire	(Cistercian)
Swine Priory, Yorkshire	(Cistercian nuns)
Tavistock Abbey, Devonshire	(Benedictine)
Tewkesbury Abbey, Gloucestershire	(Benedictine)
Thame Abbey, Oxfordshire	(Cistercian)
Thetford Priory, Norfolk	(Cluniac)
Thornholme Priory, Lincolnshire	(Augustinian)
Thornton Abbey, Lincolnshire	(Augustinian)
Tilty Abbey, Essex	(Cistercian)
Tintern Abbey, Monmouthshire	(Cistercian)
Torre Abbey, Devonshire	(Premonstratensian)
Tupholme Abbey, Lincolnshire	(Premonstratensian)
Tynemouth Priory, Northumberland	(Benedictine)
Ulverscroft Priory, Leicestershire	(Augustinian)
Usk Priory, Monmouthshire	(Benedictine nuns)
Walsingham Priory, Norfolk	(Augustinian)
Waltham Abbey, Essex	(Augustinian)
Waverley Abbey, Surrey	(Cistercian)
Wenlock Priory, Shropshire	(Cluniac)
West Acre Priory, Norfolk	(Augustinian)
Westminster Abbey, Middlesex	(Benedictine)
Wetheral Priory, Cumberland	(Benedictine)
Whalley Abbey, Lancashire	(Cistercian)
Whitby Abbey, Yorkshire	(Benedictine)
Wigmore Abbey, Herefordshire	(Augustinian)
Winchester Cathedral-Priory, Hampshire	(Benedictine)
Worcester Cathedral-Priory, Worcestershire	(Benedictine)
Worksop Priory, Nottinghamshire	(Augustinian)
York St Mary's Abbey, Yorkshire	(Benedictine)

NB In addition to the above, Morwell Grange in Devon, Saighton Grange in Cheshire and Tisbury Grange in Wiltshire are also mentioned. Morwell belonged to Tavistock Abbey, Saighton to Chester Abbey and Tisbury to Shaftesbury Abbey.

APPENDIX 2

A Survey of Surviving Gate-halls

SECTION 1 FRONT AND REAR WALL ARCHWAYS: POSITIONS AND NUMBERS

For each gate-hall are given:

a. the number of arches in the front wall;
b. if applicable, the left-hand ('l') or right-hand ('r') position of the pedestrians' front archway in relation to the position of the vehicular front archway (as viewed from the front);
c. an identification of the presence of a cross-wall, or cross-wall remnant;
d. an identification of the presence of a longitudinal wall;
e. The number of arches in the rear wall;
f. if applicable, the left-hand ('l') or right-hand ('r') position of the pedestrians' rear archway in relation to the position of the vehicular rear archway (as viewed from the front).

Notes

1 The term 'archway' above includes openings that are square-headed, e.g. beamed entrances.
2 'n/a' = not applicable; 'ni' = no information available.

	a.	b.	c.	d.	e.	f.
Abbotsbury inner	2	r	no	no	1	n/a
Abingdon	2	l	no	no	2	l
Alnwick	1	n/a	no	no	1	n/a
Arbroath	1	n/a	yes	no	1	n/a
Aylesford outer	1	n/a	no	no	1	n/a
Aylesford watergate	1	n/a	no	no	1	n/a
Barking	1	n/a	no	no	1	n/a
Battle	2	r	no	yes	2	r
Bayham	1	n/a	no	no	1	n/a
Beaulieu inner	3	l,r	yes	no	1	n/a
Beaulieu outer	1	n/a	no	no	1	n/a
Binham	2	l	ni	ni	ni	ni
Blanchland	1	n/a	no	no	1	n/a
Bolton	1	n/a	yes	no	1	n/a
Bridlington	2	l	no	no	1	n/a
Bristol Abbey Gatehouse	2	r	no	yes	2	r
Bristol abbot's	1	n/a	no	no	1	n/a
Bromfield	1	n/a	yes	no	1	n/a
Broomholm	1	n/a	yes	no	1	n/a
Buckfast north	ni	ni	yes	ni	1	n/a
Burnham Norton	1	n/a	no	no	1	n/a
Bury St Edmunds Great Gate	1	n/a	yes	no	1	n/a
Bury St Edmunds St James' Tower	1	n/a	no	no	1	n/a
Butley	2	l	no	no	1	n/a
Byland	ni	ni	yes	no	ni	ni
Calder	1	n/a	no	no	1	n/a
Canonsleigh	2	l	yes	yes	2	l
Canterbury Christ Church Christ Church Gate	2	l	no	no	1	n/a
Canterbury Christ Church Forrens Gate	2	r	no	no	1	n/a
Canterbury Christ Church Larder Gate	1	n/a	no	no	1	n/a
Canterbury Christ Church North Gate	2	l	no	no	2	l
Canterbury Christ Church Pentise Gate	1	n/a	no	no	1	n/a
Canterbury St Augustine's Fyndon Gate	1	n/a	no	no	1	n/a

Canterbury St Augustine's Cemetery Gate	1	n/a	ni	no	1	n/a
Carlisle	1	n/a	yes	no	1	n/a
Carmarthen	1	n/a	ni	no	1	n/a
Cartmel	1	n/a	no	no	1	n/a
Castle Acre	2	l	no	yes	2	l
Chester Abbey Gateway	2	r	no	no	1	n/a
Cirencester	2	r	no	no	1	n/a
Cleeve inner	1	n/a	yes	no	1	n/a
Clerkenwell	1	n/a	no	no	1	n/a
Colchester St John's	2	r	no	no	1	n/a
Cornworthy	2	l	yes	yes	2	l
Coupar Angus	2?	r	ni	yes	ni	ni
Coventry Whitefriars	3	l,r	no	yes	3	l,r
Coverham	1	n/a	yes?	no	1	n/a
Crossraguel	1	n/a	no	no	1	n/a
Dover	1	n/a	no	no	1	n/a
Dryburgh	1	n/a	no	no	1	n/a
Dunfermline Pends	2	l	no	no	1	n/a
Dunstable	2	r	ni	ni	ni	ni
Durham	1	n/a	yes	no	1	n/a
Easby	1	n/a	yes	no	1	n/a
Ely Palace	1	n/a	no	no	1	n/a
Ely Porta Gate	2	r	no	no	1	n/a
Ely Sacrist's Gate	1	n/a	no	no	1	n/a
Ely Steeple Gate	1	n/a	no	no	1	n/a
Evesham North Gate	1	n/a	no	no	1	n/a
Ewenny north	1	n/a	yes	no	1	n/a
Ewenny south	1	n/a	yes	no	1	n/a
Forde west	1	n/a	no	no	1	n/a
Fountains	ni	ni	yes	no	ni	ni
Furness cemetery	1	n/a	no	no	1	n/a
Furness inner	1	n/a	yes	no	1	n/a
Furness west	1	n/a	no	no	1	n/a
Glastonbury	2	l	no	yes	2	l
Gloucester inner	1	n/a	no	no	1	n/a
Gloucester St Mary's Gate	1	n/a	yes	no	1	n/a
Gloucester St Michael's Gate	1	n/a	no	no	1	n/a
Gloucester Lanthony	2?	r	ni	no	ni	ni
Guisborough	1	n/a	yes	no	ni	ni
Hexham	1	n/a	yes	no	1	n/a

Hulne main	1	n/a	no	no	1	n/a
Hyde	2	l	no	no	2	l
Kenilworth	1	n/a	yes	no	1	n/a
King's Lynn priory	1	n/a	no	no	1	n/a
Kingswood	1	n/a	yes	no	ni	ni
Kirkham	1	n/a	yes	no	ni	ni
Kirkstall	1	n/a	yes	no	1	n/a
Lanercost	ni	ni	ni	ni	1	n/a
Langley	1	n/a	ni	ni	ni	ni
Leez inner	1	n/a	no	no	1	n/a
Leez outer	1	n/a	no	no	1	n/a
Leigh (Buckfast)	1	n/a	no	no	1	n/a
Letheringham	1	n/a	no	no	1	n/a
Llanthony	1	n/a	yes	no	1	n/a
London Charterhouse outer	2	r	no	yes	2	r
Malling	2	r	no	yes	2	r
Malvern	1	n/a	yes	no	1	n/a
Maxstoke inner	1	n/a	ni	ni	1	n/a
Maxstoke outer	1	n/a	yes	no	1	n/a
Michelham	1	n/a	no	no	1	n/a
Minster-in-Sheppey	2	r	no	no	1	n/a
Monk Bretton	1	n/a	yes	no	1	n/a
Montacute	1	n/a	no	no	1	n/a
Morwell (Tavistock)	1	n/a	no	no	1	n/a
Mount Grace	1	n/a	yes	no	1	n/a
Neath	ni	ni	yes	ni	ni	ni
Norwich Bishop's Gate	2	r	no	no	1	n/a
Norwich Erpingham Gate	1	n/a	no	no	1	n/a
Norwich St Ethelbert's Gate	1	n/a	no	no	1	n/a
Norwich watergate	2	l	no	yes	2	l
Oxford St Bernard's (St John's)	1	n/a	no	no	1	n/a
Pentney	1	n/a	no	no	1	n/a
Peterborough Abbot's Gatehouse	1	n/a	yes	no	1	n/a
Peterborough main gatehouse	1	n/a	no	no	1	n/a
Peterborough south-east	ni	ni	yes	ni	ni	ni
Pittenweem	1	n/a	ni	ni	ni	ni
Polesworth	2	l	yes	yes	2	l
Quenington	2	l	no	no	1	n/a
Ramsey	2	l	no	no	1	n/a
Reading	1	n/a	yes	no	1	n/a
Rievaulx	ni	ni	yes	ni	ni	ni

Roche	1	n/a	yes	no	ni	ni
Rochester Cemetery Gate	1	n/a	no	no	1	n/a
Rochester Prior's Gate	1	n/a	no	no	1	n/a
Rochester Sextry Gate	1	n/a	no	no	1	n/a
St Albans Great Gateway	2	r	no	no	1	n/a
St Albans Waxhouse Gate	1	n/a	no	no	1	n/a
St Andrews Pends	1	n/a	yes	no	1	n/a
St Andrews Teinds Yett	2	r	ni	ni	ni	ni
St Benet of Holme	1	n/a	ni	no	1	n/a
St Osyth Great Gatehouse	3	l,r	no	no	1	n/a
Stamford Greyfriars	1	n/a	no	no	1	n/a
Stoneleigh	1	n/a	yes	no	1	n/a
Tavistock Betsy Grimbal's Tower	1	n/a	no	no	1	n/a
Tavistock Town Gate	1	n/a	yes	no	1	n/a
Tewkesbury	1	n/a	yes	no	1	n/a
Thetford	1	n/a	no	no	1	n/a
Thornton	1	n/a	yes	no	2	r
Tisbury (Shaftesbury) inner	1	n/a	no	no	1	n/a
Tisbury (Shaftesbury) outer	2	l	no	yes	2	l
Torre Mohun Gate	2	r	yes	yes	2	r
Tynemouth	1	n/a	no	no	1	n/a
Usk	1	n/a	no	no	1	n/a
Walsingham main	1	n/a	yes	no	1	n/a
Waltham	2	l	ni	ni	ni	ni
West Acre	1	n/a	yes	no	ni	ni
Wetheral	1	n/a	no	no	1	n/a
Whalley inner	1	n/a	yes	no	1	n/a
Whalley outer	1	n/a	yes	no	1	n/a
Wigmore inner	1	n/a	no	no	1	n/a
Worcester Edgar Tower	1	n/a	yes	no	1	n/a
Worcester watergate	1	n/a	no	no	1	n/a
Worksop	1	n/a	yes	no	1	n/a
York St Mary's Marygate	1	n/a	yes	no	1	n/a
York St Mary's watergate	ni	ni	ni	ni	2	r

Total number of gate-halls surveyed   **148**

front wall with one archway   101
front wall with two archways   36
    pedestrians' archway to left   18
    pedestrians' archway to right   18

front wall with three archways	3
front wall: no available information	8
gate-hall with cross-wall	51
gate-hall with longitudinal wall	14
rear wall with one archway	112
rear wall with two archways	17
pedestrians' archway to left	10
pedestrians' archway to right	7
(all 16 archways coincide with the position of the pedestrians' archway in the front wall)	
rear wall with three archways	1
rear wall: no available information	18

Addendum

Apart from the above gatehouses, seven gateways may be identified as each having two entrances, i.e. a larger vehicular and a smaller pedestrians' archway. These (giving the position of the pedestrians' archway, 'l' or 'r', in relation to that of the vehicular archway) are: Brecon (l), Canterbury Christ Church Mint Yard Gate (l), Dunwich Greyfriars (l), Furness outer (l), Lindores (r), Peterborough Prior's Gateway (r), York St Mary'a postern (r).

SECTION 2   CROSS-WALLS AND THEIR ARCHWAYS: LOCATIONS AND POSITIONS

For each gate-hall are given:

a. the approximate distance of the cross-wall from the front wall;
b. the number of archways in the cross-wall;
c. if applicable, the left-hand ('l') or right-hand ('r') position of the pedestrians' archway in relation to the position of the vehicular archway (as viewed from the front).

	a.	b.	c.
Arbroath	one-half	2	l
Beaulieu inner	one-half	3	l,r
Bolton	two-fifths	2	l

Bromfield	one-quarter	1	n/a
Broomholm	one-third	1	n/a
Buckfast north	one-half	ni	ni
Bury St Edmunds Great Gate	one-third	1	n/a
Byland	two-thirds	2	l
Canonsleigh	one-third	2	l
Carlisle	one-third	2	l
Cleeve	one-half	ni	ni
Cornworthy	one-half	2	l
Coverham	two-fifths?	ni	ni
Durham	one-half	2	r
Easby	one-third	2	r
Ewenny north	three-fifths	1	n/a
Ewenny south	one-half	1	n/a
Fountains	one-half	ni	ni
Furness inner	three-fifths	2	l
Gloucester St Mary's Gate	one-third	1	n/a
Guisborough	one-third	2	l
Hexham	one-third	2	r
Kenilworth	one-half	2	r
Kingswood	one-half	2	r
Kirkham	two-fifths	ni	ni
Kirkstall	two-thirds	2	l
Llanthony	one-third	2	r
Malvern	two-thirds	1	n/a
Maxstoke outer	two-thirds	2	r
Monk Bretton	one-third	1	n/a
Mount Grace	one-half	1	n/a
Neath	one-third	ni	ni
Peterborough Abbot's Gatehouse	one-third	2	r
Peterborough south-east	one-half	ni	ni
Polesworth	one-half	2	l
Reading	one-third	1	n/a
Rievaulx	one-third	2	ni
Roche	one-half	2	l
St Andrews Pends	one-quarter	ni	ni
Stoneleigh	one-quarter	1	n/a
Tavistock Town Gate	one-half	2	r
Tewkesbury	one-third	2	l
Thornton	four-fifths	1	n/a
Torre	one-half	2	r

Walsingham	one-half	1	n/a
West Acre	ni	1	n/a
Whalley inner	one-half	2	r
Whalley outer	three-fifths	2	r
Worcester Edgar Tower	one-half	2	l
Worksop	one-half	2	r
York St. Mary's Marygate	one-third	ni	ni

distance one-half from front	20
distance one-third from front	16
distance two-thirds from front	4
other known distances from front	10
distance: no information	1
Total	51

cross-wall with one archway		14
cross-wall with two archways		27
pedestrians' archway on left	13	
pedestrians' archway on right	13	
pedestrians' archway no information	1	
cross-wall with three archways pedestrians' either side		1
cross-wall with indeterminate no. or placement of arches		9
Total		51

SECTION 3 LONGITUDINAL WALLS AND THEIR ARCHWAYS: LOCATIONS AND NUMBERS

For each gate-hall are given:

a. the left-hand ('l') or right-hand ('r') position of the pedestrians' passageway in relation to the position of the longitudinal wall and vehicular passageway;
b. the number of archways in the longitudinal wall.

	a.	b.
Battle	r	2
Bristol Abbey Gatehouse	r	nil
Canonsleigh	l	nil
Castle Acre	l	1

Cornworthy	l	nil
Coupar Angus	r	ni
Coventry Whitefriars	l,r	ni
Glastonbury	l	nil
London Charterhouse outer	r	1
Malling	r	nil
Norwich watergate	l	nil
Polesworth	l	nil
Tisbury outer	l	1
Torre	r	2

longitudinal wall and pedestrians' passageway on left   7
longitudinal wall and pedestrians' passageway on right   6
longitudinal wall and pedestrians' passageways both sides 1
Total   14

SECTION 4   BAY NUMBERS

The 114 gatehouses have been classified according to the period in which they were built or when they received a major remodelling. For each is given the number of bays evident in the gate-hall.

Early Period (twelfth and thirteenth centuries)
Arbroath 4, Beaulieu outer 1, Bristol Abbey Gatehouse 2, Bristol abbot's 1, Bury St Edmunds St James' Tower 1, Canterbury Christ Church North Gate 2, Canterbury Christ Church Pentise Gate 2, Cirencester 1, Cleeve inner 2, Easby 3, Evesham North Gate 1, Ewenny north 3, Ewenny south 2, Fountains 4, Gloucester St Mary's Gate 3, Hexham 3, Kirkstall 3, Llanthony 2, Peterborough Abbot's Gatehouse 3, Peterborough main 1, Reading 2, Roche 2, Tavistock Town 2, York St Mary's Marygate 3.

Number of gatehouses	= 24
Total number of bays	= 53
Average number of bays per gate-hall	= 2.2

Middle Period (fourteenth century)
Alnwick 1, Battle 2, Beaulieu inner 2, Bridlington 1, Bromfield 1, Burnham Norton 2, Bury St Edmunds Great Gate 3, Calder 1, Canterbury St Augustine's Fyndon Gate 3, Cartmel 2, Chester Abbey Gateway 3, Dover 1, Dunfermline Pends 2, Ely Porta Gate 1, Ely Sacrist's Gate 1, Ely Steeple Gate 1, Furness cemetery 1, Furness west 1, Kenilworth 2, Kingswood 2, Malling 1, Maxstoke outer 3, Micheham 1, Norwich St Ethelbert's Gate 2½, Pentney 2, Polesworth 2, Rochester Sextry 1, St Albans Great Gateway 1, St Andrews Pends 4, St Benet of Holme 2½, Stamford Greyfriars 1, Stoneleigh 2, Thetford 1, Thornton 5, Torre 2, Whalley outer 8, Worcester Edgar Tower 2, Worksop 2.

Number of gatehouses	= 38
Total number of bays	= 76
Average number of bays per gate-hall	= 2.0

Late Period (fifteenth and sixteenth centuries)
Abbotsbury inner 1, Abingdon 1, Aylesford outer 1, Aylesford watergate 1, Barking Curfew Gatehouse 1, Blanchland 1, Canonsleigh 2, Canterbury Christ Church Christ Church Gate 1, Canterbury Christ Church Forrens Gate 1, Carlisle 2, Clerkenwell 1, Colchester St John's 1, Cornworthy 2, Coventry Whitefriars 1, Crossraguel 1, Dryburgh 1, Durham 2, Ely Palace 1, Forde west 1, Glastonbury 1, Gloucester inner 1, Gloucester St Michael's Gate 1, Hulne main 1, King's Lynn Priory 1, Leez inner 1, Leez outer 1, Leigh 1, Letheringham 1, London Charterhouse outer 1, Malvern 1, Minster-in-Sheppey 1, Montacute 2, Morwell 2, Mount Grace 2, Norwich Bishop's Gate 1, Norwich Erpingham Gate 1, Norwich Pull's Ferry 1, Oxford St Bernard's 2, Quenington 1, Ramsey 1, Rochester Cemetery Gate 1, Rochester Prior's Gate 1, St Osyth Great Gatehouse 2, Tavistock Betsy Grimbal's Tower 1, Tewkesbury 2, Tisbury inner 1, Tisbury outer 1, Usk 1, Walsingham main 2, Wetheral 1, Whalley inner 2, Worcester watergate 2.

Number of gatehouses	= 52
Total number of bays	= 65
Average number of bays per gate-hall	= 1.3

REFERENCES

Ashmore, O. (1981), *A Guide to Whalley Abbey*, Blackburn Diocesan Board of Finance.
Bottomley, F (1981), *The Abbey Explorer's Guide*, London: Kaye & Ward.
Butler, L. and Given-Wilson, C. (1979), *Medieval Monasteries of Great Britain*, London: Michael Joseph.
Clapham, A. (1951), *Thornton Abbey*, London: HMSO.
Coppack, G. (1990), *Abbeys and Priories*, London: Batsford.
Cox, D. C. (1980), *Evesham Abbey and the Parish Churches*, Vale of Evesham Historical Society.
Finberg, H.P.R. (1951), *Tavistock Abbey: a Study in the Social and Economic History of Devon*, Cambridge: Cambridge University Press.
Gifford, J. (1988), *Fife*, London: Penguin.
Gilyard-Beer, R (1958), *Abbeys: an Introduction to the Religious Houses of England and Wales*, London: HMSO.
Lawrence, C.H. (1989), *Medieval Monasticism*, London: Longman.
Mee, A. (1945), *Northamptonshire*, London: Hodder & Stoughton.
Midmer, R. (1979), *English Medieval Monasteries 1066–1540*, London: Heinemann.
New, A. (1985), *A Guide to the Abbeys of England and Wales*, London: Constable.
New, A. (1988), *A Guide to the Abbeys of Scotland*, London: Constable.
Newman, J. (1969), *North-east and East Kent*, London: Penguin.
Pevsner, N. (1961), *Suffolk*, London: Penguin.
Pevsner, N. (1962), *North-east Norfolk and Norwich*, London: Penguin.

Pevsner, N. (1966), *Berkshire*, London: Penguin.
Pevsner, N. and Cherry, B. (1975), *Wiltshire*, London: Penguin.
Pevsner, N. and Cherry, B. (1977), *Hertfordshire*, London: Penguin.
Pevsner, N. and Harris, J. (1989), *Lincolnshire*, London: Penguin.
Pevsner, N. and Wedgwood, A. (1966), *Warwickshire*, London: Penguin.
Rahtz, P. and Hirst, S. (1976), *Bordesley Abbey, Excavations 1969–73*, Oxford: British Archaeological Reports.